Books by Jack Pulaski

The St. Veronica Gig Stories
Courting Laura Providencia
Chekhov Was a Doctor
Love's Labours

Acclaim for Jack Pulaski

"Jack Pulaski has his turf, and the talent to work it."
– Andrei Codrescu

"Get the book and read it. And then shower copies on everyone you know who still enjoys moving his or her eyes from left to right."
– Sven Birkerts

Pulaski has a gift for combining the lyrical with the earthy.
– *NY Times Book Review*

Jack Pulaski writes convincingly about so many different cultures it is hard to pigeonhole him. He looks at life through the eyes of Jews, Italians and Puerto Ricans, each change of heart and mind as believable as the one that preceded it.
– *Chicago Tribune*

Pulaski has the language to capture the moment you are swept up by and into, giving you the clamorous, surreal dream that comes with being alive and knowing it
– *Milwaukee Journal*

The writing is dense, sensual, often hilarious and entirely confident; the characters are real, with sights, sounds, and smells crowding the page.
– *The Seattle Times*

…each story, each sentence … are so written; by which I mean that one is constantly aware of, admiring of, awe-stricken sometimes by the power and variety of language, and by the craft exhibited here …. This is prose as dense, evocative, and multi-referential as poetry.
– Alice Bloom, *Hudson Review*

"Mr. Pulaski is a wonderful American storyteller. His real American characters – Russian-Jewish boys, Hispanic girls – are us, this nation, from their skin on through to their souls. His tales, his book, the work that is to come, make up an abundance of funny and moving moments on the page that I do not hesitate to call a national treasure."
– Frederick Busch

Love's Labours

Jack Pulaski

Fomite
Burlington, Vermont

This is a work of fiction. Names, characters, places and incidents are either the product of the author's imagination or are used fictitiously. Any resemblance to actual persons, living or dead, events or locales is entirely coincidental.

"The Matinee" originally appeared in *AGNI* 60.

ISBN-978-1-937677-04-6

Library of Congress Control Number: 2012941840

Fomite
58 Peru Street
Burlington, VT 05401
www.fomitepress.com
Author photograph by Margarita Pulaski
Cover design by Anna Herrick – annaherrick.com

para Margarita

and in loving memory of Maria Mercado Moreno

Acknowledgements

"The Varieties of Religious Experience" from the William James lectures.

"Thirteenth Sonnet to Orpheus" by Rainer Maria Rilke

"Auschwitz was not the garden of my childhood" by Fayad Jamis

In "The Patricide" – "It's us Ma, the wretched refuse of your teeming shores" from Barry Goldensohn and Emma Lazarus.

"As in days yore and even before yore"... a line from a standup comic of the fifties whose name I can't remember

Table of Contents

The Matinee

In my sleep I saw my head resting on the Himalayas of Bubbeh's breasts. My waking leached from dreaming pictographs, coating my tongue with the residue of the language I'd lost. Clearing my throat, dredging spit as for a gut-bucket serenade, the fish fell out of my mouth. I approximated the sounds of words I'd once spoken. The large, wriggling flounder wrapped in damp newspaper, scrolled in Hebrew, the frantic pulsing of the flounder's gills swelled *Aleph Beth*; and I ran with the fish tucked under my arm. I weaved between pedestrians. Bubbeh charged ahead of me, multitudes fell away before her, like Moses parting the waters; water waiting in the bathtub in her kitchen where I could play with the fish.

My shadow tailed Bubbeh. She, legs astride, negotiated the pavement like the pitching deck in steerage. Having left the city market where I got the fish that now resided in my belly — except for the fish's skeleton that Bubbeh had extracted and set on a plate, alongside the head and tail she'd lopped off — this time we made our way down Broadway and I held a twine-leash at the end of which waddled a duck. Because I said I wanted one. With Bubbeh there were no impediments to my wishes.

The uniformed official emerged from the crowd and marched past a man with the most dolorous face I'd ever seen. The man with the wracked face had huge signboards hanging from his shoulders displaying a menu with a picture of a steaming bowl of soup. The official maneuvered around a mother pushing a baby carriage. He might have been a cop, or a representative of the sanitation department in mufti. The man with the military bearing placed himself in front of us. He said something emphatic to Bubbeh in an English whose cadenced syllables had the echoing resonance of a harp. He was tall, Bubbeh much shorter but monumental sideways. She'd almost plowed over him, but brought up short, she smiled at the musicality of his voice. I sensed his displeasure at whatever it was that undermined his authority. Again he spoke. Bubbeh began to understand. She, not yet a *citizenya*, was most law abiding; she'd feared deportation during the Palmer Raids because her son, Ruben the criminal, beat people up for money; but the deportees were members of the Amalgamated Clothing Workers, the International Ladies Garment Workers and Wobblies. Ruben – Ruby in the street, was only an unkosher capitalist and that didn't warrant banishment from America.

Later, through years of recitations, I heard from my mother and aunts how Bubbeh had beaten Uncle Ruby when she found out that the money he brought into the house was in payment for beating people up outside of the ring, as well as inside: a trade she wouldn't honor in any case. My mother and her sisters, girls then, hung on Bubbeh's arms, begging her, "Please Mama, stop! You're going to kill him." The blood ran down the sides of Uncle Ruby's head. His sisters hung on their mother's arms shrieking, "Mama, please stop, you'll kill him." And Bubbeh, wielding the cast iron frying pan said, "Yeah, either I'll make a mensch of him, or I'll kill him."

Despite the requirements of Uncle Ruby's employment (on behalf of Shiv, a.k.a. Baron Slechtman, collecting protection payments) Ruby was a neighborhood hero. His picture was in the paper. Everyone was talking, "Already, at least a contender." He'd never lost a fight in the ring, and he considered that being out on his feet, blood blurring his vision while Bubbeh knocked him around the kitchen with the frying pan, this he judged a T.K.O. and honored Bubbeh as his most formidable opponent. Bubbeh belted him, his hands moved only to fend off the words, "Bum!" "Thief!' Unlike in the ring, he didn't move from side to side but staggered straight back. Bubbeh loaded up and whacked him. He might make widows but he would never lift his hand to a woman, let alone his mother.

Ruby grew from neighborhood hero to local deity. He was the Israelite army defending the immigrant Jewish community against the Wops, Micks, and Polacks; he attained something, a quality of being nearly commensurate with menschhood.

It wasn't achieved through what Bubbeh attempted to pound into his head, but because he fell in love with a horse. It began with a delinquency, when he was almost twelve; three years before he began to fight pro, and four years before he went to work for the Baron.

Everyone knew everything. The toilets in the hall, windows open or closed, the tenements couldn't house secrets or curtail rampant influenza and tuberculosis.

My mother said Ruby was eleven when it happened, Aunt Tessie said he was twelve; the other five sisters, my aunts, supported the estimate of one or the other; but the permutations of the story didn't change in its essentials except for how each teller of the tale declaimed her innocence: her powerlessness to rescue her mother from working herself to death. There would be lifetime of testifying to what had made it impossible to forestall Bubbeh dying in a charity ward, old at fifty. The declamations were reprised at each gravesite as my aunts passed away; sometimes too, at weddings and bar mitzvahs where grief and joy cooked up blood pressure leading to stroke and heart attack.

I was at the unveiling of Bubbeh's great memorial stone, replacing the modest stone set up in hard times. I was ten and still susceptible to the wailing. I bore witness to the drama which resulted in Aunt Esther's first stroke, slurring her speech and leaving her gimpy; and Aunt Sophie's aneurysm making her forgetful about household routine. Aunt Sophie died a year later.

But as I matriculate in the language of ghosts I hear not only the guttural sounds, pith, and ruthless wit, but an expressiveness that transfigures what is – would be – banal. Everyday toil, living and dying turned into opera. And this, in spite of my having lost the language, has hammered my idiom, how I think and speak, ostensibly in English.

A policeman came to the door to inquire whether eleven-year old Ruby might assist in finding a horse and wagon that had disappeared. "The blind onion-and-potato peddler," the policeman said, "depended on the animal and wagon for his livelihood – the horse especially." Ruby's sisters, half of them shoeless, and in their homemade dresses ran into corners and translated for the courteous policeman to Bubbeh. I imagine the parabola of Bubbeh's enormous chest trembling under her chin, all the way down the slope into her lap, where I would rest. "*Oy, Moishe the Blinde,*" she moaned, "*A shande! Mein zin a gonif!*" The policeman quickly surveyed the chilly railroad flat; the mattresses on the floor, the orange crates serving as chairs, the coal-less stove, and the seven per- haps eight hungry-looking girls trying to hide from his sight – and concluded that Bubbeh was a widow. He was essentially correct. Zayde, in crossing the ocean had been turned into a specter. He prayed and he studied, was otherwise unemploy- able, and he recognized his children as part of humanity at large; any problems connected to these offspring was woman's work. His only complaint was that on those occasions when he loosened his belt buckle, his wife immediately became preg- nant. ("*Shvenget! Nokh a Mol!*") From time to time, provoked by the outrages of the man-made world, Bubbeh would re- mind Zayde that he was complicit in pumping up her belly. Then, in vain pride Zayde's spectral imminence would take on a rosy hue. Self-effacing or effaced on occasion, Zayde as- serted himself into visibility. There was in the house a scarcity of shoes. When Bubbeh had to leave for work at the com- mercial laundry and her carpet slippers seemed to have walked off on their own, Bubbeh borrowed Zayde's shoes. Whatever the Jewish aversion for idolatry, Zayde's shoes were damned near objects of worship. It was my Aunt Tessie's job to dust and shine them. Bubbeh was expressly forbidden to wear them; her courage had no bearing in the matter of the shoes. She sneaked when she needed to wear them and swore the children to secrecy. When Zayde discovered this he roared himself into existence.

Bubbeh's life remained a struggle but she had acquired a bed. Because the warfare between my parents was constant and terrible, and my mother wanted to spare me as much as possible, she allowed me to walk the one block south, to Bubbeh's house. From the age of five on, I made my way there on my own.

If Zayde was in bed with us I hardly knew he was there. I pressed myself against Bubbeh. When I was in the first grade, Bubbeh and I cuddled in bed, and read from the same primer. We laughed and struggled to recognize the words and Bubbeh, never increasing her English vocabulary beyond my first-grade primer, didn't venture to get her second papers, and never became a *citizenya*.

Once I wandered into the bedroom and saw my grandfather lying on his belly, naked, little glass cups barnacled all over his back. Bubbeh would lift one at a time – pop! – and leave on Zayde's back a constellation of little bruised suns.

My mother and Aunt Tessie agreed that it was the same policeman who came to the house the second time. Aunt Zelda, Aunt Esther, Aunt Sophie, Aunt Leah, and Aunt Ruthie, said no; it was a different policeman. But they all agreed that the man seemed patient, even compassionate.

"What happened, Ruby?" the policeman asked. "I found it," said Ruby. "Where?" the policeman asked of the horse and wagon, "did you find it?" Ruby couldn't explain. The policeman heard a note of complaint in Ruby's voice, some symptom of complicated feeling.

The inhabitants of the neighborhood gossiped Ruby into legend long before he suspected that his being in thrall to a horse was love; and this loving might not have made him, quite, a mensch, but the concomitant symptoms were kindness, devotion, and a certain confusion.

My aunts' story telling, (I was closest to Aunt Tessie, the youngest who'd shined Zayde's shoes) was unrelenting, minimally cathartic, the exoneration they sought for some crime or sin never clear to them. For the rest of my life I would work at reconciling the variations in my aunts' narratives, all the nuances in their telling and pleading that led to the same mystery. In the endless explanations I can provide for myself as to why these stories have claimed me, in the wealth of all the analysis, the abundance itself seems the body of something arcane. Bubbeh died when I was ten and I knew there would never be that much love in the world again.

When Ruby was eleven, Bubbeh went to work in the commercial laundry where the women at the tubs and machines had to ask permission to go to the toilet, and the day's work might last twelve to fourteen hours. The women were not allowed to leave the shop; but their children could bring jars of water and things to eat, so work was not interrupted. Bubbeh took pride in never having fainted, as many did; before this employment Rivke the older sister, remembered primarily for the story that surrounded her, was taken in the influenza pandemic, just before her fifteenth birthday. When Rivke was fourteen she'd caught the eye of a gangster. At that time Bubbeh generated a little income by washing corpses for burial and running a kiosk, where she sold cigarettes for a penny a piece, pretzel sticks two for a penny, and glasses of seltzer, two cents plain. Her working capital never exceeded a dollar and fifty cents. Beautiful Rivke helped out at the kiosk. The sharply dressed dandy who stopped at the kiosk a couple of times to buy the pretzels that he gave to the kids running around the street engaged Bubbeh in conversation; he eschewed Yiddish and spoke in Russian. His obvious prosperity and dandified splendor contrasted with his too-familiar manner. His effort not to stare at Rivke was detectable. About halfway down the street, a black, hearse-like automobile was parked at the curb. Bubbeh identified it as a gangster's coach.

The next time the impeccably groomed landsman who would speak to Bubbeh only in Russian came to the kiosk, he asked for a pack of cigarettes, Bubbeh's entire stock. Rivke was startled by the extravagant purchase. The gangster's oblique glance surveilled Rivke. Bubbeh studied the gangster, and placed the pack of cigarettes on the counter. He picked up the cigarettes and placed a ten-dollar bill on the counter. Rivke stared at the princely sum. The cigar box contained, in coins, one dollar and seventeen cents. Bubbeh said to the gangster, in the language that lurked in my aunt's dreams, as Yiddish lurks in mine, that she couldn't make change for a ten dollar bill. He made a show of digging in his pockets, extracting wads of currency, but couldn't find anything smaller than a ten. He smiled, shrugged, and turned his head toward the hearse-like vehicle. If Rivke would walk the short distance to the car he was sure his colleague had a pocket full of small change. Bubbeh's eyes locked on his. Girls had disappeared from the neighborhood, this part of the city a preserve for such enterprise; the police turned a blind eye. Bubbeh rested the palm of one hand below Rivke's heart, shoved her into a corner, and with her other hand reached down into a pail that held a cake of ice, and the ice pick she used to chip the ice to chill glasses of seltzer water. The ice pick in Bubbeh's fist measured the distance to the landsman's throat. He backed away from the kiosk's oblong window. He claimed innocence; this was a misunderstanding. Bubbeh extending one arm kept the ice pick in the vicinity of his face. She hoisted one hefty leg over the counter and climbed out into the street. He who had laid claim to being a neighbor in the old country (a sort of kinship) was no longer smiling. He backed away toward the car; a pistol appeared in his hand. Bubbeh kept coming. She identified him, shouting to mothers congregated on stoops, milk boxes, gathered around the fruit and vegetable pushcarts; she shouted in Yiddish, Russian, and Polish, "Whore master!" The pimp turned and sprinted for the car. Bubbeh chased after him. Women ran from the stoops, and pushcarts. Bubbeh chased the pimp; a horde of mothers ran in her wake; the pimp jumped onto the running board of the car, the vehicle sped off. Bubbeh and the gang of mothers chased after the car for the length of the block.

For Bubbeh, this was one skirmish in a long day. The event, which was told again and again and again until my aunts became curators of the myth, the event itself had an immediate and practical civic effect; the fruit and vegetable vendors, the tailor shop, the grocery, Bubbeh at the kiosk, all would continue to pay their twenty five cents a week protection money; but the pimps would no longer browse the street to replenish their houses. The mothers were alerted. And it became known, regarding this business, that Bubbeh's street was just too much trouble. Bubbeh, like Ruby, had a preeminence in the street. And Bubbeh too would have trouble with the police. Although she managed to keep the young Ruby out of jail, she couldn't do the same for herself.

Ruby was eleven when he was sent to the principal's office for misbehaving in the classroom. Mr. Doolin, the principal, removed the leather belt that circumscribed his large middle, raised the belt above his head to administer some prescribed number of strokes for Ruby's offense, and Ruby beat him up. The principal required medical attention.

With the aid of a social worker – an uptown young German-Jewish woman of formidable dignity who could speak Yiddish – Bubbeh pleaded, begged, and bargained to keep Ruby out of reform school. She knew her Ruby. If he were caught up in the penal system, given his relationship to authority, any authority, his chances of getting out were minimal; he was likely to kill someone, or be killed himself. Finally the matter was settled: eleven-year old Ruby left school for good. When they got home Bubbeh smacked Ruby's face. He regarded the blow as a rhetorical flourish. The ringing in his ears diminished with sundown.

Bubbeh would go to jail for a day and a night. Eventually, Ruby would go to jail for a year and a day; as it was a felony for Ruby to use his fists outside of the ring. The man Ruby damaged had been mistreating a horse.

The junk dealer who would be subject to dizzy spells for the rest of his life had a reputation as a mild man. He'd never lifted a hand to his wife or children. To alert customers and assuage the tribulations of his life he beat, furiously, the bell suspended from an L-shaped wooden frame attached to his seat in the wagon. Customers approached to sell buckets without bottoms, rusted wash boards, basins, broken knives, all manner of metal debris. The junk man maneuvering his horse and wagon through the traffic of cars, trolley cars, vendors pushing pushcarts, would in the misery of his life (a first wife he loved who had died, a son who had died, eczema) beat his horse with a whip to purge his anger and retain a tenderness for God and the human race. When in the bye and bye, Ruby became wealthy, he provided Yosip the Junkman with a lifelong stipend, not only because he had injured him, but because Yosip would also introduce Ruby to the scrap-metal business which became the basis of Ruby's fortune.

Despite Bubbeh's well-founded concern, Ruby got through his prison term well enough, but with a greater aversion for human creatures. Upon release Ruby declined the Baron's offer of continued employment. They remained cordial. Ruby apprenticed himself to a farrier, and Bubbeh was arrested for participating in a rally supporting Margaret Sanger.

Ruby took to the trade just as horses and wagons were disappearing from the city streets. Pounding steel on an anvil, sparks exploding from his hammer, in the terrific heat the molten U-shaped plates took form, and no one ever fitted a shoe to a horse with such care, with such powerful caresses.

Ruby's shoulder hoisted the animal up a little, as needed, and he made loving sounds. I remember the sounds uncle Ruby made at weddings. He would play the two sticks splayed between the fingers of each hand, beating the sticks on his knees, head, and chairs, compounding complex rhythms, the sticks whirring into invisibility; he did the same with spoons, the acoustics ringing a different song. He played the harmonica, and he could tap-dance. He wouldn't, or couldn't talk much, but how he could dance. The nimble bear of the man beating music from the floor with his feet, the syncopation wrung joy from my aunts and uncles, who gasped as Ruby's feet flew, the great bulk of him hovering just above the floor.

When the Sanger clinics were set up around Brooklyn, Bubbeh took each of her grown daughters to receive counsel on birth control, and instruction on the correct insertion of the contraceptive pessary. As each married daughter gave birth Bubbeh would arrive shortly after labor to say, "Well, how did you like it? Don't forget. One is enough, two is plenty. A woman shouldn't make soldiers for the Czar!" My aunts repeated to their daughters, "Don't make soldiers for the Czar!" The injunction has remained in the family. My mother in the early stages of Alzheimer's disease, at the point when long-term memory urgently disgorged itself, shouted at a young pregnant, Portuguese mother (three little ones trailing the mother down the hallway), "Don't make soldiers for the Czar!" The teenage mother was baffled by her elderly neighbor, who shouted the strange injunction at her; until my mother grasping each recalcitrant phrase, each fleeing word, willed coherence and explained to the girl, "Don't make soldiers for the Czar!" The Portuguese girl didn't hear Czar, but cigar, which she associated with her husband, and she understood.

Bubbeh spent a day and a night in jail for her participation in the rally in support of Margaret Sanger. My mother and Aunt Tessie recall that there weren't any coins in the cigar box and they tried to fill up on the stock of pretzels and soda water. This made them sick. Ruby was at the farrier's hammering a shower of sparks, stepping out of that blistering rain to stand eye to eye with a mare; the mare's nostrils flaring, Ruby's nostrils flared, they picked up the same scent, shared a way of knowing. As best as Aunt Tessie and my mother can recall, on the days Bubbeh failed to provide a meal, Zayde felt no hunger.

The consensus of my mother and aunts is that Bubbeh had fifteen, perhaps sixteen pregnancies. One of Ruby's brother's was stillborn, another died after two weeks, another went with Rivke during the influenza pandemic. Bubbeh also had a couple of miscarriages and an abortion. The greatest injury my mother sustained was the knowledge that Bubbeh, desperate, considered giving her away for adoption to a rich lady uptown, who wanted an elder sister companion for her younger adopted daughter. Bubbeh reckoned that whatever her industry, she couldn't feed all her children;

and my mother, Molly, was well-spoken, the most charming storyteller, and in Bubbeh's estimation, my mother's plain looks didn't make her a promising marriage prospect. Bubbeh worried constantly about how she'd marry off so many daughters without dowries. As often as she was told dowries weren't the custom in America, she was incapable of believing it. In any case the arrangement that had seemed certain fell through and mother wasn't given away. From that time on, my mother became acutely aware that she was fair-skinned and had reddish hair, while her sisters were dark and had black hair; and despite male attention, and any evidence to the contrary, believed herself homely. The image she spied in the mirror conveyed something sour she couldn't expunge, or cover with cosmetics.

The oldest brother Ezra's name came down from the scribe and prophet. In spite of Ezra's living until he was twenty-two, he was mentioned obliquely, as when Bubbeh traveled upstate to visit him. The stigma of the sanatorium was more powerful than the notoriety of Sing Sing, where Ruby did his time. Tuberculosis warranted shunning as death was borne on the air, breathing a hemorrhage, the consumptive and his family always a suspect contagion. But the legend of Ruby's extraordinary strength, his invincibility in a fight, was community property, and this helped obscure the memory of Ezra in the neighborhood. When Bubbeh set out to visit Ezra, she did it discreetly, on Sundays; and only the family knew where she had gone.

Bubbeh got a job as a janitor in a tenement with a coal furnace. The job didn't carry a salary, but did provide a rent-free apartment on the fifth floor. Bubbeh shoveled coal into the furnace, hauled up, out of the basement, trash cans full of ash. She washed the five flights of stairs and landings on her hands and knees. She still sustained her employment at the laundry. When a corpse needed washing the Rabbi notified her. My aunts took turns maintaining the kiosk. Still, with all this enterprise, each week contained a quota of hungry days. However stealthily Bubbeh made her journey to visit Ezra at the sanatorium, she appropriated whatever money there was, blatantly, and wouldn't tolerate any argument or pleading to the contrary, as far as she was concerned Ezra would have, in his young, short life, luxuries. Fancy pajamas, a bathrobe like an emperor's coronation gown, fur-lined slippers, books, pencils, crayons, and paper, (Ezra loved to draw and scribbled Yiddish verse), also caviar and linen handkerchiefs to cough blood into. When Ezra died, the staff burned his drawings, books, pages of verse, and garments, fire being the most trustworthy hygiene. Bubbeh had, my aunts maintained, always favored Ezra, even before he'd contracted tuberculosis. If Ezra had represented a refinement too good for this world, Ruby represented to Bubbeh, all the barbarities of the new world.

Bubbeh couldn't forget that Ezra was one of the charity cases taken in at the sanatorium, and she slipped coins into the pockets of the white-coated attendants in the hope that the care given to Ezra might be as diligent as that given to wealthy patients.

The aftertaste of hunger could never be assuaged and when the time of plenty arrived at last, gluttony became an expression of filial piety. The children's grievances were expressed as comedy only when my aunts were grown; and telling it at a plentiful table they laughed, convulsed, as in, and accompanying, coronaries; Ruby didn't laugh, when Aunt Esther recalled the day they realized they were eating the pigeons Ruby had been keeping in a coop on the roof. He loved the birds almost as much as he loved the horses. When Bubbeh confirmed that their mouths were full of the birds he loved, Ruby swallowed, then cried for the second and last time in his life.

From all that couldn't help but be revealed, as my aging aunts discussed their failing bodies, inventoried their aches and pains, ridiculed inadequate medicines, they also gossiped about their marriages. None were happy, a few were resigned and almost content, and a couple tolerable. The union of my parents was a misery. The marriages were unhappy for every reason in the world but want.

Many of the marriages, if not arranged by Bubbeh, were strenuously promoted by her. Aunt Tessie, not married until she was eighteen, was considered in danger of being an old maid. Aunt Esther, a beauty with a predilection for nineteenth-century Russian literature, was courted by Sammy the grocer's son. Sammy's family, Bubbeh reminded Esther, was well-off. The grocery was a thriving business; no one in Sammy's family was likely to go hungry with shelves of food near at hand; also the Berkowitzes owned a two-family house, and every summer they took a bungalow in Coney Island.

Bubbeh didn't need to say that such a marriage might also be a resource for Esther's sisters, an auspicious first step to a better life for all. Esther said she felt nothing for Sammy, despite his attentiveness, industry, and his oddly emotionless confession that Esther's beauty had affected him more powerfully than anything else in life, and that he couldn't imagine denying her anything. Esther was put off by all she imagined Sammy could never imagine. Bubbeh countered, saying that he was quiet, serious, and not altogether ugly; he would provide a fully furnished apartment of Esther's choosing, in a more desirable neighborhood, and he'd promised to help Esther's sisters. Bubbeh argued that there was something wanton in denying such devotion. What were a woman's options? Hadn't she herself married out of some romantic impulse she'd never understood, mistaking Zayde's unworldliness for something lofty that must inevitably enhance love on earth. Bubbeh swore that she hadn't any inkling that in marrying Zayde she'd enlisted to serve the man's reputed genius, so that he might derive sublimity's true existence through mathematical and Cabalistic proofs, while he barely noticed her children were hungry; and to make his periodic earthly connection, climb on her, as this too was her duty. Sammy, whatever he couldn't imagine, could provide, and had promised to insure an easier life for Esther; that, Bubbeh said, was the true beginning of marriage.

Esther returned from her honeymoon in the Catskills weeping. She told her mother that Sammy had been kind, patient, and the marriage hadn't yet been consummated. Sammy, Esther cried, was a soulless materialist and she couldn't bear his touch. She begged Bubbeh, asked if the marriage might be annulled. Esther said she couldn't return to him. Bubbeh commiserated, and she said that Sammy "Pischer," however puny his soul would always dote on Esther, and as for the other, Esther should close her eyes and dream of what her children's lives could be. With the exception of my mother and Aunt Tessie, Esther's sisters gave the same advice. After a week, Esther returned to Sammy.

—⁓—

Bubbeh paused, looked over her shoulder. I stood with the twine-leash in my hand and watched my duck waddle. The avenue was crowded, people hurriedly side stepping the quacking duck they nearly trampled. My sixth birthday was drawing near and Bubbeh had promised a surprise. I wondered whether it would be a cake, or one of the wonderful hats she could fold out of newspaper. The uniformed official from the sanitation department who'd placed himself in front of Bubbeh went on and on about some law we were breaking because of my strolling on a city street with a duck. He'd raised his voice, as if shouting would make Bubbeh understand. Finally she did understand; the official was presuming some authority that allowed him to interfere with her grandson's activity. She mouthed something that sounded like, "*Nyet* – not you biz-nyess," and with one broad arm moving in a swimmer's butterfly stroke swept the official into the passing crowd.

It was a warm summer night. The duck, which I knew would soon be a meal (and I felt no remorse at the prospect, as I was completely taken by the delights and transformations that flowed from Bubbeh's hand), the duck was teth-

18

ered to a rail on the fire escape, where I would sleep the night. The mattress, pillows, and blanket made a comfortable bed. There were wooden cheese boxes with morning glories all around me. Perched five stories above the street in the cocoon Bubbeh had made I floated in the dark, watched the stars, listened to the melancholic sound vessels hooted from the East River, and opened my mouth as Bubbeh fed me figs.

Bubbeh's present for my sixth birthday was something completely new. It yielded wonders in another darkness, fantastic as anything I saw dreaming on the fire escape. Occasionally it occurred to me that I'd been away from home for some time. There had been an unexpected silence there, more frightening than the curses my mother and father hurled at one another; a silence threatening to explode into something more awful.

Bubbeh took me by the hand. The duck remained on the fire escape. Bubbeh had pointed to the morning glories, the flowers opening with the light. We made our way through the streets. Bubbeh pointed to various stores, a furniture factory at a corner where we turned, pinched her nostrils as we walked the thoroughfare of slaughter houses, past the gas works, and a store front where gypsies lived; there were two large windows with a purple door in between. On one window there was a giant painted eye, and some writing with a number of words I recognized; I assumed the writing was an invitation. On the other window the enormous palm of a hand. I wondered why the gypsy families made their homes in stores rather than apartments. Bubbeh pointed out the gypsy residence as a landmark; she marked it all for me emphatically in the language of ghosts, and the pictographs her hands shaped in the air, so I could find my way back to her house. Unlike Hansel and Gretel I was meant to find my way home. She caressed the top of my head and murmured, "Life to your head."

Outside the movie theatre, standing near the ticket booth, she put coins in my hand. I counted fourteen cents. She was delighted with my ability to compute, and kissed me. I could tell time, and this also seemed miraculous to Bubbeh; and as she found it miraculous, so did I. At her urging I bought my ticket.

In the lobby I walked up an incline, moved in a medium lighter than water, inhaled a perfume thick and sweet, as though the air were composed of liquefied candy, and underfoot, soft, mushy, the wine-colored carpet gave off the odor of mildew. Bubbeh summoned the manager who was also the ticket taker. I handed him the ticket; he tore it in half. He must have been a landsman because she spoke to him in Russian. I surmised that she'd said, "This is my grandson, check up on him, make sure no one bothers him." He nodded his head, and dropped the half of the ticket into a tall, black, vertical box. The landsman-manager was wearing a suit, shirt, and tie that appeared bloated and wrinkled, as though he'd just been retrieved from the ocean. The movement of his hands, his head, was mechanical, accomplished by rote. He had a lost, remote look, reminiscent of Zayde, but concentrated in the present and eternal function of taking and tearing tickets. The face, which had never been young, lapsed into the language of ghosts, and I gleaned, "I make a living." Bubbeh responded in the language saying, she was well, and wished him strength. His eyes had the fixity of the blind. He nodded. The arches of red, yellow, and blue light bulbs surrounding the colored posters on the walls of the narrow lobby on either side of me, pulled my head to the right and left as I trod up the incline of the lobby: a cowboy in a ten-gallon hat, sitting on a rearing stallion brandished six-shooters, a giant gorilla sat on top of a skyscraper with a screaming girl in the palm of his hand, a man in a cape with mad, gleeful eyes and a smile of brilliant teeth thrust a sword toward the sky; I glimpsed a sinking ship, the panorama of a burning city. I clutched the soiled, comic book the lady in the ticket booth had given me. She'd said that every boy and girl who bought a ticket before noon would get a free comic book.

Bubbeh grasped the elbow of the manager and pulled him along; they accompanied me to my seat. She kissed me, gave me a brown paper bag containing a slice of pumpernickel smeared with chicken fat, a smaller bag inside the bigger bag with raisins, and a jar of tea, and two cents for candy. She hugged me. I knew she believed in my ability to find my way back to her house. I wasn't afraid.

I sat in a dusk as rank as the dawn of creation and watched children hatching in the dark. In front of me, in the distance, loomed the great surface of a screen, dim and pocked as the mountains of the moon. Down to the left of the screen was a concession stand attended by a shadow. Sweet smells drifted from the stand, and from somewhere behind the stand the smell of frying potatoes, sauerkraut, and hot dogs. Also wafting in the air, the distinct odor of unflushed urinals. My seat too, springing coils of hairy stuff gave off the scent of something putrefying. Thin beams of light fell through the roof, illuminating dust motes. Looking up toward the roof I could see clusters, transparent bubbles, swelling and trembling, the fat drops of water fell soaking the head of a man as derelict-looking as the one I'd seen on Broadway with the great sandwich board hanging from his shoulders, advertising soup. He snored. I wondered whether he'd bought a ticket to come in and sleep, or if, as an act of charity, the manager had let him in to snooze in the back row where his smell could be washed away by the rain that fell through the ceiling.

The dark filled up, became riotous. The great tabula rasa at the end of a long smoking cone of light teemed with stampeding cattle, mooing in the swirling dust; a cowboy on a magnificent white stallion galloped after a wagon dragged by a sextet of berserk horses; a girl in the careening wagon screamed. The cowboy plucked the girl onto his saddle just before the wagon plunged over a cliff. The triumphant cheers in the theatre drowned out the sound of the cattle. A vendor made his way up the aisle hawking ice cream. Another hawked hot dogs. Their voices, ballooned and gravelly could be heard above the bedlam. I followed the cylindrical cone of light down to the concession to the left of the screen, saw the silhouette of my head darken the chest of Johnny Mack Brown's stallion, and purchased two sticks of licorice for a penny, and for the other penny a thin filament of paper with pink sugar drops on it. When in time, I'd learned Johnny Mack Brown's name, I wanted it; Benjamin Seymour Schanofsky is a mouthful, although within the year, in the schoolyard, I became Benny.

I watched Tarzan wrestle a crocodile. All the sounds of a jungle rose, bird calls trilled in the dark, elephants trumpeted, an amphibian roar swallowed the hours and I munched the pumpernickel smeared with chicken fat. Tarzan strangled the crocodile. I coughed, bread crumbs caught in my throat. My eyes teared. I took the last swallow of tea. My head jerked sideways and again I saw the beautiful, bandannaed gypsy lady sitting next to me, smoking her pipe and bouncing an infant on her lap. The baby began to cry. The gypsy lady opened her blouse and popped her breast into the baby's mouth. I put a raisin on my tongue. The baby sucked. My vision listed toward the gravitational force of the milk-filled moon; the baby sucked; I swallowed the raisin. The gypsy woman took her breast from the baby's mouth, the plum-colored nipple at my nose, bosom in her palm, she smiled and offered me a sip. I choked. Her smile widened into a gold mine, teeth giving off fireworks of light, clamped around the bit of her pipe, grinning, billowing smoke.

I learned, and like everyone else, quickly forgot the name of the movie house; it was simply known as 'The Dump". By the time I was fourteen the Puerto Rican kids called it "*El Meaito*", I asked my pal Hector Perez what that meant. He said, "A place where one may piss."

Faithful, wedded to years of matinees, Hector and I attended every Saturday. The ambrosial stink was the same. Saturday morning in the lobby, Bubbeh's landsman was still there (Bubbeh four years gone), the ticket taker no older than he'd been the first time I saw him. Still looking as though he'd just been fished from the sea, he tore the admission tickets in half.

In the semi-dark of the theatre, Hector and I and the packed audience waited for the show to start. Hector explained to the boy sitting behind him, who sneezed on his ear, and refused to step outside, "Either you got valor or you a piece of shit." He had to shout to be heard over the stamping feet, clapping, and whistling.

The theatre darkened. There was thunder outside, and thunder in; on the screen the Wolf Man stalked through the mist. Someone's hat was launched, a shadow lobbed again and again with cheers, the shape of some attenuated flying thing, wingless, passed through the projector's cone of light just in front of Wolf Man's gnashing teeth; Wolf Man menacing an old gypsy woman. Hector shouted encouragement and genuflected. Wolf Man's furry brow metamorphosed with the waning of the moon to suffering, thoughtful flesh, the old gypsy woman escaped. I thought of my mother and father, each fearful of the other in their ordained madness.

Meanwhile, a large, chaste, bumbling Lon Chaney Jr., subject to the merciless moon, begged to be locked up; rage and carnage some deity's test of his innocence. The howl came from the balcony. "You pissed on my shoes! You pissed on my shoes and you say you're sorry?" The sound of the scuffle coincided with the most pious moment, Wolf Man dying into human form, the face contrite, at rest, a rapture of peace and death. Between the main features we saw a Three Stooges comedy. I watched the Stooges bang one another over the head with hammers; heard the *buffo* tune of perpetual calamity, the mocking sound of horns at The End.

A pocket of silence, surrounded by riot, traveled down the aisle. I turned to see what was passing. Hector turned. It was Cookie. She fingered the crucifix at her throat, pinkie running over the body of Jesus, arms outstretched, pulsing on her throat. My face turned among the ranks of profiles, staring, mouth wide open. Cookie looked, laughed, and said, "Whatcha doin', catchin' flies?" My ears burned, I closed my mouth and thought of Lon Chaney Jr. staring at the hair growing on his knuckles. "Ay what a barbarity," Hector said, as he perused Cookie's spectacular anatomy in the tight skirt and sweater. Hector's scream wailed through delight, horror, the permutations of all sexes. "*Ay Mami!* What a barbarity, a woman making such a show of what God gave her."

Popeye quaffed a can of spinach. Buck Rogers traveled to a star. The sound system sounded water logged. Buck Rogers' voice gurgled. The dark shot through with beams of light, bright blue threads of spring funneled through the holes in the roof, illuminated flocks of galoshes and caps, flying about: and cheers, pandemonium, gangs of boys limp ing Wolf Man-like into the aisle, wizards of peripheral vision they lurked in the vicinity of Cookie. On the screen, a sol- dier of the French Foreign Legion staggered, alone, under the blazing sun. Love had sent him into the desert. The roof of The Dump was porous as a sieve, all weather blew through the dark. I could smell spring and one unremitting wind of winter. Great thunder from outside. On the screen the legionnaire staggered across the technicolor desert, crying, "Water, water." The rain came through the roof, my head soaked, I cried, "Water, water." The legionnaire crawling across the desert cried, "Water," with everyone in the house taking up the cry, "Water, water," and the flood fell through the roof.

El Damage: a novella

Bisabuela Consuelo, my mother-in-law, is a month shy of her ninety-ninth birthday. She has been living with us for three years. My wife Laura is climbing the stairs to her mother's bedroom. Laura rarely complains, except for the pain in her knees, still, if I put a Tito Puente record on the stereo she can't resist dancing, no matter what activity she's engaged in; she moves beautifully, the girl inside the body betraying her enchanting. Likewise, the trajectory of her stories, as linear as the mambo: epics within the symmetry of each moving part, hips, knees, shoulders, belly and ass, and keen dreaming head. Now she's trying to get a word in, temper the story her mother's telling, insinuate the truth or mitigate it; I am not sure. Our daughter Maria has inherited her mother's gift for storytelling and is trying to interpose her version, perhaps for her daughter Alicia's sake: a hedge against destiny. Our granddaughter who has completed her first year of college, listens avidly to the story she is heir to. She's been listening for years. It began not long after "Little Red Riding Hood". She's overheard a lot, and learned more eavesdropping. Later she was captivated by the tales her mother couldn't resist telling. Maria replicated the richly broken English of Alicia's Puerto Rican and Russian Jewish great-grandmothers: the stories of each fantastic, horrible and funny.

I hear them, upstairs in Bisabuela Consuelo's bedroom. Rowdy, laughing, so far they are having a good time. The clamoring Scheherazades intrude on one another, claiming that the latest episode that each is ready to divulge is the news that will change our understanding of the story. Alicia struggles to stifle her laughter. Bisabuela allows Laura to interpolate while she pauses to bite a cookie with her two remaining teeth, one above and one below, aligned beneath the tip of her sharp nose. She says the two teeth are all she needs to defend herself against enemies. Bisabuela masticates the coconut cookie and meditates on the martyrology wherein her eldest sister Teresa, also known as Tia or Titi is preeminent. Titi passed on five years ago. She was three months shy of her one-hundredth birthday. Bisabuela announces each time she awakes, day or night, that she is determined to live to one hundred; moreover, the three months not spent by Titi are her inheritance, and the Virgin Mary is arguing her case to the Lord. In prayer she reminds Mary that Titi was also a virgin when she passed from this world. To everyone within earshot, temporal and supernatural, Bisabuela declares that two of her octogenarian cousins can attest to the provenance of Titi's innocence. I imagine the relic membrane veiling Titi's maidenhood more authentic than the Shroud of Turin. But because Bisabuela isn't on good terms with her cousins, she has decided, again, to testify on their behalf. She will say that when Teresa was sixteen she was betrothed to seventeen year old Rodolfo. Rodolfo made promises but was seduced by and married his cousin Celia. Teresa came to the quick and emphatic understanding of the weak character of men, never married, remained pure, and was deeply involved in the raising of her sister's and brother's children, thus becoming Titi. Titi, as befits a virgin was buried in a white bridal gown. But careless functionaries at the funeral parlor had allowed a man to wash her body in preparation for burial. Remediation for this injustice Bisabuela claims also accrues to her, and she is entitled to the compensation of the three months not lived by Titi and the better part of a year for the sacrilege of the man washing Titi's nude body. Laura says, "But." Bisabuela shouts, "*Recuerda*, in the United States, Titi went to night school for three weeks, long enough to learn to say in English, 'Don't touch me.'"

Bisabuela says, "Every Sunday morning Pedro..." and falls asleep in mid-sentence. She wakes in twilight, alone in her room and yells, "Pedro was a good boy. Every Sunday morning he made his mother coffee and served it to her in bed. As if I were a queen." I clear the supper dishes from the table. Laura shouts, "Mami, *tienes hambre? Quieres* sweet potato, rice and beans?" Silence. Laura hollers, "Banana?" And we hear the whistling exhalation of Bisabuela's robust sigh. "Coffee, *pan blanco*, soft."

Yesterday, when I brought Bisabuela breakfast she peeped out from the quilt she held like a veil beneath her eyes, and said, "I'm freezing." It is July. The thermometer on the wall read eighty degrees. The electric space heater was on full blast. The quilts, blanket, and bed sheet that reached her knees were piled into a mound; her shanks, two sticks, topped by her bunioned knees stuck out of the bed clothes. "*Guapo*," she said, smiling, "feel my knees, they're ice." I stared at her fleshless shanks, and pale reptilian feet with their thick, horny toenails. Bisabuela said, "It's okay. I'm the same like your mother. Feel my knees." I touched them." See," she said, "Ice." I rubbed her knees. She moaned and I rearranged the bedclothes so all of her was covered.

Laura says, "I'm being summoned. And it's time for her evening meds." Upstairs Bisabuela interrogates her. "*Dónde están* Maria and Alicia?" Laura explains they had to go home; it's a three hour drive to the city. "And your sister Sylvia, when?" "Maybe next week." "Maybe" says Bisabuela, dredging phlegm from her throat and spits. "Mami, *por favor* not on the floor. Use the tissues; drop them in the pail by the bed." "Your father," Bisabuela says, "loved you most of all. You can't remember. We lived in Puerto Rico then, on Columbus Landing. A very noisy street. You were a baby. The shouting woke you and made you cry. Your father ran out into the street with a *pistola* and threatened to shoot anyone who spoke louder than a whisper."

When Laura told it, her father was wielding a machete. And she said that later, Papi had a shoe repair shop in the United States. He was skilled at his work and charming and the business should have been a success. But too many of his customers were women he found attractive and as his hands caressed the refurbished shoes, the women lingered as he closed the shop and accompanied each into what would be, for him, yet one more domicile. Laura said she has an unknown number of half-brothers and sisters in the five boroughs of New York. She described her father as a cavalier racist, brown as an old penny, sporting a thick black mustache, the furry valence augmenting his smile of handsome white teeth. He was thin, finely made, magisterial in his posture and not so much handsome as beautiful. Almost always he was smiling, as if he'd just learned something funny and true which he was willing to share, and the getting of wisdom was after all an affable business. His sense of his innocence was unassailable. He'd explained to Laura, when she was an adolescent, that if his consciousness had been taken hostage by beauty, he was not to blame. Nature rules supreme. And as God had set all this in motion, He would understand. Moreover, Papi wrote poetry in his youth, considered himself a poet, and thinking no less of the Almighty, assumed his maker capable of poetic justice. Papi, whose name was Francisco, had become Frank shortly after the family had emigrated from Puerto Rico to the Lower East Side of New York. Papi said that Laura was his most beautiful child, but because of her *café-con-leche* complexion it was necessary that she protect herself from the sun, as she quickly turned chocolate brown. Laura believes that her mother Consuelo's ivory-white skin was a moral force in her father's life; it accounted for his frequent visits and extended stays with Consuelo, his first and foremost wife. His lifelong project was the eugenics of his profligacy, mixing his blood with pale women and bleaching his offspring so that finally they'd be white, and being white, they'd have access to the kinds of prosperity inherent in whiteness. Nevertheless he was not immune to the charms of dark women.

Now, after so many years I'm less jealous, even empathetic when I think about the men in my wife's life. First and foremost Papi and Pedro. I never met Pedro, but when Laura and I had been lovers for three weeks, she told me about him. Our talk poured out in the aftermath of lovemaking, astonishing us almost as much as the desire that had us groping at our clothing to make bare the parts that would join us. We did it on tenement roofs, in dark hallways, my apartment if we could wait to get there, and one night pressed against a tree in Central Park. Gangs prowled the park at night. Joined, Laura's legs clamped around my hips, we slid down the tree trunk. On the ground in *flagrante delecto* Laura heard the horse's hooves before I did. We fled, wet, stumbling, pulling our clothing in place. We heard but didn't see the cop on horseback galloping close by in pursuit of crime in the dark park. In less than an hour the other floodgates gave way, and we were exchanging histories, all at once astonished by our lives. We'd met while taking night classes at City College. In Finley Hall lounge among our friends, Laura was the only woman to take part in the rarefied bullshit sessions: Schopenhauer, Freud, Marx, and especially Camus. The world which Schopenhauer described as blind, obstinate, impetuous will, became more impetuous when Laura appeared and participated in the discussion. It was an event when she entered a room. Although she didn't trade on her beauty and worked hard not to have what she had to say trivialized, the half dozen young men, me included, began to show off, preen, entertain and woo her, rhapsodize the moment she arrived at the table; the ostensible subject under discussion "The World As Will and Idea", or the argument for or against suicide as an honorable option became comedy, dada, and other dumbfounding things. Maybe because I was stripped bare fastest, the impossibility of pretense expunged from my face, while the other boys continued to wiggle and flounder, and I stumbled away – somehow, Laura and I found each other, divested one another of virginity, got lost and found our way, recuperating in actual conversation. The first time we made love in my apartment. Afterward, just as we were about to leave and stroll about the spring besotted city, Laura reached under her skirt and dabbed her maiden blood on my nose. She said she was a lapsed Catholic, I said I was a vestigial Jew.

That was in a previous life – quite aside from the numerical consistency of the accumulating years. There were the first four transfiguring weeks. A month later, on the day we walked the streets adjacent to the East River, the air smelling like coffee from a nearby warehouse, Laura, silent and angry, wouldn't let me hold her hand. She stepped away from me. Couldn't bear to be touched. She was tired, exasperated; as if she'd made an enormous effort to make me understand something I was too dull to grasp. I did sense that I was part of something she had to repudiate. She told me, vehemently, she couldn't see me anymore. I had a presentiment of dying alone. And she screamed, "Pedro is dead."

I understood what was being said to me in the most perfunctory way. I saw mouths opening and closing, the mobile features of faces turning into abstract shapes. On the job in the warehouse my body did the work. I attended my classes at night recognizing the nominal meaning of the words spoken by the lecturer, but had no understanding of the lecture. Laura had vanished from the college. Riding the subway to the warehouse during the morning rush hour or to college during the evening rush hour I was aware of the bodies pressing against me, but didn't feel them. The faces an inch from my face breathed on me and I saw them with such clarity, I saw through them, was blind to them. My sleep was oblivion or episodic nightmares.

I couldn't remember if I had locked the door. A shadow searched the dark for something worth stealing. Many apartments in the building had been burglarized. It occurred to me that the phonograph could be sold or pawned. If I had been capable of speech I might have directed the intruder to drift to the right, where the phonograph sat on a table. I heard a "poof" and saw the small ring of flames illuminate the top of the gas range. The thief was brewing a cup of coffee. In my moribund bed, mouth shut, the yammering in my head was let loose again; the arguments and entreaties, that of their own accord blathered for some part of my nights resumed. A lunatic suitor pleaded to Laura's mother, father, and brother repeating that he was serious, and truly loved Laura. The aureole of light from the gas range revealed the beautiful face of a boy who could have been Laura's twin. The flame from the cooking range illuminated his face in purple and gold, a saint in a church window whose sympathy was for humanity in general.

Her weight lay on my back like a cloud. I inhaled the piquant scent of her skin and stirred. Her fingers probed the vertebrae from the back of my neck all the way down my spine, caressing my back as if it were a Ouija board that could remind me of the last thing she had said, before she'd said we had nothing more to say to each other. She whispered, "I never returned your key." And she was touching, tickling me everywhere. I wriggled out of the mummifying bed clothes, and wondered if Lazarus had giggled upon his resurrection. And I was in awe, and grateful for my life being something more than I could have imagined. Laura said, "I made coffee."

From that time on making love had to remain her initiative. If I touched her first I'd provoke a pause. When I'd been a ghost with a hard-on I had an intimation of the perseverance required of Laura to sustain some crucial aspect of her being. The rebuffs hurt, but were something I learned to bear, not always with grace.

The following day, until this, I can't remember whether we made love before or after she resumed justifying herself, explaining that she'd never heard of Vietnam, and in any case the shooting hadn't begun, as far as most citizens knew. She said again and again she couldn't imagine what else she might have done. She reviewed Pedro's street career just prior to her urging him to join the military and get away as quickly as possible. Her assumption that Pedro would be safer in the Marines than in the neighborhood made her laugh and gag. She wouldn't have to guess about what he was up to. Alfredo Molina like Pedro, was a member of "The Outlaws", and Alfredo had declared his love to Laura, although she'd told him that she could never reciprocate his feeling. Because she couldn't dissuade Alfredo's persistent courtship, she told him that her secret ambition was to become a nun. There was an element of truth in this. For a time she had wanted to be married to Jesus. His languid beauty on the cross pulled at her, not the torture and suffering, but the ascension to another world. She longed to be wedded to transcendence. Alfredo was humbled. Still, he needed to demonstrate his capacity for devotion. He violated the vows he'd made to the Outlaws, and confided Pedro's gang activities to Laura. He asked Laura to be discreet, not because he doubted her discretion, she knew, but to make plain that he was putting his life at risk for her sake. Her worst fears were confirmed. Pedro's initiation had required that he participate in an armed robbery; the money from the holdup of the liquor store went into the gang's war chest. He was also in the turf battle with the Italian gang in which one of their number was killed. Alfredo said with so many shots being fired, they couldn't be sure whose bullet snuffed the Italian. Several Outlaws claimed credit, but Alfredo said, in the hope of comforting Laura, that Pedro, a guy with plenty of heart didn't vie for such honors, he was a serious person. Alfredo paused, looked grave and mumbled, "He was skin poppin' heroin on account of he couldn't stick a needle in his veins, and it's only been a couple a months, but he's on his way to a habit. *Lo siento mucho*, Laura." And Alfredo pantomimed Pedro slack faced, sitting in a meditative posture. "Like he thinks he's becomin' some kind a wise man. He was supposed to be sellin' product, not usin'. I guess he got curious." Laura could see Pedro, horse surging in his blood, warm all over, having intimations of shamanistic calm, as every human need diminished into one. Alfredo kept saying he was sorry.

Laura had wondered about the source of her authority over Pedro. She was only two years older than her brother. Her power hadn't been so complete that she could govern Pedro's wild life in the street, but her terror and care for what would become of him had jurisdiction, and when she told him it was time to get as far from the neighborhood as possible, as soon as possible, he accepted her judgment. She remembered that when they were children, and she had initiated their exploratory touching and time stopped in the fervid pleasure that was in them, but not of them, the intimate and most impersonal thing they'd ever experienced, and as she was the one who started it, she was also the one who had said when it was time to stop. And he had accepted that too. Why, she wondered. For all of Pedro's lawbreaking, he never rebelled against her. It had all begun long ago in their prescient childhood, a bond durable as the vocabulary of a forgotten dream. They didn't feel the need to discuss the delirium of that first touching, neither did they confess to a priest, although Pedro assumed Laura had confessed something nearly commensurate in its place, absolving them both, as he'd acknowledged his sister as the keeper of the calculus of mortal and venial sins. Tethered by an incorrigible faith, they believed they were entitled to at least some secrets God had no need of knowing. And Laura recalled that she and Pedro had danced together at the Palladium and won a contest. Pedro's ability on the bongos and conga drums was also legendary, and he was invited to sit in with the Machito band.

Except for the times when her father was visiting, Laura, Sylvia, and their mother slept together in the bed in Consuelo's bedroom. When their father was present, Laura and Sylvia slept on the convertible couch in the living room. The living room was also her mother's workspace, and there was a sewing machine and a headless mannequin against the wall beneath the large velvet, moonlike likeness of the late President Kennedy. Consuelo had a small thriving business making garments for brides, and for the dying, who knew how they wanted to be attired in the coffin. During the day Consuelo worked in the blouse factory and at night she labored at her own enterprise. Her children were well provided for, and the immaculate three room apartment decently furnished. Consuelo managed tuition for parochial school so that Sylvia would be spared the chaos of the neighborhood public school, where twelve year olds were recruited as couriers for the drug dealers. Nevertheless, Sylvia begged to be liberated from St. Ann's. She lived in terror of the Sisters whose teaching method was grounded in humiliation; Sylvia thought of her time in the school as punishment for sins she hadn't yet committed.

Sylvia was fourteen and still slept clinging to Laura. In the dark of the living room, Laura could hear the bedsprings wheezing in her mother's bedroom. Moonlight illuminated the headless dummy in the glittering wedding gown. President Kennedy rendered in fuzzy velvet appeared to be hibernating on the wall. Again Laura was surprised that her mother never denied her father. He might be absent four or five months but when he appeared they retired to the bedroom as if this were a nightly routine in the most staid and sumptuously weary marriage. Laura wondered if her mother hadn't found her martyrdom an aphrodisiac; quite aside from conjugal duty, Consuelo viewed martyrdom as an honorable state, a worthy vocation. She was proud and devoid of irony. Frank's earnings from the shoe repair shop were never adequate for the increasing number of children he fathered. When he asked Consuelo for a loan, she never denied him, and he never repaid the money. However tired from her day and night labors, Consuelo took pride in being an infallible provider, and in regard to her plentiful work, she knew the Virgin Mary favored her.

Laura lay in bed. Sylvia like some marsupial creature clung to Laura's belly, their mother at Sylvia's back embraced the child, and Sylvia sandwiched between them, snored. The death of Pedro aged Consuelo. Her black hair had turned white within a month, startling Sylvia. In the month since they'd been informed of Pedro's death, Consuelo had taken to sleeping with her eyes open. Her gaze was fixed on the ceiling where the patch of light cast by the votive candle from the altar below trembled. It seemed to Laura that her mother had extended her vigilance through the night against stealthy ill will, and Laura rose from the bed to close the window so that the breeze wouldn't blow out the flame of the candle. The night ticked on. Laura dreamed of sleeping alone, a voluptuous surcease, the void's ultimate luxury. In the bed Laura's, Sylvia's and their mother's legs touched and crisscrossed at the knees and ankles. Laura tried to disengage her leg from the tangle of limbs. Sylvia hung on tighter and drooled on Laura's neck. Laura turned her head and stared at the ceiling. She confided to herself that Pedro was dead, and yet the memories clamored, as if what they said could forefend any further hurt to her brother.

However Pedro had tried to get the attention of his father, Laura saw that her father remained impassive. She came to understand that Pedro's wound wouldn't heal. Her mother had commented on the startling physical likeness between Frank and his son, "Like one drop of water resembles another," she said, even so, Frank's eyes seemed not to regard Pedro at all. One night, before drifting off to sleep, her mother told Laura that Frank's blindness to Pedro's mirror likeness to him was the beginning of the self reproach growing in Frank's soul, an aversion to himself he would have to face in this life or the next. Laura recalled that during Pedro's first year in high school, he won a medal at a track meet. Pedro had waited for his father to pause in his long disquisition focused on Laura as to why independence for Puerto Rico was folly. When his father had at last stopped speaking to allow Laura time to respond, Pedro said that he had won a race representing his school, and extended his hand with the medal resting in his palm. Without turning his head, and in the most neutral voice, his father said, "A horse can run." Laura quickly interjected that there was a good chance that Pedro's athletic abilities could win him a scholarship to college. Her father said that Laura was a person of generous sympathies.

While Laura had been obsessed with the imminent danger to Pedro's life, persuading her brother and mother of the only solution she could think of, and going so far as to accompany Pedro to the recruiting station, she had been uncharacteristically forgetful of Sylvia. Then, on the Monday morning when Laura remembered that she'd forgotten Sylvia's fifteenth birthday, Sylvia was ill and couldn't attend school. Laura stood outside the locked bathroom door and heard Sylvia retching. She knocked on the door and called "Sylvia, Sylvia." At last Sylvia unlocked the door and stumbled out. Laura put her hand on Sylvia's forehead; she didn't feel feverish, but she was shaking. Laura put her to bed, covered her with a quilt, adjusted the pillow under her head and said, "You're probably coming down with the flu." Sylvia said, "No, I'm not."

Laura was shocked that it could happen without her sensing something. Her mother, who had sniffed the "strange *muchacho*" on Laura's neck, also had been insensible to what had been happening in Sylvia's life. Consuelo, at the sewing machine announced that "*el damage*" had occurred; Laura was no longer a virgin. Consuelo swayed her head like a fighter trying to shake off a terrific blow, and continued to push the hem of a dress under the swift bobbing needle. After a minute she said that the disgrace of "*el damage*" was one of the hazards of education she'd anticipated. Her smile was an exertion propagating wrinkles up through her cheeks, under her eyes, and a blue vein pulsed in her milky left temple.

They quarreled on and off for the remainder of the week, saying things to each other that shocked them. They wept as they said the terrible things. After her mother had reminded Laura numerous times of the dishonor she had imposed on herself and the family, and repeated that at least she'd bequeathed her daughters the dignity of having been married in a church. Laura asked her mother if she'd ever tried to tally her husband's infinite infidelities. Consuelo sighed and said of her husband, "*Está enamorado de una mujer que nunca ha existido* and all men are unfaithful in this way." By week's end the combatants, exhausted, and a little in awe of each other looked on one another with compassion.

Laura knew her mother had to know; Sylvia was ill in the morning, and when she and Sylvia argued they didn't whisper. Consuelo went to work at the factory, returned, worked at home and remained silent, except when her clients came to the apartment for measurements or to pick up a garment. When Laura attempted to talk to her about Sylvia's condition, her mother screamed, genuflected, and sunk into her chair behind the sewing machine.

It was close to noon, and Sylvia was napping after having been ill. Laura stood at the bedside. After a time she realized that she wanted to sit down. The straight-backed wooden chair felt unaccountably comfortable. She couldn't imagine Sylvia a mother. With her eyes closed, she could see Sylvia hugging herself, standing slightly pigeon-toed, her thin arms across her budding breasts, her long fingers grasping her sides. Sylvia, Laura thought, was a good student or at least a competent one. Her report card was invariably all "A's" and "B's". But when on various occasions Laura asked, "What is your favorite subject; what do you like?" Sylvia could only shrug. But she was interested in Eduardo, the janitor's son, who was nineteen years old. Serious, circumspect, and ambitious he was attending Fordham University on a scholarship. He'd spoken of a future in law and politics. Laura had allowed Eduardo to take Sylvia to the movies. She was stunned; how she could have been so wrong about Eduardo? But if Sylvia had to get in trouble, maybe it was best that it was Eduardo. Sylvia said, "It ain't Eduardo."

However, Sylvia said Felix and Laura reeled. Felix! How could she have forgotten Felix? He'd appeared when they were in seventh grade, one autumn morning in the schoolyard, before the whistle was blown to signal that it was time to stop all play. Laura stood off by herself, looking at the two quarters in her hand, one new and shiny. The money was to pay for that week's school lunches. Felix came up to her and said, "What you got little girl?" Laura closed her hand. He smiled, "What you hidin'?" She said, "None of your business." "Yeah sure, that's 'cause you got nothin'." "I got my lunch money; I'm not a charity case." Felix said, "Oh yeah, at least I was born in this country, and I know you're lyin', and that's why you can't open your hand. You got nothin'." She stuck out her tongue at him and opened her hand. He slapped her hand, the coins flew, and he snatched them out of the air. He turned one cursory glance toward Mr. Cochran, the gym teacher in the far corner of the school yard, breaking up a scuffle between two boys. Felix plunged the coins into his pants' pocket and puckered his lips. "Give me a kiss and I give you the money." Laura said, "You're disgusting." Felix touched his cheek with his forefinger, "Kiss me here." Laura said, "Never." "Laura, *linda un beso aqui.*" She glared at him and he said, "An' I axed you nice." "You better give me my money." "Yeah, what you gonna do, squeal to the teacher?" "No, I'll tell my brother." "Your brother? You don't want me to hurt your little brother." She thought about it. Felix was three years older and a head taller than Pedro. And Pedro didn't know how to back down from a fight. Felix was right. She wouldn't tell her brother.

That week Laura went without lunch. She was very hungry when she got home and gulped down a glass of milk and gobbled fistfuls of bread. During the hungry week she watched Felix reconnoiter the schoolyard; making sure the teacher was preoccupied elsewhere, he stalked the weakest and smallest kids, extorting nickels and inflicting gradations of humiliation.

Within a day of his absence all thought of him vanished, although before his disappearance she heard rumors; a neighbor had heard from her sister-in-law that Felix had stolen money from his foster mother's purse and tormented the woman's ten year old son. Felix was remanded to reform school.

A year later, when Pedro returned from the wake for eleven year old Rafael, he explained that the word "wake" was a recent acquisition; he still heard in his mind, "*velorio*" – the watching; and he and Alfredo, Benny, Louie, Angel, Jesus and Shorty were at the watching. Felix watched also. Rafael, laid out in his coffin wore his Communion suit, his New York Yankees baseball cap, and sun glasses. The apartment was packed; the whole street attending the velorio. On one side of the coffin Rafael's mother, father, and three sisters, sat on kitchen chairs. On the other side, people passed by the coffin one or two at a time to say goodbye and pray. Photographs of Rafael were tacked along the length of the coffin: Rafael the baby in a gown at his baptism, in his mother's arms, Rafael in his Communion suit in front of the church, Rafael on the roof at his uncle Emiliano's pigeon coop. In every photo, except for the one at his baptism, he wore his Yankees baseball cap. Pedro said, "Felix helped. He ran to Rissoto's Ice & Coal Warehouse to bring back more ice to put under the coffin. All of us who saw what really happened said nothin'. But we paid respects to Rafael's family. It should 'a never happened. We was on the pier, watchin' the tugboats on the river. It was terrible hot. We took off our clothes; everythin' but our underpants and dived in. It's a long way down. You go far under and can't see good; the river's dark. Alfredo says the East River is so full of stuff from the medicine factory, the beer breweries, the shoe polish factory and all kind a garbage, that swimmin' in that soup makes us atomic; like we too strong to catch sickness, we don't need no injections. Anyhow, even though Rafael's a little kid we let him tag along. He was too embarrassed to take off his clothes. He said he didn't know how to swim. Said he just wanted to watch. We teased him a little bit, cause we saw he was scared. Man it was hot. Pretty soon we quit teasin' him, jumped into the water and just had a good time. But every time Felix climbed out of the river to the top of the pier, he laughed at Rafael, called him chicken. Kept raggin' the kid. After, Felix swore he was just tryin' to give Rafael confidence. Hardly touched him. More like a pat on the back. We saw Rafael falling. He made a tiny splash and was gone. *Rapido.* We wasn't sure where he sunk. We swam under water searchin'; but he was disappeared. Like maybe it wasn't the river that swallowed him."

Laura couldn't be sure, it could have been a year, maybe longer, after Rafael drowned, and there was Felix walking toward her, and the hiatus since she'd seen him last ceased to exist. She felt his appearance as some failure on her part, a flaw in her character that conjured and drew him to her. He made his customary furtive glances to the left and right; his face a smiling taunt, he spoke to Laura and it seemed that only moments had elapsed since he'd accosted her, and she could still see the coins he'd slapped from her hand spinning in the air. "Someday," he said, "you gonna be my old lady." She said, "You're crazy."

Several days passed and Laura found herself thinking that Felix appeared like a troll in a fairy tale. Within a week, perhaps two, Felix was arrested. She heard two stories: Felix had snatched the purse of an old woman as she stepped out of Luis' Bodega, the strap of the purse twisted and caught around the woman's wrist; the old lady was dragged on the sidewalk, and her arm broken. The talk among the Outlaws disdained Felix; not only was his activity contemptible, he didn't know enough to do his thing in another neighborhood. "You don't shit where you eat," said Alfredo Molina. "And anyway, Felix was never really a member of the Outlaws." The other story was that the police, who knew Felix well, caught him driving a stolen car.

In the intervening four years Laura forgot Felix. Her academic and artistic talent was recognized by her teachers in junior high school, and they encouraged her to apply to the High School of Music and Art. She was accepted and flourished there.

On a night in April of her senior year, when she should have been studying for a history test, she couldn't resist returning to the painting she'd been working on. The source of her composition had come from a family photo. The photograph had been taken shortly after the family's arrival in the United States. Her mother and father posed standing in front of a splendid new automobile that didn't belong to them, their proprietary sense clearly in evidence in their faces, as they now lived in the realm of American optimism. They were dressed in their best clothing, her father was smiling, and Laura saw that even her mother's austerity had been mitigated; she wasn't smiling, but her look was benign, as though she had just awakened from a long and satisfying sleep. In Laura's painting, the windows of the tenements behind her child-like parents were inhabited by a quality of light that made vision possible, and blooming clusters of children cradled their parents in their arms, the fire escapes were copious gardens of corn, the providential plenty vaguely ominous, like the fulfillment of the third wish in a fairy tale, when insatiable desire finally brings doom.

She had worked on the painting all night. The street was dim and silent, and if the inhabitants of the tenements were awake, any sound they made didn't penetrate the tomblike buildings. Laura's footsteps whispered along the pavement. There were few moving vehicles in the street. The shadowed shapes of the buildings and stoop fronts, the sky above and between the roofs began to fade toward light. A low, gyrating whine turned out to be the wheels rotating on the rusted axle of a child's red wagon. The person pulling the wagon was no longer a child. As he came closer she saw that she knew him. Again she had the feeling that some failure of hers drew him to her. Felix greeted her joyfully. In his red wagon was a television set and a pile of dresses. He stopped and his hand went to his crotch, the emblematic touch of his preening was also comforting. Laura stepped back. Felix said, "I been looking for you." "I forgot all about you." "That's okay, see, I'm here now." "But for how long?" As one might touch wood, Felix's hand again went to his testicles with a slight lifting motion and he was reassured. "Don't worry," he said. "You should worry." "I ain't got time for it. Just look at the present I got for you, especial." He held the dress with elaborate lace work across the bodice and gauze-like sleeves up to her shoulders. She took another step back. "*Que linda*," he said. She said, "Not my size." "Take it," he said, "maybe it's gonna fit your sister." She turned and ran. He called after her, "What about a TV?"

Following the dawn when Laura saw Felix moving toward her, pulling his red wagon, she anticipated seeing him again. But it didn't happen. Two or three weeks passed. Now that she thought about him when he was absent, she believed he existed only in memory. The rumors of Felix in the neighborhood marked his maturation into a felon, and graduation from reform school to an adult correction facility. As the memory of Felix faded, Laura tended to think of him (when she thought of him at all) as a creature of sociology, a paradigmatic illustration. Thinking of Felix this way annulled him more thoroughly than any lapse of memory.

⸻

Not until Sylvia said, "Felix" did he exist again. Sylvia's resourcefulness in maintaining the clandestine romance was a shock. It was midweek, Consuelo was at the factory. Sylvia's nausea had abated. Laura made an effort not to sound shrill, but heard the high pitched desperation of her voice. She warned of the danger, the certainty of calamity (providing well known examples to which various people in the neighborhood could testify) and followed Sylvia's gaze to the clock. She realized that she'd been ranting. Her throat hurt and her head ached. Sylvia inched toward the front door. Again Laura attempted to recapitulate what was most important and heard herself begging. Sylvia, crying, cornered in the vestibule, within arm's reach of the door, screamed. Laura attempted to hug her. Sylvia pushed her away and cried, "Felix!" They grappled at the front door. Laura clung to Sylvia's sinewy arm, "Please," she said, "Please." Sylvia screamed, "*Sueltame*," and thrashed against the wall. Laura let go and begged, "Stop, please stop." Sylvia grasped the doorknob. She pushed and the door opened into the hallway leading to the stairs, down to the street, and Felix. Laura

49

swung, stumbled and found herself with her back to Sylvia; her left hand was throbbing. She looked over her shoulder and saw Sylvia sprawled on the hallway floor, her nose bleeding, her eyes lifeless.

Señora Perez from the apartment next door, Lily Rodriguez from across the hall and old Mr. Lopez stood closest to Sylvia's body. Sylvia's howl hadn't been sufficient to bring the neighbors, but Laura's wail carried the unmistakable note of keening, and neighbors were crowding into the hall. Mr. Lopez, head bowed, leaned on his cane. Lily Rodriguez swayed, her hands covered her face. Señora Perez kneeled and tried to rouse Sylvia. Laura heard someone whisper "*Muerta*". She stumbled back into the apartment, made her way to the kitchen where the wall telephone was located, called the police, and said, "I just killed my sister." She gave her name and address, repeated the information, shuffled back to the hallway and stood at the rear of the crowd.

Two policemen preceded the two ambulance attendants who carried a stretcher; one policeman listened to the various accounts of those neighbors willing to talk to him. From what he could gather the sisters had a jealous quarrel about a boyfriend each claimed exclusively and the quarrel had escalated to physical violence. "And," the cop said, "she ran away?" "No, no," several of the neighbors said. They turned and looked around and Laura squeezed between the bodies to the inner circle where the paramedics bent over Sylvia. The younger policeman tried to clear a path to the stairwell. Laura's left hand was throbbing and swollen. She was thankful that she hadn't injured her right hand, the one she used for drawing and painting. She experienced a partial numbness, her thoughts occurring apart from any feeling. She was overcome with fatigue, and also aware that normally the presence of police in her life would have signified the sordidness she loathed. She felt clear in her mind, but her legs would no longer support her. She sat down on the hallway floor next to Sylvia's splayed feet. The paramedics stood up, apparently there was nothing more they could do, and they weren't going to remove the body just yet.One of the paramedics whispered to the older policeman, and they both smiled. Sylvia sat up and rubbed her eyes. There was applause; someone cried, "*milagro*." One of the paramedics removed Sylvia's shoes. She smiled, removed a sock from her foot, and dabbed at the blood dripping from her nose with the sock. Laura sat there, stared at Sylvia wiping blood from her nose, the golden light penetrating the hallway window collected in a radiance around her: and Laura weeping, laid her head in Sylvia's lap. Sylvia stroked her head, and whispered, "Shush, shush *hermana*." Laura lay curled up, her thighs close to her belly, arms wrapped around Sylvia's waist, her head resting on Sylvia's lap. Sylvia caressed her brow, her coiled body; her hand soothed Laura's shuddering away. The older policeman said, "It ain't nice for ladies to fight, you behave now." The younger policeman said, "Definitely." Neither Sylvia nor Laura replied. The medical orderly resting the rolled up stretcher like a flag pole against his shoulder, repeated to Sylvia that she might have a concussion, and it would be best to examine her at the hospital. Sylvia said, "Go ahead; we'll follow you in a cab."Laura mumbled,

"There's money in the pocket of my sweater hanging on the bedroom doorknob." "You're sure," the paramedic said, "you're well enough to get there on your own?" Sylvia said, "Yes, yes," and Laura noted that she ought to be grateful for Sylvia's thoughtfulness, she would have been mortified to arrive at the hospital with a police escort. She was content to lie there, the hallway floor gave back the warmth of her body. Sylvia's skin emitted a peppery aroma and Laura was able to review the events of the previous three weeks as though it was all something she was reading.

When she had asked Sylvia if she felt ready to be a mother, Sylvia said, "No." Then, once more, Laura summarized what she knew of Felix's criminal career and asked, "Can you imagine him a father?" Sylvia, face shining, said, "Wait" and left the room. She returned with a packet of letters. Laura was astonished; they had carried on a correspondence while he was in prison. Sylvia seated herself on the bed, her back against the headboard, legs outstretched, ankles crossed, she loosened the string around the packet of letters and let them fall into her lap. She favored Laura with a tolerant gaze, and plucked a letter from the pile. "Just listen," she said.

Sylvia read the poems Felix had written and dedicated to her. "Forgive me for wanting you so, but I'm burning inside, my heart cries for you, you are the key to my prison door." Laura endured, listened, and recognized the lines Felix had pilfered from popular love songs. Sylvia read, "I'll love you 'til the mountains disappear." Laura foresaw terrible things. Sylvia read, "When you speak, I hear music divine." And

Laura recalled her panic of the previous week. For one day Sylvia had conceded almost everything Laura said. Laura had reminded Sylvia that Felix had already abandoned another teenage girl with whom he'd had a son. She assumed Sylvia knew. Sylvia hadn't known. Stricken, she acquiesced with a nod to everything Laura said. Laura, remembering how her best intentions had lead her to inveigh against love, and advocate that Sylvia kill what was living in her womb, was suddenly fearful, as Sylvia read, "I turn for light to you."

The following day Sylvia's faith in love rebounded; she recanted all she had agreed to and enlisted her mother as advocate. For the first time in years Consuelo didn't go to work. They gathered in the living room where the headless mannequin stood between the mute sewing machine and the blank television screen. Sheaves of white satin were folded and stacked on the couch and on an armchair. Shafts of sunlight came through the two living room windows and played over the large velvet tapestry of President Kennedy's face as over a meadow. Sylvia said that Felix had never before had anyone who truly loved him. Her mother interrupted her and apologized, saying that she loved Sylvia no less than her other children and she was sorry for what she had done. Consuelo asked Sylvia to try to understand. Sylvia had been too young to understand then, but now if she tried she could understand – should understand. Consuelo spoke of herself in the third person. "Your mother was worried about the rent and grocery money. Her husband had disappeared. You were very little, maybe five. You were laughing." Sylvia said, "It's okay, Mami." "Your sister was entertaining you.

You were looking at me and laughing. Laughing, *mi amor.*"
"Mami, I don't remember." Laura said, "I remember." Sylvia
turned to her. Consuelo said, *"Comprende por favor."* Laura
recalled the scrupulous cleaning of the apartment. A lady
was coming, a prospective customer needing a wedding
gown for her daughter. Sylvia, bored, trailed after her big
sister all that afternoon while her mother and sister dusted,
washed the floors, and polished the furniture. Laura worked
and attempted to keep Sylvia amused by telling her stories.
They were in the living room. Laura made funny faces while
on all fours, scrubbing beneath the radiator. Her mother was
removing the newspaper path from the kitchen floor now
that the washing and waxing had dried. Laura crossed her
eyes. Sylvia convulsed with laughter and peed on the floor.
Her mother walked to her, bent over and wiped the puddle
of urine from the floor with a rag. She straightened up and
mashed the piss sodden rag in Sylvia's face. Now Consuelo
said, *"Hija, lo siento mucho,* you don't have to kill your baby,
and I'll make you a wedding dress."

Every time Laura thought she had accepted what she
lacked the power to change, she envisioned some unspeak-
able aspect of her sister's future, and tried again to persuade
her mother to oppose the marriage. She reminded Consuelo
that because Sylvia was only fifteen, she would need her
mother's written permission to marry. Laura said, okay, Sylvia could have the child but that didn't mean she had to
marry Felix. Why should Sylvia tie herself to someone who
would ruin her life? Consuelo said, "They will be married in
church." Laura shouted, "That's stupid! You want her to be a

martyr like you, and put up with a lifetime of abuse? She's too young to know better, but you're the fool who will help destroy her life." "And daughter, you are the egoist who thinks she is boss of the house, and can tell everyone how to live. Go, read a book, paint a picture." Sylvia stood and listened, reassured, she stole glances at her bosom, growing more ample and womanly.

There was little change in the arguments. Back and forth. All week. Each restatement more searing than the last. They were wounded, and strange to each other, and they had seen clearly, unmercifully, one another's failings which they had shouted loud enough for the world to hear. Although Laura continued to believe the truth of all she said, beneath her mother's scrutiny she felt trivial. Finally they were exhausted.

Consuelo, Laura, and Sylvia bundled in bed each night, convalesced, and nursed each other with somnolent caresses. Consuelo slept with her eyes open, her hands traveling like the adept blind making their way through darkness, measuring Sylvia for the wedding gown. In the following days they prepared. Laura and her mother moved around each other shyly, glancing at one another solicitously, but unable to retract a word, or offer any comforting explanation that either could believe. Consuelo worked on the wedding gown. Laura cleaned the apartment, borrowed extra chairs from the neighbors, shopped for food, cooked, and enlisted neighbors to prepare special dishes. She ordered a wedding cake from the bakery. Consuelo made the arrangements with the priest who would conduct the marriage ceremony, and she borrowed two hundred dollars from the Beneficial

Finance Company.

Consuelo negotiated with Alfredo Molina and allowed him to pay for the beer, wine, rum, and the flowers that would decorate the apartment. Alfredo had risen to second in command of The Outlaws, and taken on executive duties, including responsibility for the expanding drug market. Angel, titular head of The Outlaws had moved uptown, and once a week drove to the Lower East Side to confer with Alfredo and the hierarchy of The Outlaws. Alfredo wore at all times, a tie, suit, sported a diamond ring on his pinkie and toured the neighborhood in his Mercedes Benz. He had insisted on taking care of expenses for Pedro's funeral. He'd claimed the privilege as long time family friend, and Pedro's best friend. Consuelo acceded to Alfredo's help with thanks, and was aware that allowing him to act as benefactor was balm for his longing for Laura, although he was living with Maria Diaz, the former Miss Bronx. On his own initiative he found an apartment for Felix and Sylvia in a building just two houses south of the building where Consuelo and Laura lived, and he'd paid the first month's rent and security.

Laura noticed that along with the thick, black mustache Alfredo had grown (which did make him appear older) he'd taken on patrician airs. She thought the manner was another factor that favored her ability to keep him at a distance. As far as she could see, he was esteemed in the neighborhood. The fact that his money came from the heroin trade, which was destroying many young people in the community, didn't seem to detract from people's admiration for his success. And Alfredo had decreed that The Outlaws abandon that name, and remain nameless.

During the weeks leading up to the wedding Sylvia's happiness made her radiant and beautiful, and she moved in an aura of royal prerogative. She observed her mother and sister working at the preparations for the wedding party. Consuelo sewed tiny pearls to the sleeves of her wedding gown. Laura hung paper lanterns in the hall, nailed sconces on the living room wall that housed colored candles; she obscured the cracked ceiling with a rainbow of streamers, and washed, waxed, and buffed the floor to a golden light. The flowers would not arrive until the morning of the wedding. Sylvia's only tasks were to try on the wedding gown as her mother made adjustments, and to attend with Felix counseling sessions with the priest who would marry them. When Felix had occasion to be at the apartment, or when he attended rehearsal for the wedding ceremony at the church, he was polite and courtly. Laura had seen the jailhouse decoration, the demons and angels tattooed on his forearms, the snake creeping above his shirt collar. He read Laura's mind and said with the solemnity of one giving legal testimony, "I'm workin' at the supermarket and payin' for the ring on the installment plan, ax anybody." Consuelo nodded to indicate she'd heard what he'd said. Sylvia held out her left hand, the engagement ring with a small diamond on the finger next to the pinkie, sparked a tiny glow. Laura hoped that what Felix said, and Sylvia believed, signified a caring and respectful marriage. She held her breath as in a baptism that required being plunged into deep, dark water.

Laura sat on the window sill, her legs dangling into the

living room, the rest of her outside, four stories above the street. She gripped the bottom of the frame with her left hand, and with her right, washed the windowpane. A warm breeze blew over her as she peered inside and watched Consuelo stitching Sylvia's tiara. It seemed to Laura that her mother was taking as much time with the tiara as she had with the gown. The telephone was still ringing. Consuelo refused to answer it. Before Laura went to work on the windows, she took the calls and responded to the questions of relatives and friends preparing special dishes, or those inquiring whether they were invited to the church, or the party, or both. Eduardo who had taken Sylvia to the movies several times called to apologize and say he was studying for exams and couldn't attend the wedding; then Eduardo's father, Julio the Janitor called to apologize for his son and said he would be attending the party and promised to bring more chairs. The baker called and the priest called. The muted but persistent ringing of the telephone penetrated the window and for an interminable moment Laura struggled against the compulsion to return inside and answer the phone. When at last the ringing stopped she felt she'd accomplished something. Four stories above the street, with the soles of her bare feet not quite touching the living room floor, her bottom on the sill, and her head and torso outside in the breeze, she floated above the sound of traffic, scraps of music drifting from windows stirred in the wind a meditative whisper and she felt herself borne toward some inevitable understanding. Through the window reflecting the clouds she saw Consuelo in her chair blind to everything but stitching the tiara, the graceful sweep of her hand above her head, thread and needle invisible, her face a propitiating grimace.

Titi, bell-shaped, in an ankle length black frock, her pendulous white braid bouncing off her backside, and not much taller than the two eight year old nieces and a nephew in tow, entered the apartment smiling. No one in the family was required to knock. At Titi's approach doors unlocked themselves. The children chased around the room screaming and laughing. Laura perched on the window sill, her nose an inch from the windowpane, heard the children's shrieking as the first notes of the celebratory bedlam that was only three days away. It occurred to her that she hadn't yet asked her fourth floor neighbors, all of whom were invited to the wedding, if the guests could use their bathrooms; the one bathroom at home was inadequate; four bathrooms would almost suffice. She didn't doubt that her neighbors would oblige, but she did have to ask beforehand. Looking through the window she caught Titi's eye and blew her a kiss. Titi nodded yes and held her sister's hands still. The phone was ringing. "Francisco," announced Titi. Consuelo hesitated. Titi said, *"Si, si verdad, es Francisco."* Consuelo rose to her feet, placed the tiara on the table and marched to the telephone. Stoically, she listened. Unable to believe in the efficacy of the instrument she held to her ear, she shouted into the speaker, "Ay Elena, I have more important things to worry about, adios." She then walked to the hallway closet, took out the lavender spring coat she'd made for herself and left.

That night Consuelo, Laura, and Sylvia lay in the king sized bed that would have to be dismantled and stored in a neighbor's apartment to make room for the wedding guests. Laura thought, amazed yet again, that Titi was correct, it was her father calling; although it was Mami's cousin Elena on the other end of the line. After so many years Laura only knew Elena as a fantasma of one of her mother's least told tales. Nevertheless, it was Papi, present all at once, by means of Elena, by way of Carmen, Papi's most recent paramour, all foretold by Titi. As best as Laura could remember, her father had only come to see her mother once the previous year, and not yet this year, already half gone.

Sylvia snored and recoiled as Laura adjusted her pillow, as if her sister's touch would deprive her of the realm of sleep. Laura sat up in the bed, unable to sleep, listening. As Consuelo dozed, she cursed Elena, not calling her a whore, but a weakling and a contagion of calamity, who would pollute Purgatory and Heaven so that the only accommodation that could abide her without contamination was Hell.

Consuelo communed with herself, and Laura feeling once more like the child she'd once been, eavesdropped; her mother said that it was an early betrayal, the marriage was still young. The pain that continued to the present day might be dormant two, perhaps three days in a week, but was never completely absent. Consuelo, interrogatory, then importuning admitted that she'd contributed to her own humiliation. She and Cousin Elena had been childhood friends. When Elena, her husband Nestor, and their two little boys moved from Puerto Rico to New York, Consuelo found an apartment for them. In the first job Consuelo found outside of her home, at the pants factory, she recommended Nestor to her boss, Mr. Neussbaum, who valued her judgment, and Nestor was taken on as a presser. He made good money. A month later Nestor disappeared with a woman from the factory and Consuelo felt sorry for Elena. Often she took care of Elena's two little boys. She couldn't bear the thought of the children being hungry and sent Francisco to Elena's house with boxes of groceries.

The drone of the sewing machines stopped. She had been struggling with a zipper as if her hands had lost their wits in anticipation of what the floorlady, Angelica was about to tell her. Standing behind her, bending to her ear, Angelica said, "Lunch break, hurry, you can catch him there." Consuelo looked at the clock; she had twenty-seven minutes before she'd have to be back to work. Elena's apartment was one block away on East Broadway. One block there, five flights up, five flights down, and one block back. She'd have to run. And there was the difficulty of El Bosso. Mr. Neussbaum wasn't a bad boss. The ladies were on salary, not piece work. Everyone was paid time and a half for any week that exceeded forty hours; but there were no rest periods, the lunch break was a half hour, and Consuelo had seen how desperate Mr. Neussbaum looked when any of the ladies went to the bathroom; every minute a lady was away from her sewing machine was torture for him. It was obscene, Consuelo thought, to see a man so desperate. Angelica said, "*Avansa.*" Consuelo couldn't decide whether she herself was the fool, the only woman in the factory who didn't know, or a coward who didn't want to know. Again Angelica said, "*Avansa,*" and patted her shoulder. Consuelo, on her feet, decided that Angelica, always the bearer of bad news was gratified by what she conveyed, not because she was malicious, but because disasters yield piety.

She ran all the way. Breathing heavy after the five flight climb, she pushed the door which opened on the sparsely furnished kitchen. Consuelo took in the room as though seeing it for the first time. She didn't remember the peach colored walls. There was the small folding table and two kitchen chairs. No dishes in the immaculate sink, no curtains on the window. There were neither images of saints, nor a crucifix, nor a clock on any of the walls. She wondered where Elena's two boys were and then recalled that they would be in school. A radio from one of the two adjoining rooms was playing a lamenting ballad. Yesterday Frank had come home late in the evening, and there were stains of peach colored paint on the knees of his trousers. The odor of the freshly painted walls mixed with the scent of Frank's cologne pervaded the air like the coming of bad weather. Elena, standing next to the caribbean blue ice box, wore a tight red dress. She was barefoot, her toenails painted silver. Consuelo thought her a pretty woman with a mournfully provocative face. Elena said, "I regret the loss of our friend-ship." Consuelo waved her hand in the air as though sweep-ing away a trifle. Elena said, "*Quiere café?*" Consuelo could not find her voice. "He left minutes ago," said Elena; "Frank comes and goes as he pleases." Consuelo thought, yes, there are days when he doesn't bother to open the shoe repair shop. He is a free man. I feed our children. Elena said, "Frank is his own boss. He said he never married you."

Later, at the factory, Angelica and the other women told her she'd returned to work with a minute to spare. Consuelo remembered it as the women had told it to her. Titi, who knew almost everyone who lived in Elena's building, most of them being relatives, told Consuelo that she had acted with dignity. And she agreed that Consuelo's returning the next day and showing Elena the marriage certificate proclaiming Consuelo Alvarez Vega, the wife of Francisco Rivera was what honor required. Moreover, Consuelo's discreetly leaving the ten dollar bill on the kitchen chair for the children's sake was the act of a Christian lady. Titi assured her sister that the calumny that Consuelo had threatened Elena, pressing a fork to her throat was promulgated by Elena's side of the family, people incapable of believing anything but their own lies. Consuelo believed Titi. She trusted what the women in the factory had told her. And that was the way she remembered it, having forgotten that she had forgotten, or had been extinguished the moment Elena said, "He said he never married you." The following minutes and hours, that afternoon and night obliterated until restored by Titi's repeated recitations. The obliteration itself worn away as rocks washed by an eternal ocean.

Consuelo couldn't forget that when she answered the phone the voice was that of the young Elena. She'd said, "Frank needs you." Again Consuelo waved her hand in a farewell gesture, this time to decline her place in the episode of the everlasting novella that would return her to the kitchen with the peach colored walls. The voice of young Elena conjured the miasma of the kitchen, and a vision of

Elena as an oracular vapor in a red dress with toenails like mirrors, who had, after all, provided reliable information.

Carmen, Elena's niece, a woman half Frank's age, was waiting just where Elena said Consuelo would find her, in front of the shoe repair shop. Consuelo approaching the young woman on the street she'd avoided for twenty-five years, felt her return as destiny's retaliation, instigated no doubt by Elena, or Elena's mother. And there was the shoe repair shop, where Frank restored the shoes of his female clientele setting their feet moving toward him, a pied piper not enticing them to doom, but to care for him, pleasure him until it was no longer a pleasure for them or him; and he engendered a score of children and unfailing chaos which would teach the children to be resourceful.

As Consuelo came closer to the young woman, she saw that this Carmen's resemblance to Laura was superficial, and she was relieved. Pretty, dark complexioned, Carmen held two fat books to her chest, offered no salutation and looked like she was about to cry. Consuelo said, "I am Señora Consuelo Alvarez Vega, the wife of Francisco." Carmen nodded her head toward the shoe repair shop behind them. "He," she said, and her voice petered out. Consuelo said, "I know, he is in the apartment behind the shop." Carmen hiccuped. Consuelo cooed a deep, soft sound, innocent as a moan, a mother coaxing a child to sleep. At last, Carmen said, "I can't anymore. It is barbarous but I must be strong." Consuelo said, "*No te apures mi amor*, I understand. You are a student." "Yes again, after five years. I have a class this evening." "What are you studying?" "Someday I hope to be a nurse. And I have taken care of Frank; he will tell you that himself. Pero now, he needs too much." Carmen held the text books before her like a shield and swayed on her feet. Consuelo embraced her, and Carmen holding the books as a wedge between them, allowed her head to rest, briefly, on Consuelo's shoulder. Consuelo almost said "daughter", and Carmen hearing the thought, and wanting to be more precise explained, "Everyone concerned with my honor, mami, papi, my brothers, uncles, and Enrique." She laughed. Consuelo said *"Mi amor"* and felt suddenly as if somehow she'd had a hand in the things that had oppressed the young woman's life.

Carmen recounted her life, the telling itself making distance. Consuelo listened, as anonymous as a priest, knowing and tolerant; she was attentive and intimate as only an ordained stranger might be.

Nothing Consuelo learned surprised her. Cousin Elena had introduced Carmen to Frank at a party. He was immediately obsessed with the girl who was not quite sixteen. Carmen noticed Frank's uncanny resemblance to her uncle Luis. But Frank was different from Uncle Luis; he was gallant, courtly, even when besotted. Elena had also introduced Frank to Carmen's husband, Enrique.

Carmen was not sure how Frank found out that she and Enrique would be at Club Paraiso. Perhaps his presence there was coincidental. The place was crowded. The dance floor packed. Enrique and his friends Ernesto and Miguel had just returned from the bar when Frank came up to their table. It was clear that he had also been drinking. He ignored

Carmen's husband Enrique, didn't bother to ask his permission, but asked Carmen to dance. Enrique, Ernesto, and Miguel were incredulous. Frank bowed extravagantly and again asked Carmen to dance. Alarmed, she declined. He recited a poem. She heard the rhyme but not the words, as her husband and his friends dragged Frank away.

Enrique and his *compañeros* kicked Frank down two flights of stairs. Carmen considered that Enrique had only danced with her once, when they had first arrived. For most of the night her husband remained at the bar drinking with his friends. Though many men looked at her, not one asked her to dance. She sat alone. The hours passed. The band was very fine and she enjoyed the music but longed to dance. Close to midnight an older woman, similarly abandoned, asked Carmen to dance. They danced together for about a half hour, thanked one another demurely, and returned to their tables. Carmen hoped that Frank was not seriously hurt; thinking about him brought Uncle Luis to mind. It was after one in the morning and she thought she wouldn't wait much longer, but would go to the bar and tell Enrique that she wanted to go home. It was then that she saw the man with regal bearing, wearing what looked like a turban, approaching her. Frank, with his head wrapped in bandages and one arm in a sling stood before her. He took his arm out of the sling, bowed, and asked her to dance. She begged him to go. "Please," she said, "now things will get serious." He refused to leave until she consented to meet him the next day for coffee.

Carmen became suspicious when Enrique became less

vigilant, then indifferent; finally, without a farewell he moved into his girlfriend's apartment in El Barrio. Carmen was relieved, it seemed that neither she nor Frank would be casualties of their romance. The anticipation of violence that had lived in her stomach quieted. Although Frank's gentle touch sometimes precipitated the vision of her father throwing Uncle Luis off the roof. She saw it, again and again. Papi, legs bent at the knees, arms over his head like an acrobat who had just launched his partner into the air; Uncle Luis fell, arms flapping, legs churning like a clown on a unicycle. She was sorry she told. She'd been playing on the roof, as usual with Mami and Papi's permission; and she was a little embarrassed to still be playing with dolls now that she was almost fourteen. It was a humid Sunday in August. The occluded sun stewing in the clouds. Uncle Luis who lived in the same building was also on the roof enjoying the scant breezes and the canopy of shade cast by the towering seltzer bottle factory. Uncle Luis was affectionate. He often hugged her. She liked Uncle Luis, but this time he touched her where he shouldn't have. She knew he wasn't supposed to touch her there. She was not frightened; she picked up her favorite doll, walked down one flight, opened the door into the kitchen and told Papi, as she knew a good girl must. Papi, like Father Logan, who spoke excellent Spanish, demanded to know everything. Papi didn't say a word. He put his can of beer down on the kitchen table, ran out of the apartment and up the stairs to the roof. She followed him. She thought Papi would scold Uncle Luis as Father Logan scolded her when she confessed that she'd touched herself where she shouldn't have. Sometimes Papi came into her bedroom at night. It was darker than in the confessional. She made believe she was sleeping. Through the slits of her eyes, she could make out Papi's trembling hand. His hand came close to touching her where it shouldn't, but didn't. Some nights she fell asleep waiting.

"Señora," Carmen said, "I tell you what I didn't tell Frank, never told anyone. *Por favor*, understand, I no longer confess. I'm Pentecostal. I clap, shout, dance, but I don't confess. Anyway, Mami was upset when I left the Catholic Church. I don't know if she confessed; but I know, like the others in the building who knew Uncle Luis hadn't fallen from the roof, Mami lied, me too, everybody, all of us told the police it was an accident. After that day we didn't talk about it. But a year later it almost happened; I thought we would speak of it. It was after the party for my fifteenth year. I got a lot of presents. Papi bought me a wrist watch. The guests had left, neighbors, aunts, uncles, cousins, everybody, and Papi's friend Enrique. Mami said, I must speak to you of a serious matter. Papi stood close by also looking serious. I thought that Mami was about to say something about what happened on the roof. Uncle Luis was Mami's favorite brother. First Mami said that because it was my special day I didn't have to wash the dishes. Papi told my brothers, Paco, Hector and Jose to go play in the street even though they were still wearing their good clothes. Mami lowered her voice, although there were only the three of us in the kitchen. She said that now I was fifteen, and had actually been a señorita since I was fourteen. Also I was a great temptation to men. One must respect the dangers that nature presents. The time had come for the protection and the honor that marriage could provide. Papi nodded his head vigorously, in agreement.

And this is the one thing I haven't told Frank. This secret and one thing more; when he touches me, I see Uncle Luis falling from the roof. Uncle Luis was Mami's favorite brother, and my favorite uncle. And, see, there have been no lies between Frank and me; only this, which I've kept hidden, and it is now, a burden. Truly, for two of the three years I've been with Frank, I've been happy. He is a sweet and sympathetic man. I'm not a jealous person. He told me without remorse, that in the three years we've been together he's only been with another woman two times, each time with a different one. And oh, Señora, he said he respects you, as he did his mother, that much. He said you are formidable, wrapped too tight to weep, he's never seen you cry and he never cries, though he yells and breaks things. As Elena no doubt told you, he cannot leave the apartment unassisted. Three months ago he could no longer tell day from night. What little vision he has is completely dependent on memory, which he distrusts. He cannot handle a knife well enough to cut a slice of bread from a loaf. He can't pour coffee from a pot into a cup. He has difficulty finding his mouth with a spoon, spills food on himself, and rages, flinging whatever his hands find, smashing things, and often he falls to the floor. Standing a foot in front of him, I am a shadow within a shadow. When at last he accepts the help I offer, it is for him, a bitter surrender. Then, after a time he will ask me to describe myself. I try and he denounces me; he says that if I truly loved him I'd find the words that would allow him to envision me. He is drowning in darkness. Recently he accepted the cane I bought for him months ago, and at last consented to see a doctor. He calls doctors "death's ambassadors", and believes he'll live longer if he avoids them. The only reason he finally agreed to see a doctor, is because the knee he injured in a fall would not heal, and the pain he'd endured for six months had become unendurable; neither aspirin nor rum brought relief. The doctor prescribed a medicine that obscures the pain, and calms him, but leaves him confused. The doctor said Frank's knee requires surgery; he also took blood from Frank and explained that Frank is diabetic, and this has led to an infirmity called glaucoma, which has deprived him of his sight. Frank will not be able to attend his daughter's wedding without assistance. This is why Elena called you. Now I must hurry. I must take a test. If I pass I'll receive my high school diploma."

—∿—

The velvet tapestry of President Kennedy, the sewing machine and the mannequin were stored in a neighbor's apartment. The picture of Jesus with his heart aflame remained on the wall. The four foot statue of the Virgin Mary, who appeared to be praying for the celebrants, stood catty-cornered and adjacent to the sideboard loaded with food and drink. The apartment was crowded with guests. Laura hardly recognized the room she created. She had distributed flowers in vases and under the cardboard trellises she had made and taped to the walls of the living room. Paper lanterns were hung about the borders of the ceiling. The colored light bulbs, the candles on sconces on the two walls without the trellises cast rose and butter colored shadows, the rainbow of streamers just below the ceiling, the breathing belly of heaven. Many people were smoking and Laura hoped the place wouldn't catch fire. She sat in a chair, tired, and steeped in a vigil, studying the scene as she would a painting, waiting for it to confide its secrets. She sipped her third glass of wine, more than she had ever drunk before, and watched the fluid movements of the dancers, the different shapes and sizes of their bodies, the colored shadows following them. She heard the joyous blare of trumpets, a mambo coming from the phonograph; in the hallway two young men pounded bongos and a conga drum. The contrapuntal rhythm melded the multitude of laughing voices. The party spilled out into the hallway and a nearby apartment. Some of the guests had climbed out of the living room window with plates of food and cans of beer and sat on the firescape. They called to people passing on the street and invited them to the party.

Hidden in a cluster of men studying Laura, close enough to hear her, I couldn't bear being identified as just another male of the species, scheming how to differentiate myself from all the others. Laura studied her father. Later she would say that his hair wasn't any grayer, nor had his features changed, yet he appeared old. Perhaps it was the cane, and his tentative movements. In his blindness his gestures resembled Consuelo's hands searching the air as she slept with her eyes open. Her father said, "Laura, do you see your cousin Rita?" Laura spotted her dancing with a young man she recognized, but whose name she didn't know. She was about to say "Yes Papi", when her mother said, "*Ay*, I see her; oh Frank she's grown so fat, she looks like a pig." Her father continued to question Consuelo about the pretty women in the family. She described each one as having suffered some blight, turning them ugly.

There was applause, and the crowd of dancers parted, clearing a space; and there, at the center the bride and groom danced. The guests applauded Felix and Sylvia executing the most intricate steps within a three foot radius which their grace made spacious. Watching the splendid couple dancing, Laura was struck by the absurdity of her intrusion. However horrific the bride and groom's future, they were also subject to the power of their beauty; their dance, Laura thought, also attesting to their ephemeral glory.

And I was there. Laura had invited me. She said, "Come if you want to" – a dubious invitation. In the two months leading up to the wedding I'd only seen her twice. On the telephone she sounded harried. Late one Sunday afternoon she showed up at my apartment. I was glad, relieved to see her. She explained, "I'm busy; busy, busy." We went to bed. She told me a little about what was going on. I learned more, months and years later. When she spoke of the things that concerned us it was as though I were part of a story she was telling somebody else. I held her, she cried and fell asleep.

She woke an hour later and left. The second time she visited I embraced her the moment she came through the door and began to unbutton her blouse. Her sigh of enduring patience stopped me. Then, looking apologetic, she started to slip out of her skirt. I said, "It's okay," and we sat on the couch. Laura's part in our minute long embrace was strenuous.

Nevertheless, I attended the wedding party, as a quasi ghost. Still, the guests greeted me decorously. Laura had introduced me to her parents, and they acknowledged me politely, as one of the guests they were unacquainted with, welcome in the expansive beneficence that seemed to be sweeping up everyone in the neighborhood. Consuelo's dignity was more an aura than deportment. There wasn't a hint that she recognized me as the muchacho who had committed *el damage*. Laura's father sat in an armless wooden chair nodding greetings to people he couldn't see. Consuelo stood beside him and repeated, "*Encantada*" to all who danced by or paused to embrace her, Frank and Laura. I hovered near Laura's side. She said, "Titi," and inclined her head in the direction of a small round, white haired woman in a grey dress, moving among the guests, chiding and caressing children, admonishing men; just as Laura had described her; Titi, buoyant in her sovereign circuits, ameliorating the manmade world.

I'd had a lot to drink and wandered about the party, silent, anonymous, watching. I entered a room filled with middle-aged, and old women. I was the only male in the room. All the other men and boys were outside dancing with or watching the young women. The aging women, forgotten, having their own party, danced with one another to a rumba playing on a portable phonograph set on a coffee table. They ate, drank, and seemed to be having a fine time. As I came through the door they applauded. I said, *"Encantado."* A large, wide woman swamped me in a hug. She said, "I'm the widow Gracia," sat me down in an arm chair, and brought me a plate of ink-colored rice with what turned out to be diced squid. It was delicious. The women told stories to each other, laughed and cried. A woman somewhere in the room, amending Gracia's recitation shouted, "Gracia is the widow of Juan, Arturo, and Manuel. Pepe the poet built a hut with a door too small for Gracia to enter. When she squeezed through a window he ran away." Gracia laughed and her three chins, mountainous bosom, and the hanging flesh of her upper arms trembled. I finished eating and she took the plate from my lap and brought me a glass of beer. I drank the beer. Gracia took the empty glass from my hand and said, *"Baile."* I said, "I'm sorry, I don't know how to dance." She pulled me to my feet, and enveloped me. Cushioned and surrounded by Gracia, I felt tremors of movement, symbiotic undulations, and I no longer worried about where to put my feet. She said, *"Si muchacho, rumba."* In a whisper heard throughout the room Gracia told me that in her previous life her allure drove men wild, including a village priest whose day and night dreams of making love to her destroyed his vocation, but deepened his appreciation of God. Pressed against her I said that I too was grateful. She said she could feel my sincerity. Obedient, weightless, we let the music move us amid the swaying thickets of ripe and aged women. The walls slid along with the framed pictures of St. Lucia offering her eyes on a plate to God, St. Jerome and his loitering lions, and Jesus perched on a wave of the Galilee, all dancing as Gracia rumbaed me out the door.

The bride and groom disappeared. The crowd thinned out. I stood in plain view of Laura, and Alfredo, whom I might have been introduced to. Laura hadn't said a word about him. When she did I recalled a tall, handsome black man in a white suit, white shirt and white tie, presiding over the sideboard, dispensing glasses of wine and plates of cake with the elegant gestures of a magician. Two smiling old women passed me carrying plates heaped with cake. One glanced back at Alfredo and said to her friend, "The pope." The other said, "Like a fly in a glass of milk."

I turned toward the shouting. Titi, knowing where political argument could go hurried to the sideboard and wedged herself between the two men, one middle-aged and stout, the other tall and quite young. The debate, the little I heard of it, concerned Puerto Rico's status vis a vis the United States. The young man in the blue suit, hands in his pants' pockets, said contemptuously, "Of course *Señor*, we'll be saved by the Chamber of Commerce or not at all." Titi crammed between the two men, bent over the sideboard, grabbed the knives and threw them out the open window. The debaters recoiled from her hips. Alfredo, behind the sideboard, ducked. The guests sitting out on the fire escape covered their heads with their arms as the cutlery rained down. There was a suspension of voices and only the bolero coming from the phonograph, and the congeros in the hallway thumping the drums, the melodic pulse of the protracted seconds until the knives chimed off the sidewalk.

—∿—

The baby was born seven months later. Felix insisted that his son be named Felix Junior; Sylvia agreed, but bargained that her son's middle name be Carlos, for her maternal grandfather. Felix called his son Junior, Consuelo and Laura called him Carlitos, and Sylvia called him Nene. Consuelo cooked Frank's favorite dishes and accompanied him on walks. Frank tried to retain the vision of the lovely women he had known, but lost them in the dark, as he receded into sorrow. Laura dropped out of City College and attended the Art Students League three nights a week. She would devote the year to exploring the shades of one warm color and one cool color; and she worked part time in a bookstore in Greenwich Village. Felix had been working at the supermarket four months when the manager, Mr. Romero, impressed with his diligence and knowing that Felix would soon be a father, offered him management of the produce section and gave him a raise. Felix had been manager of the produce section for two months when his co-workers began to gossip about his standing in a trance and scratching himself, or disappearing into the bathroom for long intervals. Customers complained that various fruits and vegetables that they'd always been able to find were unavailable. Mr. Romero spoke to Felix about being more steadfast in his duties. Felix was agreeable. Three weeks later the manager was still getting complaints from customers and his staff. Mr. Romero said he was sorry, but fired Felix, who appeared to be asleep on his feet.

When Sylvia came home from the hospital with the baby, Felix was still unemployed. For a while they got by on his unemployment insurance and Consuelo and Laura's contributions. But when Sylvia searched the dish cabinet she found that the money disappeared almost as soon as it arrived. Felix suggested that she report to a social worker that her husband had deserted her, and sign up for welfare. In the evening Sylvia took the baby and visited her mother. She told Consuelo what Felix suggested. Consuelo cried, "*Por favor*, no! To live on the *cuento* is a disgrace. He must find work. In the meantime your sister and I will help."

Felix continued to argue that Sylvia sign up for welfare. One afternoon when the baby refused to nap and cried, and Sylvia told Felix to lower his voice, he slapped her. He apologized immediately, and was remorseful and tender.

Some weeks later, Sylvia looked in her slipper for the grocery money she'd hidden there and it was gone. She screamed, "Junkie!" at Felix and he hit her again.

Sylvia stopped visiting her mother and sister. After four days had passed, Consuelo walked to her daughter's door and knocked. Sylvia opened the door a crack and said, "The baby is sleeping." Consuelo couldn't make out her daughter's face in the narrow crack. Sylvia started to push the door and Consuelo quickly slipped the envelope with money in it into the narrowing gap, and managed to pull her hand out before the door slammed on her fingers.

The next evening Consuelo asked Laura to accompany her. They took turns knocking and they heard muttering on the other side of the door. They cried, "Sylvia, Sylvia, *por favor!*" Tenants climbing up or down on the stairs glanced at them knowingly.

Two days later, Señora Gomez, a friend of Consuelo's, who lived across the hall from Sylvia visited Consuelo and told her that she heard Sylvia crying. Consuelo and Señora Gomez rushed out and down five flights of stairs, ran the short distance to Señora Gomez's building, scrambled up two flights of stairs, and pounded on Sylvia's door as though they were the police. Señora Gomez deepened her gravelly voice and shouted, "Open up." The door opened and Sylvia stood there, the baby in her arms; one of Sylvia's eyes was swollen shut, and her cheek was bruised. Consuelo stood there and shivered, and then said to the grotesque girl who didn't resemble her daughter, "We must call the police." She peered into the apartment. Felix was not at home. Sylvia lifted the baby to her shoulder, patted his back and said, "Me and Felix can take care of our own problems." Señora Gomez turned to Consuelo and said, "She has to be willing to sign a complaint."

That night Consuelo prayed for Felix's death. Frank snored. She considered *La Bruja Rubia*; but potions and spells took time. She thought of the tragedy of Señora Diego's daughter. She had married a young man of sincere intentions who could not overcome his addiction and eventually Señora Diego's daughter succumbed to her husband's blandishments, tried the drug, became addicted, and sold herself to support both their habits. That girl had died or been killed before her twenty-first year. There were many such stories. Consuelo was awake all night. She reviewed the fate awaiting her daughter.

Laura hadn't slept well. She saw Sylvia as her mother had described her. She thought that she'd make a complaint to the police despite Sylvia's wishes, but Sylvia would have to sign a complaint to get a restraining order against Felix. Then she remembered Alfredo. All she needed to do was ask. He would help. But she wasn't sure she'd be able to ask, and she didn't want to think about what asking would mean.

In the morning Consuelo served coffee and toast to Frank in bed. She and Laura sat down at the kitchen table, sipped coffee and stared at one another. They both began to speak at once. They exchanged what each had thought throughout the night, not because they didn't know the other's thoughts, but to prolong the hesitation, although they spoke with haste. They repeated their justifications, which they expressed as the narrative of what had happened to Sylvia. Laura felt her own reluctance, and let her mother persuade her. "Go, go now," Consuelo said, "You know where his office is?" Laura had never been there, but she knew which street, which building.

The office was an apartment in a grand building with an elevator and a canopy out front about nine blocks west of where Laura lived. Maria Diaz, the former Miss Bronx answered the door, seated Laura on a white leather couch and left the room. About a half hour later she returned, served coffee and cake and asked Laura if she'd like a cognac. Laura declined and Maria left. Laura recalled that she hadn't seen Maria at Sylvia's wedding. For a moment she was tempted to remind her that she had been invited. But such an assertion, Laura knew, would only betray her nervousness. She also realized that in all the years she knew Alfredo, this was the first time she'd sought him out. She waited for a long time in the room with white and pink leather furniture, white carpet, a bar, gilded mirrors on the walls, and a golden chandelier hanging from the ceiling embossed with moon and stars.

At last Maria Diaz ushered Laura into Alfredo's office and left. Alfredo sat behind a massive desk in a spartan room containing a metal filing cabinet, a table with an electric type-writer, a wooden chair, and a club chair into which Laura lowered herself. "Laura," Alfredo said, rising out of his chair, "*encantado.*" She was unable to speak. Seeing her difficulty he talked about the wedding. He joked about hiring her to paint a mural. She remained silent. He laughed and said that Maria had presided over the decoration of the apart-ment and her taste was abominable. Finally he said, "You have a problem." She said, "Yes." He said, "Felix." She nod-ded. He said, "There's little that happens in the Barrio that I don't know. And you want me to fix the problem." She said, "Yes," and felt herself trembling inside. Alfredo began to describe all the things that had happened to Sylvia, slow and in detail, and he ventured to say how Laura felt about it. His voice was coaxing, like a judge who wanted to make sure he had all the facts right. Then he said he needed Laura to tell it in her own words. She didn't know where to begin, but thought that in all the years of Alfredo's gifts he'd remained circumspect, honorably distant. Now she reminded herself that she'd never before explicitly asked for his assistance, and certainly never attempted to be charming when in need of help; nevertheless his gifts and assistance were always opportune. "So?" he said, waiting. Laura described her sister's marriage. Alfredo's manner was didactic, his face close to something like a leer. Laura continued, shrinking into the story she was telling. Alfredo interrupted her from time to time, he said, to be sure she wanted him to take care of her problem. Laura tired of the story, its sordidness made her feel ill, and finally she thought the intimacy Alfredo imposed was her recognition of what his taking care of the problem would mean. And this, she saw in his face, was more satisfying to him than the deepest touch.

A day later, Felix was found dead on the landing just below the apartment where he had lived. The police said he'd died of an apparent overdose. The chief detective said he was sorry, but he needed Sylvia to make a positive identification. She followed him down the stairs. A policewoman stayed in the apartment watching Carlitos asleep in his crib. The landing was crowded with neighbors. She recognized the janitor and his wife, and Señora Gomez. Felix half lay, half sat, his back propped against the wall. He wore a beret, and had grown a beard. Sylvia stared at him. The detective waited for her to identify her husband. Sylvia bent over to get a better look. Once again she recognized him in the Che Guevara disguise, grabbed his beard with both hands and slammed his head against the wall; the beret fell and his body slipped to the floor. Two policemen struggled to pull her away.

The scream that had taken her wouldn't quit; the yelp in it, the sound of a language she didn't yet understand. Señora Gomez volunteered to take care of the baby, and the police-woman and another officer took Sylvia to Bellevue Hospital.

Consuelo arranged for Frank and Laura to exchange beds. Laura lay beside her mother, baby Carlitos slept, his face pillowed on his grandmother's bosom, sucking his thumb. Light from the votive candle slid over the bottles, cans of formula, and a pile of cloth diapers on the dresser. Laura could hear her father's cane tapping as he'd risen from bed and was finding his way to the bathroom. Consuelo was whispering, repeating that the doctor at the hospital had said that Sylvia might be able to come home in a day or two, he couldn't be sure, it might take longer. Consuelo waited for Laura to respond. Laura wanted to, but speaking seemed to require an enormous effort, as anything she might say about anything would be perfunctory. Consuelo said, "Don't worry daughter, I absolve you, and God will absolve me."

In The Park

"Herbie is a little slow," his mother, Sophie Mintz hollered, "and nobody should take advantage." And in case anyone should forget, as she tended to as the day wore on, she'd thrust her head from the fourth story window, and yell, "Herbie, Herbie." When he didn't respond, she shrieked, "Swifty, Swifty!"

No one could remember who named twelve year old Herbert "Swifty". None of the street's wits claimed credit. The nicknaming, a baptism, during which his head was doused with cream soda, flooded recall and Swifty had difficulty remembering that his name had been Herbert. This was a time when truth couldn't be veiled by euphemism, and on the same street lived Frankie-One-Eye, Sammy the Gimp, Moshe the Gonnif, and Vinnie Pazzo.

Swifty's father, Sol, wasn't so much taciturn as overwhelmed by the one great truth of his life; to all questions he answered, "I make a living." The statement had sufficed for a marriage proposal, and if there were greetings or inquiries that required mouthing something more, he never noticed; but, when confronted with a question regarding a plumbing problem, his trade, he would describe in vivid detail, clogged pipes, and sewage flow, recreating, when words failed, the sound of unimpeded water, the flushing of a toilet.

Old man Levine, weathered into the stone stoop, rested his head on his arthritic fist grasping the handle of his cane, and said to Sophie Mintz on various occasions, "Not to worry Sophie, Swifty lives in God's time." Swifty, lingering under the blows of astonishment, eyes and mouth agape, stared at the luminescent marble in the palm of his hand. The boy he was playing with crouched at the curb, one knee on the pavement, the other lowered on the asphalt, his shadow straddling the pavement and the gutter. He squinted, forefinger and thumb cocked, aimed, and shot his marble, a red jumbo. He looked up and called, "Swifty, yo Swifty." Swifty studied the marble in the palm of his hand. He heard faintly, "Swifty, yo Swifty," as his vision gathered in a mother further down the street squatting at the edge of the pavement and holding between her knees, a baby girl above the curb, the child's dress gathered up, panties around her ankles, the palms of the mother's hands cradled the undersides of the kid's thighs; the little girl's legs, from the knees down, dangled; her bare bottom hovered over the curb and she peed. The vision of the golden rivulet trickling down obscured Petey's claim on Swifty's attention.

Regarding stick-ball, Swifty could hit when he remembered to swing. One day he connected with what looked like a two sewer home run; the ball flew high and arched, floating between roof tops and Swifty stood watching the ball chase a cloud. The other boys were shouting for him to run the bases. He stood and watched. A teammate shoved him. He stumbled, regained his footing and examined the sky. His teammates yelled. He heard a voice he was susceptible to, loped suddenly, and was nearly hit by a car. The vehicle veered toward the opposite curb and screeched to a stop. Swifty hardly noticed, never rounding third he continued to trot straight down the middle of the street and followed the cloud that had swallowed the ball until he and the cloud disappeared in the vicinity of the docks. When his mother remembered him, and cried, "Herbie – *oy* – Swifty," from the window, and there was no reply, neighbors pointed in the direction where Swifty had run until he was an illusion dwindling into the haze near the East River. Sophie charged down four flights of stairs screaming out of the building and searched for her son. Swifty perambulated in a mystery. Sophie and Swifty's circuits traversed, although they never met. Later at night, they encountered one another in the apartment. Sophie wept with relief, Swifty wept in sympathy.

On a Saturday late in the autumn the scent of snow could be detected among the smells of the shoe polish factory, the sugar factory, and the beer brewery. A group of boys had gathered to choose sides for a game of punch ball. Swifty wouldn't be chosen to play on either team. He stood, unperturbed, staring at Cosmo Leznick. Cosmo studying the dregs twisted his mouth in distaste, any selection foreordained defeat. Cosmo pointed to a boy staring at his feet, standing next to Swifty. Swifty, mouth agape, in what may have been taken for a smile, stood, his vision riveted on

Cosmo. During the choosing of sides Cosmo had been scratching his crotch. He interpreted Swifty's smile as presumption, unspoken, but plain enough, and Cosmo wouldn't endure the insult alluding to his family's hygiene. He stopped scratching and popped Swifty. Swifty blinked, and continued to stare. His nose throbbed and he stuck his tongue out to taste the blood. Sophie happened to be at the window. She appeared in the street. Cosmo had been about to lay down a flattened garbage can lid to serve as first base. She grabbed two fistfuls of his hair and yanked his head east and west, north and south. From the stoop Mr. Levine leaning forward on his cane, called to her in Yiddish saying she was creating a disgrace for the eyes of the gentiles. She ran back upstairs, locked herself in the apartment, and didn't appear at the window for the rest of the day. Cosmo's mother stood outside the locked door and spewed curses in Polish on the Mintz family. From that time on whenever Mrs. Leznick passed the Mintz family's door she paused to curse them; however as she knew they were already an accursed people, she also entreated Jesus to remember his responsibility and punish them.

Buzzy Demarco, a countervailing spirit to Cosmo Leznick, was often the captain of the opposing team: stoop ball, stick ball, punch ball, and all the variants of baseball. Buzzy's authority derived from a supernatural grace. A pink Spaulding bouncing off the roof of a moving car, gaining altitude would appear to halt in midair and wait as Buzzy's flight described the symmetry of larger winged birds, and obedient gravity brought the ball to his hand.

There was also the ritual of Buzzy's summertime beneficence. Buzzy's friends, admirers, and the envious would seat themselves on the steps of the stoop to watch. Old man Levine mounted there, grimaced, watched the feral children and thought that surely the coming of the Messiah couldn't be far off. As Tony's ice truck slowed for a delivery, Buzzy trotting a car-length behind the truck, accelerated, and within three strides leaped onto the flat bed of the truck, and slid a cake of ice off the tailgate, which exploded shards all over the gutter. Tony slammed on the brakes, and shot out of the cab of the truck brandishing the ice tongs he swore would someday impale Buzzy's head. Buzzy was nowhere in sight. The ice man, who had once made an unwelcome advance toward Buzzy's widowed mother retrieved the largest piece of ice from the street and swore revenge against Buzzy, a maiming worse than death, and touched his crotch in analogous genuflection. Everyone knew Tony meant it, and Buzzy, a fugitive, most often in plain sight took this danger as just one more responsibility. When Tony and his truck were gone kids bounded from the stoop steps, grabbed the gleaming wet chunks from the black hot asphalt, and sucked the cold diamonds.

Swifty was among Buzzy's worshipers. Although Swifty couldn't speculate, as many did, on whether fourteen year old Buzzy, honing his extraordinary talent, would two years hence box in the Golden Gloves. Buzzy would reappear in the street as the kids bent to harvest the ice from the gutter. Swifty, always a little too late, never would have snatched a piece if it weren't for Buzzy, who handed Swifty the melting gem. Swifty licked it. His eyes fixed on the slits of Buzzy's eyes, shaped like smiles, the dark light of his irises shining in his umber tinted face. Swifty gaped, suckled by ice.

On a Sunday, church bells ringing, Buzzy, pinnacled on a scrap of floor jutting out of the side of a tenement recently destroyed by fire, called to his followers climbing through the charred ruin. The half dozen boys had progressed up above the fourth story and clung to the ladder and firescapes attached to what had been the front of the building. Buzzy hadn't given Swifty permission to join in. He shook his head and said, "No Swifty, stay here, on the block," and pointed to a group of younger children gathered in front of Swifty's building. Still, Swifty tagged along, ambling a distance behind the group led by Buzzy. The game was "Follow the Leader" and it was up to Buzzy to determine the level of risk all would try to meet. Swifty followed the gang at a half block interval.

Three stories above the rubble piled in the street, Swifty opened a door to a chasm. The remains of the stairway that had shuddered under his weight trembled behind him, gaping space on either side of the steps. Suspended there, Swifty stretched his neck and looked below. Acrid wisps of smoke made his eyes tear. Looking down he saw the tenement's coal bin, like a jewelbox, glowing. Others were calling from the ladder and firescapes attached to one of the tenement's two remaining roofless walls. The wind moving the clouds surrounding the five story high wall made it appear to sway; the smashed windows dribbled ribbons of smoke. Vapors of mortar dust drifting from between the bricks blew in the air. The wall, and the firescapes and ladder attached to it seemed to list in the wind.

Swifty heard them calling his name. He saw Buzzy riding the scrap of floor among the clouds, exhorting the boys below, frozen to the ladder and firescapes. Buzzy hollered for them to continue the climb. A fragment of a vestibule made a narrow bridge between the two walls. A kitchen at the further end of the bridge rested on what looked like the outcropping of a giant, concrete mushroom, spawned from the blackened brick walls. The kitchen, with the four chairs and table was inhabited by pigeons strutting and pecking on the table. At the outermost lip of the kitchen floor one could view the East River and the Manhattan skyline; and hanging from below the concrete outcropping an entanglement of wire mesh, a network of girders and pipes the boys could climb down leaving a twelve foot drop to the sidewalk. But to reach the bridge the boys would have to continue their climb up the ladder and firescapes to join Buzzy on the floating scrap of floor and then, one at a time, leap into the air.

Swifty stood in the doorway of sky. He was aloft as Buzzy was aloft, saying his name. Swifty couldn't remember how he got there, but he was comfortable as he was in the playground, standing on a swing, grasping the narrow links of chain on either side, bending his knees and pumping himself higher and higher into the sky. Now he bent his knees and rested the palms of his hands on the doorframe, navigating his flight. Buzzy was yelling, "Bennie, Joey, keep goin'." Swifty felt wind whoosh by his ears, the sound like Mama's lips at his ear pleading, "Give me loving." He'd reach his arms around her, far as they would go, hug her hips, his face sinking into the great cushion of her belly. "Give me loving," she wept. He'd maneuver his head so that he could breathe and repeat "loving", the tip of his tongue touching the roof of his mouth. Poppa only said, "Nah!" heaping food on his plate, and "Nah!" handing him a slice of bread. Sometimes Mama screamed, "Give me loving." Then Swifty was scared.

The prism of Swifty's seeing framed Louie falling from the ladder; the fathom of sky that framed him empty in the instant his cry dissipated. Louie would never walk again. People blamed Buzzy. The boys who had climbed the ruin of the burned building said that the fault wasn't really Buzzy's. They said everyone had become distracted by Swifty in the doorway of sky; he had caused the accident. Swifty knew the word "accident". It felt like his mother's breath brushing his ear, when she pleaded, "Give me loving." Within weeks the boys' assertion that it was Swifty who had caused Louie to wind up in a wheelchair became the prevailing belief. Everyone said that Swifty had hexed Louie, not deliberately; but he was a jinx, susceptible to the malocchio, the tumult of cacodemons at play in the shadow of his dumb wonder. The gossip reached Sophie. She would have argued against it but her waxing unhappiness convinced her of the futility of opposing such talk. However, she did take the precaution of dropping a pinch of salt in Swifty's pants pocket to weaken the force of blaming.

Sophie under siege behind her locked door heard Mrs. Leznick curse, "*Paskuddniak!*" But Sophie knew her apartment was immaculate. She scrubbed the floors on her hands and knees. Stood on a ladder and washed the walls. The odor of disinfectant was the perfume of her home. The accusation and curse "Filth" that Mrs. Leznick spat at her door was ameliorated by Sophie's scouring, and knowledge of Sol's labor that kept faucets running and toilets flushing.

Sophie cried and confessed to the simmering pot roast that she couldn't remember Swifty every minute of the day. She considered tying him to his bed but decided that was too cruel.

—◌◌◌—

As Swifty approached a group of boys, they faded and reappeared at a greater distance. Mothers pulled their children away when Swifty came near, and the distance between Swifty and other children remained constant. He saw the mothers' faces whispering, and knew it was about him. Only old man Levine mounted on the stoop made coaxing sounds. And it began to snow.

The bus was moving slowly through the slush, the chains on the tires ringing. Swifty thought he saw Buzzy. The runner outpaced the cloud of gas he was striding in, and leaped onto the back of the bus. His feet resting on the rear bumper, he clung to the rim of the bus's oblong rear window, and bent his knees, riding the undulations, letting every bounce shape his posture. Voices from the stoop called out in scofflaw affirmation, "Hitchin' on the wagon, hitchin' on the wagon." And Swifty was off, chasing the bus as it slowed to a stop.

The wheels clanged. Swifty rode, clinging to the back of the bus, his legs flexing and thrusting like a swimmer riding the swell of a wave. From inside the bus a kid pressed his face against the rear window, the boy's nose flattened against the glass into a pig's snout; he rolled his eyes. The boy's cheeks ballooned and his eyes squeezed shut. The face gnashed teeth. Swifty looked away, up at the gray sky shedding snow. A surf of clouds raced along with the bus, invisibly tethered to Swifty's vision. The rooftops sped along, and a flock of pigeons rolled out of sight carried by the wind. And thick, wet snowflakes fell.

The boy clinging to the back of the bus wasn't Buzzy, and he jumped off after two blocks. Swifty tightened his grip on the metal rim that bordered the rear window. Gas fumes wafted around his head. The breeze buffed his cheeks. He thrust his head out of the cloud of gas and gulped air. A quivering radiated up his spine, humming the ride in his bones.

The knocking inside the rear window was urgent. The boy unpressed his face from the window, shouting warning, rapping on the glass. An old woman seated next to the boy scowled. Swifty knew what to do. The wheels hissed. The bus rocked to a stop.

He was halfway down the street when the bus driver gave up the chase several paces beyond the rear bumper, as was always the case; the driver stood, shouted warning and returned to the inside of the bus.

Swifty strolled along a street of neat brownstone buildings. Everything had turned white. He smelled something delicious. Under the rolled up awning the store front window of "Ernie's Rib Joint" was open. The savory breeze pulled a stream of brown men through the doorway. Swifty stood for a while in the mouth-watering aroma, and then wandered on. His hands hurt with the cold; he crossed his arms over his chest and sheltered his hands under his armpits.

"Hey snowflake, stop where you at." The three boys came up to him. Two were smiling. The one who wasn't smiling stood close to Swifty and said, "You woofin' at me?" Swifty looked at the two boys who couldn't stop laughing. The angry one grabbed the front of Swifty's jacket and said, "I ain't jokin', what you doin' paradin' your dumb ass on my street? Where you from, little ofay?" Swifty recited his address. The two laughing boys convulsed into a dance around Swifty. The angry one shouted, "I'm serious," and cuffed Swifty's ear. "Lemme see," the angry one said, "what's in your pockets." The two who had been laughing became attentive. Swifty turned his pants pockets inside out. From one pocket salt drifted down. Swifty raised the hand that had pulled out the pocket and tasted the tips of his fingers. The boys howled, "Nasty!" The angry one pantomimed a punch he didn't throw.

The stout, brown woman carrying the shopping bag stepped between Swifty and the boys. "What you up to here?" The angry one said, nodding toward Swifty, "He lookin' for trouble." One of the laughing boys said, "Sheeet, anyone can see he a born fool." The woman rested the clinking, shopping bag full of empty bottles on the sidewalk, and said, "Boy, when you talk around me you better mind your language." The boy said, "Sheeet" again. "Smell that" the woman said, and put her fist under his nose. The boy took a step back. "I was jus' sayin' anyone can see he dumb by nature." The woman studied Swifty's face. "Child," she said, "you can close your mouth." Swifty did. "And wipe your nose." Swifty raised his sleeve to his nose, and the woman said, "Wait." She opened her purse, removed a tissue and handed it to Swifty. She guided his hand with the tissue to his nose. "That's right," she said. "Now," she said, looking away from Swifty, standing there with his jacket and pants pockets turned out, "was you all gonna rob this child?" "We jus' playin' with him," the two who'd been laughing said. The angry one said, "Maybe he jus' some kind a runty nut, but he best keep to his home block anyways. He don't belong here." The woman took a closer look at Swifty as he appeared completely absorbed watching her. "Listen," she said, "whether he be a little simple or just carried away appreciatin' ain't no cause for robbery. Now you boys be on your way, and stay out a mischief, you hear?"

The stout brown lady told Swifty to stuff his pockets in, and loaded three empty milk bottles in his arms. She pointed to a grocery store. "Now, you give the grocery man these here empties, and he give you six cent, a nickel to ride, and a penny for what you want. You know your way home, child?" Swifty recited his address. The lady said, "Go now." Swifty lingered, wanting to stay in the warm eddies of the woman's voice. She smiled and pointed at the grocery. They stood looking at one another. She started to walk away and Swifty followed her. She stopped, turned and said, "Go on now," pointing, once more, at the grocery.

Seated in the bus Swifty watched the snow covered streets roll by. The rushing sky and rooftops lashed to his scrutiny by the thinnest membranes of light; again, he recited his address. A man seated across from him raised his head from a newspaper, looked at Swifty and ducked back behind the newspaper. The bus turned and went down a steep street.

Looking through his breath on the window he saw the faint reflection of the boy that was him, the falling snow, and two boys fencing with large, frozen fish. Passengers on the bus shouted,"Look." Boys all over the street threw fish at one another, and whacked each other over the head and shoulders with fish. The bus maneuvered through the narrow street slowly. Fish were strewn all over the gutter: heads and tails, and glittering ice. A spiral of fish scales swirled, shining among the snow drops. A man seated in the back of the bus began to shout angrily in a language Swifty had never heard. Someone yelled back in English, "Believe me, the little bastards ain't orphans. It's the parents they should put in jail!" The bus driver said, "Amen to that." Snowballs thudded against the windows and sides of the slow moving bus. A woman passenger screamed and ducked her head toward her lap as a snowball splattered against the window where she was seated. Nuggets of ice and fish heads bounced off the bus. Swifty saw the boys take aim. Gleaming, somersaulting through air the fish guts flew like something alive, and smacked the window where Swifty stared; his head recoiled as though he'd been punched. The entrails slithered down the window. One round, stumpy *babushka* adjusted her kerchief, tightened the knot under her chin, and with a paper shopping bag hanging from her hand tottered to the rear door. "Stop," she wailed. The bus rocked to a halt. She swayed. The doors whooshed open. "Leo!" she cried, "Leo!" The bus driver yelled, "Give it to him good! Warm his pants." A fish head landed on the floor near the *babushka's* feet. She howled, "Leo, don't come home or you'll make me a murderer." All the passengers, except for the man reading the newspaper were yelling. The *babushka* stepped down and moved toward the melee. At the opposite curb there was a truck parked halfway up on the sidewalk, tilted to the driver's side, the right rear tire pancaked. Two boys stood on the tailgate and emptied bushel baskets of fish and crushed ice into the gutter. Swifty looked for Buzzy. Fish thumped off the side of the bus. The driver maneuvered the bus around the truck and the kids pounding each other with fish. At the corner the bus turned and picked up speed. Swifty reached up and pulled the cord. The bus didn't stop. He stood up, held onto a pole with one hand and with the other pulled the cord again. The bus sped on. Swifty looked toward the bus driver; he couldn't think of what to say. He saw unfamiliar streets flying by. At last the bus stopped. The rear doors opened. Swifty stepped down, off the bus.

The air was dense with snow. The corridor of trees, white. Next to a boarded up snow-domed kiosk was an entrance to a park. The paths and the benches were empty and white. Swifty had never heard such quiet. Except for his chilled feet he wasn't very cold. He tasted his salty finger tip, stuck his tongue out and lapped in the moisture. He looked behind him and saw the long trail of his footprints disappearing near the hedges where he'd entered the park. He walked in the quiet, following his shadow and exhaled little clouds of breath. The path turned; Swifty turned with it. Through the white flecked silence he heard wheezing. The sound grew louder. He came closer. He passed the breathing body heaped on the bench under a rug. The face had the pink sheen of a lollipop wrapped in cellophane. The lips trembled. The man's arms hung down, his fingertips sunk in the snow. Under the bench a brown bottle with a picture of three roses on it peaked a hillock of slush. The snow made all of the man white, except for his glistening pink face. Between the upright slabs of his shoes and the ragged cuffs of his pants, coils of newspaper squeezed out over his milky blue ankles. Swifty walked faster. The man's puling wheeze followed him. Swifty ran until he could no longer hear it.

Footprints in what had been the smooth expanse of snow appeared; he stopped, lifted his leg and placed his foot into the recess and his foot fit exactly. On either side of him the white sloping grounds swelled, untouched. His feet inside his sodden shoes were damp and chilled. He walked in slow motion placing his feet in the indentations as if he'd made these footprints earlier, and now he was playing follow-the-leader, carrying himself somewhere he'd started trudging to long ago. Gingerly he lowered each foot into each footprint, following the trail laid out in front of him. After a while he strode less carefully, exploding the footprints into white dust, but kept to the path that led him toward the sound of barking.

The seal was perched at the top of a stone pyramid, head lifted, barking. There was no one else at the iron railing that encircled the pool of water. A breathing hump rose from the surface of water, floated for an instant and sunk. The seal on top of the pyramid leaped, gliding in the air, it rode the arc it shaped down into the water, splashed and vanished. Swifty studied the water. The seal didn't reappear.

Beyond the pool and the cage with the largest black cat Swifty had ever seen was a towering cage with a giant tree inside it. Swifty studied the caged, birdless tree, walked on and thought he saw, not too far away, a uniformed park attendant disappear into a great stone house, from which came the sound of creatures he couldn't imagine.

It was getting near to dusk. He was shivering. The three boys walking toward him waved. He stood still, waiting for them to disappear, but they came nearer, gesturing for him to join them. As they turned into another path they called to him, whistling. Heavy footed in the snow, he trotted after them.

The tall one wore a leather aviator's cap, goggles, and was wrapped in a tent-like military coat, festooned with flaps, buckles, and brass buttons. The littlest one, in a red sweater, shivered. His eyes were watery, and he gnawed at his raw fist. The third was short, round, every part of him seemed swollen; he wore a flannel shirt, unbuttoned, corduroy pants, and sneakers. On top of his head, a baseball cap with the visor turned behind his head; he was sweating and smoking the stub of a cigarette. The tall one raised the goggles and placed them on his leather encased forehead. "You got a cigarette?" Swifty shrugged. The fat one said, "This little pisser got nothin'." The tall one said, "It's snowy Saturday and we own the joint; but don't worry we ain't gonna hurt you. You come to see the hellephants? Big sons of bitches ain't they?" Swifty looked beyond the railing down the deep stone incline that led to a trench filled with water; beyond it, a cobble stone hill climbed to a plateau, where two elephants raised straw in their curling trunks to their mouths. Behind the elephants stood their immense house. Swifty had never seen any living thing so large, so imperturbable. The enormous fans of their ears moved slowly. Steam rose from their haunches. "Lissen," the tall boy said, "You're gonna trade your jacket for my brudder's sweater. Okay gimmee." Swifty watched the elephants. Monumental, they moved ever so slightly, like motion in the fluid tempo of a dream. The tall boy unbuttoned Swifty's jacket. Swifty turned obligingly. He pulled his arms out of the sleeves. For a moment he couldn't see anything as the sweater that the little guy had been wearing was pulled over his head. But then he saw the elephants again, the legs like tree trunks, enormity moving.

The snowball looped out of the sky. The littlest one wearing Swifty's jacket, took his bloodied knuckle from his mouth and pitched a snowball, high. The three were throwing. The snowballs curved in the sky, splashed into the trench of water, and plopped near the elephants, tranquilly eating. Swifty turned from the immense quiet of the elephants to the murderous faces of the boys: such concentrated vehemence in their intention, rehearsing slaughter they bellowed "Fuck! Bastard! Bitch!" and Swifty cried. As if the size and imperturbability of the beasts had offended them, the boys let go barrage after barrage and cursed. Swifty turned his head from the boys to the elephants, back to the boys; frantic, dizzy, his eyes retained the image of their ferocity; the turning of his head blurred the sight of the huge indifferent animals with the splotches of snowballs melting down their sides; Swifty at the center of the boys' war dance, they howled "Fuck! Bastard! Bitch!" Swifty's weeping wracked his body.

The tall one in the aviator's cap and goggles hollered "Cease fire!" The boys froze in place, grinning. "Look at that," the one in the goggles said to Swifty, "Look at that," he commanded, pointing to a purple Jelly Baby under the iron railing, sheltered from the snow. Next to the purple one was a yellow one, the size of a nickel. Slowly Swifty's tremors ebbed and he watched the boy peel the candy from the ground, kiss it, hold it up to the sky, and say, just before he put it in his mouth, "Kiss it up to God." He pointed to the yellow Jelly Baby and directed Swifty to do the same. Swifty held it in his hand. "Go on, go on. Kiss it up to God." Swifty kissed it, and raised his hand with the candy above his head. "Yeah, awright, you can eat it now." Swifty put it in his mouth. It was sweet. "See you around," the boys said and marched away, while Swifty searched under the rail for more candy he could kiss up to God and eat.

The dark warmed him. When he looked up through the haze of falling snow he saw the white ball of the moon extricating itself from the tree's branches. Home was far away, and anyway he didn't want to go there. He walked deeper into the park, wading in the white dunes that had swallowed the streets and buildings, the billowing white going on and on until it was everything.

Fraternity

Ben climbed the steps out of the unending dusk of his basement apartment into a morning nearly as dark, walked two blocks, and descended into the gloom of the subway. Well, he thought, as he took the books he'd need for that evening's classes from under his left arm and tucked them under his right, at least my relationship with Brodsky has improved. A year ago, when he'd begun working at Elite Fabrics and Textile Waste, he could feel Brodsky watching him. He thought the foreman might be dissatisfied with his work; it had taken him the better part of the morning to learn how to operate the baling press safely. Ben took to sneaking glances at Brodsky, but turned away when Brodsky caught him staring. Once, their eyes had met and they recoiled as though each had been slapped. They continued to study one another surreptitiously. Working alongside Brodsky required getting used to his overwrought silence. Brodsky, with Kafka's neurasthenic face perched on the body of an ox, worked at a terrific pace. His strength lived its own life within him, and he was indifferent to it, as some obtuse thing that may have allowed him to survive, but couldn't free him. Standing side by side, washing up at the trough-like sink at the end of the day, Ben saw the indelible blue of the numbers tattooed on Brodsky's pale forearm.

On a cold, wet February morning, Ben, about to enter the warehouse, came upon Brodsky staring down at the street drunk sprawled in the doorway. Brodsky said something in Yiddish to Ben. Ben said, "What?" not because the smattering of Yiddish that he understood was insufficient; Brodsky's chronic look of melancholic stupor was so incongruous to the contemptuous tone in his voice, that Ben looking at him lost the meaning of what he'd heard, and asked again. Brodsky repeated what he'd said, and Ben heard the interjection "nu" and then, "a goyish holiday, no remedy exists for it." Ben bent to the drunk and shook his shoulder. Brodsky shoved him and said, "Fool, not even God can rouse a corpse."

After the police and an ambulance had arrived and taken away the body the routine of the work day went on as usual. As Ben loaded bolts of cloth into a crate, Brodsky approached and said, "You should wash your hands; please now." Ben couldn't begin to fathom the contagions Brodsky imagined spawned from the corpse. Brodsky stood there, plaintive, neglecting his work to attend to the imminent threat and Ben headed for the washroom.

Except for the corridor, about twenty feet wide, near the freight elevator, metal bins loaded with bolts of cloth extended from floor to ceiling and along the length of the parallel walls of the third floor loft. The work crew took their lunch break in the corridor adjacent to the freight elevator's gate, where piles of burlap bags stuffed with remnants of cloth were stacked, making a kind of amphitheatre some eighteen feet in diameter. The air was dense with multicolored textile particles. Each worker had fashioned a nylon stocking head cap to protect his hair from the colored dust that permeated everything. Their eyebrows were miniature rainbows and they sneezed clouds of gold, violet and red.

Now, during the lunch break, Ben and Brodsky sat together on the floor, their backs and bottoms cushioned by sacks stuffed with textile remnants. Tony, Jose, and Murphy sat facing them twenty feet away within the semi-circle made of bagged rags. Ben sipped coffee from his thermos. Brodsky offered a plum. Ben knew better than to decline the gift. Brodsky would press the plum against Ben's chest until juice dampened his shirt. Ben took the plum and said, "Thanks, I'll save it for dessert."

They unwrapped their sandwiches. Tony, Jose and Murphy, Ben's contemporaries, sat pillowed and sprawled against the humped tiers of burlap bags, as Tony proclaimed, "It was my Aunt Nina, my mother's sister for Christ's sake." Murphy flushed as he peeled the shell from a hardboiled egg. "Tony, that's what you tol' us the last time, and she took your cherry, right?" "She don't look nothin' like my mother. Otherwise I wouldn't a been able to do it. That was four years ago. I was fourteen. What the hell did I know?" Tony glanced at Jose. "Know what I'm sayin'?" "Me?" Jose said, "I'm movin' outa of my girlfren's apartment, gonna move in with Mami. She's a long time widow, was takin' care of my grandfather. Mami is his favorite daughter. She always been religious. Stric' Catholic. Mami loves the old man. A couple a years ago the alleluia people got him. Pentecostal, somethin' like that. Abuelo's eighty-five, maybe eighty-six, nobody knows for sure. A lot a' the time Abuelo's out of it. Poor Mami couldn't have no company. One time Mami's fren' Señora Ramirez come to visit anyhow. There in the kitchen was Abuelo, sittin' in a chair, jerkin' off, sayin' 'Thank you Jesus, thank you Jesus'. Mami gave him to the Sisters in the nursin' home."

Ben nodded in agreement to something Brodsky had said, although he hadn't been paying attention. Like the others, the stories garnished his lunch and abetted his appetites. Tony said, "I ain't claimin' to be like innocent, but Aunt Nina got this knockout body and she caught me starin', a lot 'a times. Now whenever I tell her we gotta stop, she cries and says she'll put her head in the oven and turn on the gas. Lucky thing Uncle Frank's a degenerate gambler, he's so busy studyin' the odds, he got no time to notice what his wife's doin'. And don't forget, there's Marie. She wouldn't let me do nothin' below the waist until we got engaged. Now she can't get enough." "Tony, you braggin' or complainin'?" "Murph, they're wearin' me out. You hear what I'm sayin'? And Aunt Nina says she's a year younger than my mother. Mama says Nina is three years older than her. I gotta believe my mother. Right? Now I ain't said a word about this before. But Aunt Nina maybe goin' through her changes. That's like the comin' attractions for becomin' a hag. She got a mustache. It ain't thick, but it's black and wiry. When we kiss it hurts, feels unnatural. What am I gonna do? Ask her to shave? She's dryin' up. I gotta chapped dick." "Bullshit." "Murph, you can't understand cause on account of your sprained wrist, you got no sex life." "I got more important things on my mind, Romeo; like I ain't gonna be haulin' bales 'til my back's broke. I'm startin' night school soon, gonna study bookkeepin'. I'm good with numbers." "Si, you gettin' serious, man; good for you. Me too. I'm gonna turn pro. No more Golden Gloves. Last year that guy Mendoza got the split decision over me in the City Finals. He was a contender in the nationals. I gonna have my dream. Be welterweight champ. It means sacrifice. That's why I'm movin' outta my girlfren's place. Gonna live with Mami. I be helpin' her with grocery money and rent anyways."

Jose rose to his feet and shadow boxed, his movement swift and beautiful. Tony swore, "I ain't stupid. I know the mess I'm in can all of a sudden not be funny, like blood. Like tragedy, man."

During the lunch break, Ben, immersed in a discussion about Dostoevsky with Brodsky, turned his head, unable not to look at Jose shadow boxing, the fluid movement of his body like a man on ice skates. Brodsky had been saying, in contradiction to what he claimed was Dostoevsky's implicit belief, that it is rare for people to be improved by their suffering. When it became obvious that Ben's attention had wandered, Brodsky, nodding his head in the direction of the gentile world, whispered, "And what can we learn from them Ben, how to beat our wives and become drunkards?" Ben winced; he heard in the refugee's voice a condemnation like his mother's. And it occurred to him that he hadn't telephoned or visited his family in over two months. The subway ride to Brooklyn seemed not so much a journey as a regression. Remembering made him drowsy; as if he were a kid again and only his fighting off sleep and readiness to intervene prevented Mama and Papa from killing one another. He'd kept the promise he made to himself when he was eight and moved out of the house two weeks after his eighteenth birthday.

Just in time. He and Pop had come close to blows. In the instant he'd raised his fists, enraged yet mindful, he knew he had to throw punches; Pop was too strong to grapple with: and Ben found himself clairvoyant, as if he'd always known this moment would come. There was the never ending operatic crisis, buffo but dangerous. It began, Ben told himself, before I was born. At the top of her voice Momma was wishing diseases on Pop that would kill him and liberate her. Pop was busting up the furniture. Ben's fourteen year old brother, Josh, who would be diagnosed borderline schizophrenic, stood in the center of the wrecked kitchen wailing. Josh had, earlier that day, told Ben about the tug boat captain who had been sending him telepathic messages. The captain said that Josh and Ben could join him as apprentice smugglers. Josh said, "Benny it'll be almost as good as being orphans." Pop paused, surprised to find the leg of a kitchen chair in his hand. Josh wet his pants. Pop turned to him, "What are you bawlin'? Nobody laid a finger on you." Momma in the bedroom, screaming afflictions on Pop, hesitated between cholera and cancer to threaten, "God is my witness, touch the little one and I'll put poison in your food." Pop considered, and said to his wife indignantly, "You gonna shiver over the pisher all his life?" Josh trembled and the puddle around his shoes widened. Pop's eyes closed; he swung the leg of the chair and took out the kitchen window. Josh ran to Momma in the bedroom. Ben felt something in him giving way and said to Pop, "You goddamn tin Mussolini." And they were at each other. Momma's scream, devoid of melodrama was unlike any scream they had ever heard. Ben's right hand sucker punch halted in midair, the momentum toppled him into Pop's arms. Startled in that embrace, they turned to search the apartment for the intruder who had howled and interfered with family business. Now Ben was shaking. The prophetic capacity that this latest drama had bled into his consciousness allowed him to know that if he had punched out his father, he'd be haunted. But Pop was looking at him sympathetically, almost pleased, as if the violence, nearly consummated, was only his son growing into a fuller range of expression.

And it had been only a week since he and Pop went to the Russian baths and had a good time. In the locker room they had a couple of belts of schnapps. Togaed in the cleansing fog, they talked politics. Ben made Pop laugh as they lamented the death of progressive politics and Ben, quoting former President Truman, said of Congress, "Those people are going to give hypocrisy a bad name." "The apple of my eye got a mouth," crowed Pop. And his father kissed him there, the place from which his words fell into the world. The old Lefties dissolving on the stone benches, grunted approval. Moans, groans, and orgasmic sighs, they liquefied, resigned. Indistinct in the steam, the margin between body and soul melted, and one of the chorus, uttering the thought of another said, *"Neshuma."* Which Ben took to mean the source of breath.

In the kitchen amid the debris, with damp October spitting through the smashed window, Ben watched Pop, startled by the wreckage, reach for a broom and consider sweeping the broken glass and shattered crockery into a pile, change his mind, and lean the broom against the wall. Pop looked into his eyes and said, "Only God is perfect, and He kills people."

Brodsky, frightened by his show of anger, couldn't stop apologizing. Ben, for his part, didn't offer the explanation that would only have confirmed Brodsky's dire assessment of the moral possibilities of the human race. Boxing remained one of Ben's infatuations. Ben's uncle Ruby had fought professionally and a lot of the old timers at Stillman's gym still spoke of him with awe. Ben's hero worship of Uncle Ruby persisted. And when he was fifteen, he went to Uncle Ruby's gym in Queens and sparred with his cousin Morty. Uncle Ruby had instructed Ben in the fundamentals. Now Ben wondered if he could spar with Jose, and hold his own. He couldn't imagine how he might convey to Brodsky that Jose's speed and grace were more than a physical accomplishment without invoking Brodsky's judgment that he, Ben, was after all, only an American, consumed by trivial pursuits and thrilled by violence. Brodsky had seen the texts that Ben was reading for his classes at City College: Kant's

"The Fundamental Principles of The Metaphysics of Ethics", Dostoevsky's "Crime and Punishment" and an anthology of the major English Romantic poets. Brodsky, spying the books in Ben's locker, looked wistful. He avoided Ben's eyes, and as though confessing something absurd and shameful whispered that he had read Kant in German. Their discussions went forward like an uncertain romance. Brodsky spoke more animatedly than usual, but still in the tone of partaking of something illicit, something that must inevitably end in humiliation. Brodsky acknowledged that Kant's categorical imperative was logical: "Act as if the maxim of your action were to become through your will a general natural law." "*Nu?*" Brodsky confided, "The problem is that the moral imagination of humanity requires scapegoats, and scapegoats, Ben, exist a priori to be slaughtered."

But Brodsky had also helped Ben with an algebra assignment for a course in which he struggled to sustain a C average. The refugee had been patient. In coaxing Ben's confidence Brodsky reminded Ben that the letters of the equation carried a greater mystery than the numbers. Even in proximity of the gentile workers Brodsky's clandestine whisper, usually the closest speech could come to silence, surfaced, mellow and clear. As he guided Ben through an equation he lapsed into something capacious, untainted by humanity's barbarities; overjoyed by the sweet relic of rational principle, Brodsky smiled. He helped Ben prepare for an exam and Ben scored eighty on the midterm.

Ben was grateful. Warm feeling and his sense of indebtedness spurred his recognition of Julius Brodsky as kin —

"*mispoche*". Although, Brodsky, a German Jew, had a certain reserve, a grotesque dignity unlike Ben's family of Russian Jews; Brodsky was not imbued with their dramatic expressiveness. Nevertheless, Ben knew, he was caught in inevitable kinship. Brodsky might have been a distant uncle, recently discovered and rescued; or an older diaspora cousin brought back from death. And *mispoche* is *mispoche*, a cousin tantamount to a brother. A brother might do anything for you, and expect naturally, that there was no limit in what he might expect of you.

When Ben turned his head he saw Jose smiling, skipping rope in the rainbow mist of textile dust. Tony had tuned a small portable radio to a mambo and he parodied the syncopation on invisible bongos. As Ben watched Jose skipping rope, glistening with sweat, beating a rhythm with the balls of his feet, the tap tap tap of the rope skimming the floor, whistling through air, the arch of the rope rotating round and around Jose, a bower of wind he made circling himself from head to toe, Ben, remembering the line of a poem he'd read somewhere but couldn't recall the title, or the author's name, recalled the line now, "Auschwitz was not the garden of my childhood."

Brodsky was absent from work the day after Jose won his first professional fight. His sister-in-law had died after a long bout with cancer. Joe Levine, Brodsky's father-in-law, boss and owner of Elite Fabrics and Textile Waste, was absent as well. The day's work progressed at the usual tempo despite the horsing around that the absence of the foreman and the boss allowed. Harvey, Joe Levine's other son-in-law, was nominally in charge. Joe Levine the self-made man, barely over five foot three, and nearly four feet wide possessed a huge voice. All day he chewed on the stub of a cigar, paced the floor of his office and issued work orders within an on-going stentorian soliloquy which included his wonderments, consternations, and nonplussed rage. As Joe Levine's voice filled the office and the first floor loft, but only penetrated the second floor loft as a throbbing, Harvey the hapless son-in-law, whom Mr. Levine called the button hole maker, since Harvey like Brodsky had failed to provide Joe Levine with any male grandchildren, Joe Levine the father of three daughters and a son who hadn't returned from his military service in World War Two, dispatched Harvey as an echo on legs to communicate his instructions to the second, third, and fourth floor lofts.

Mr. Levine's lament, growing day by day, enumerated his burdens. He was hostage to his own beneficence, supporting a host of relatives who were unable to support themselves because of stupendous ineptitude, mental and or emotional frailty, criminal tendencies and creeping narcolepsy. Joe Levine worried aloud about what would happen to all of these people if his business failed or he should die. Harvey, whose consistent bungling astounded Joe Levine, had on various occasions made overtures of friendship toward Ben. He implied that despite appearances they shared certain affinities; they were both, he said, serious people.

Harvey stepped out of the freight elevator. A large hand-kerchief folded into a triangle covered his face from beneath the rim of his eyeglasses, past his chin, like a Wild West outlaw in the movies. The mask was meant to protect him from inhaling the dust. He wore a gray, pin-striped suit, and a maroon tie; his wavy black hair lacquered in place gave off the aroma of lilacs. He walked briskly to Ben, who was busy at the shipping table, cutting cloth samples to be mailed to various garment manufacturers. Harvey said, "Hello Ben," puffing out the handkerchief mask with his breath. Ben said, "Hello." Harvey said, "You know I'm supposed to keep an eye on things when the old man's away. Like supervise." Each of Harvey's words inflated the mask. Ben said, "Why not?" and wondered whether Harvey acknowledged that although Mr. Levine insisted that he take on the role of supervisor, the old man dismissed anything Harvey had to say. There were occasions when Ben, riding the freight elevator heard the echo of Mr. Levine's lament thrumming in the elevator shaft. "What business is you can't learn from night school, Harvey. That you make my daughter happy I don't object. I wouldn't begrudge my children pleasure. But whatever they're teaching you in the night school – which also comes out of my pocket – is only making you more confused."

Tony, Jose, and Murphy said, "Hello Harvey" and went on with their tasks moving around him. Harvey cleared his throat. "Ben, how do you get to work?" "How do I get to work?" "Yeah, how?" "Why?" "Never mind why. Just tell me how." "I take the subway, from East Broadway." "Me, Ben, I take a cab from Kew Gardens." "Nice." "You bet it's nice. Look Ben, I got a right to take pride. Right?" "Right, of course." "Sure I've got to cope with the old man's *mishegoss*, but every winter my wife and the little one vacation in Miami. In the summer it's the Catskills. What's so bad? I'm crazy like a fox." Ben sneezed. "Ah, see, that's a sign I'm saying the truth. I'm working on the future." Harvey lowered his voice. "Also I invest. I got a portfolio. I tell you Ben cause I see you're watching things, thinking. And I hear from your vocabulary when you talk. You won't be here forever. Now my brother-in-law, your friend Brodsky, he belongs in a warehouse. Don't get me wrong. I understand it's a pity. It's not his fault he's weird. The terrible things in Europe, losin' his wife and all. He can't get back to normal. Can't overcome. No way. He's in this country already more than ten years. And Mr. Doom and Gloom is making his new wife and kid miserable." Harvey placed his hairy hand with the glossed fingernails on Ben's shoulder and said, "Keep up the good work," gave the third floor loft a cursory look and headed for the freight elevator. Ben cut the last of the cloth samples and felt the weight of the huge shears in his hand radiate up to his elbow. It was true, he thought, that Brodsky's unhappiness seemed unpatriotic, un-American in its depth and persistence. Brodsky occasionally mentioned his "*American*" wife and daughter, only to say they knew how to shop, talk on the telephone, and play mahjong.

Brodsky and Mr. Levine were away from work for a week observing the requirements of mourning; sitting shiva. Work was not neglected, but a kind of frivolity reigned that surprised Ben; when Brodsky was present Tony, Jose and Murphy hadn't seemed inhibited, but now Ben realized that their levity in the presence of Brodsky's disapproval had required effort. They regarded Brodsky as an alien creature. Their awareness of Twentieth Century slaughter was like the memory of an old horror movie, which now and then, Brodsky evoked as he trudged from task to task looking behind him, as if he were being followed. And with Brodsky away, there was an ease that they all enjoyed, Ben noticed, including himself.

On the third day of Brodsky's absence, during the lunch break, Jose announced that he was scheduled to fight another four rounder at Saint Nick's after the main event. Ben, Murphy, and Tony said they'd attend the fight. Ben was aware of a shift in the mood among his co-workers, a quiet derived from Jose's discipline, a palpable awe as Jose skipped rope and did sit ups during the lunch break. Up at first light, Jose ran the four miles through the subdued city streets to work, and at the end of the work day, ran the four miles home through the bedlam of traffic, breathing in the gas fumes and growing stronger. At night he went to the gym to work out and spar. Feeling shy, it took Ben three days to get up the nerve to offer himself as a sparring partner.

Jose took a pair of boxing shoes out of his gym bag, and a set of eight ounce gloves, a stop-watch, a towel, and a jar of Vaseline. He handed the watch to Murphy. Murphy said, "What happens if Harvey finds out? After all, this ain't a gym." Tony waved Murphy's words away; "For Christ's sake Murph, stop worryin'. Harvey'll take another of his two hour lunches. After he eats he goes to the barbershop for his manicure. Besides, nobody's cheatin' Levine, one' o'clock we're back to work like always." Tony nodded at the gym bag. "What else you got in there Jose? A rabbit?" "No, a ham sandwich." And Jose stretched out his arms as he scanned the amphitheater made of the ascending tiers of burlap bags, stuffed with rags. "It's eighteen maybe nineteen feet, just about regulation size for a small ring." He motioned for Ben to come closer. "Take your shirt off." Ben stripped to the waist. Tenderly Jose smeared the Vaseline over Ben's face. Ben thought, okay, I'm anointed. Jose called over his shoulder, "Like I told you Murph, when I got my boxin' shoes on and Ben laces up his sneakers we're ready. You're the time keeper. Pay attention to the watch. You say 'time in' for us to start, and after three minutes call time. If Ben wants another round we get a one minute rest."

They circled one another. In orbit they appeared attached by some gravitational force, although they didn't touch.Jose remained directly in front of Ben, bobbing and weaving, the movement of his upper body constant and in harmony with the tempo of his legs. He appeared to be gliding. Ben extended his left arm and probed the air in front of Jose's face. He tucked his chin behind his left shoulder and shuffled in a half crouch. Close, they kept a discreet distance apart and traveled round and round. Ben's mouth was open, already he was breathing hard. Jose remained in front of him, up on his toes, dancing. Gulping air, Ben thought, he's inviting me to punch. Maybe he just wants to practice his defensive skills. Ben stepped in to close the gap between them, threw a jab and got hit flush in the face. He tasted blood in his mouth, but was breathing better, some obstruction knocked loose. He couldn't tell whether he'd actually thrown the jab or had been hit the instant he decided to punch. Jose carried his left low; his stance didn't reveal whether he was set to hook or jab to the body. Nor did Ben see the punch that hit him. Again he tried to get in closer, smother Jose's punches, and throw a short straight jab, aiming at Jose's chest which offered a bigger target. Again Jose beat him to the punch, bouncing his left jab off Ben's forehead. Ben kept trying and kept getting hit. He was aware that he was punching at Jose, not only in the hope of hitting him, but to entice him into more reckless aggression. In the infinitude of the three minutes he struggled. Nothing else present in his mind.

Ben never heard Murphy call time. But he found himself on his feet, looking at Jose smiling through the drizzle of textile dust. Tony and Murphy were shouting and applauding. Jose was congratulating him. "You make me work a little bit, that's good man. Maybe tomorrow you make me work harder. Enough for today. Tomorrow two rounds if you want."

The first round on Friday was like the first round on Thursday. But sometime during the second round Ben realized that he should not lead; his only chance to land blows someplace other than Jose's shoulders and arms was to counter punch. Still, Jose hit him with two and three punch combinations each time Ben landed a blow. Jose's gliding paused and he hit Ben with a left right combination and moved straight back, his only mistake. Ben caught Jose with a left hook that made him wobble. But he wasn't fast enough to capitalize on the opportunity and Jose tied him up, hung on and then hit him with something so swift and hard that Ben found himself on all fours, a void in his head. Later Ben would recall that in the clinch some reflex of surmise, a suspicion returned to yield what he had seen before he had thought, or thought before he had seen: the danger he possessed was the disparity between Jose's talent and his own rudimentary skill. Jose'd had too much time. Dancing, he had become smitten with a vision of himself, and posed for God.

As Ben wiped the sweat and textile dust from his neck and chest with a towel, Jose asked if he wanted to spar on Monday. Ben said, "Definitely." Tony and Murphy applauded and said nothing. Looking into the mirror in the washroom, Ben saw that just below his nose his upper lip was swollen and split and he had a mouse under his right eye.

On Monday morning Brodsky returned to work. Mr. Levine was away on a business trip. Ben had punched in and was hanging his windbreaker in his locker when Brodsky came in. Ben said, "Good morning." Brodsky nodded. Ben put his books in the locker, removing from the pocket of his windbreaker a paperback edition of Rilke's "Sonnets to Orpheus", which was not required for any of his classes. The book was curled, the spine broken, and the pages dog-eared. Ben placed it on top of his required texts. Brodsky hung his jacket in his locker, turned and glanced at the book in Ben's locker. He looked pained. Ben attributed Brodsky's expression to some dark spasm of memory unleashed by the previous week's formal mourning. Brodsky snatched the "Sonnets to Orpheus" from Ben's locker and spoke in a mumble, the intonation not unlike the Hebrew prayer for the dead. Jose arrived and shouted to Ben that he'd been able to borrow a pair of boxing shoes. "You're size nine, right?" Ben shouted back, "Right. Thanks." Brodsky hung on to Ben's sleeve. He tossed the "Sonnets to Orpheus" back into Ben's locker. Workers were clustered at the time clock, punching in. Jose put the boxing shoes in Ben's locker. "Try them on, Ben." Ben said, "Sure, thanks." Brodsky whispered; Ben couldn't make out what he was saying, but Brodsky looked like he was sharing his most shameful secret. The loft crews and the office staff had punched in and the day's work was beginning. Brodsky clung to Ben's sleeve. He was reciting something in German. The only words Ben understood were *"apfel"*, *"spricht"*, *"tod"*, *"und"*, *"leben"*. He decided to get himself fired; the anxiety he felt about not commencing work was humiliating, and he was especially ashamed as Brodsky's turmoil had taken the form of a recitation; he was declaiming a poem in German as Ben stood there, at war with himself. And then Ben knew: sonnet thirteen! Brodsky was reciting the thirteenth sonnet to Orpheus! "Full round apple, pear and banana, gooseberry…all this speaks death and life in the mouth…"and Brodsky was nodding "yes". He held Ben close and divulged that once upon a time he had written poems in German.

When the lunch hour came, Ben and the rest of the crew were on the loading dock. They had just finished hauling and stacking an out of town shipment into the back of a trailer truck. As they walked to the freight elevator Jose called to Ben, "Try on the shoes, make sure they fit good." Ben lingering behind the others, Brodsky at his side said, "Sure, I'll be with you in a minute." Brodsky resumed his confession. The strangled locution of his speech made his head tremble and he whispered that his father had been an academic, and that in his parent's house Goethe and Schiller had been revered. He, Papa and Momma spoke German at home. Yiddish was shunned as jargon. Brodsky and Ben stared at one another, neither able to look away. Brodsky waited. Ben hoped that what he couldn't say didn't show in his face. Brodsky, traumatized by the language he thought in, dreamt in – 'I think, therefore I am', a curse. Jose called, "Ben, come on, we're wastin' time." Ben shouted "Okay." Brodsky's face registered betrayal. In the Yiddish he preferred to eschew he said, "Go, go, your colleague is waiting."

Exaltation

Purgatory was located in the basement of the church. The walls of the oblong, windowless room were a jaundiced white. There were rows of metal folding chairs and a lectern at the front of the room. Clouds of cigarette smoke saturated the air, which also reeked of germicide. Behind the lectern, a blackboard. Sometime in the past the church had maintained a parochial school. Ben couldn't dispel the feeling that in this room, children had been fearful and punished. Men and women welcomed one another. At a coffee urn set up on a table in a corner, two men looking worn and penitent embraced. Ben remembered looking into the mirror that morning and becoming reacquainted with his face: the broken nose, livid and bent pointed toward the right ear, the left eye half hooded by the bruised pouch of skin; what could be seen of the eye suggested the contemplation of something the right eye, looking out at the world was blind to, and his right hand was swollen. It would be a week before he could close his fingers around a pencil again. He would never have come here if the judge hadn't made his attendance the condition for the suspension of the drunk and disorderly charge. At first, what he couldn't remember struck the judge as insolence and Ben was threatened with a contempt citation, and a longer stay in jail. He did remember the laughter, mocking laughter echoing down a flight of steps. He'd gotten to his feet, collapsed, and on his belly dragged himself upward. Anesthetized as he was, still the sudden pain in his hamstrings toppled him, and he tumbled down the stairs. As he stood before the judge, the deep bruises on his thighs and shins ached. The judge, mentioning his youth, suspended the sentence on condition that he embark on the program that offered rehabilitation. Ben had sufficient presence of mind to thank him.

Released from court he walked toward the subway and parts of the night in question came back to him, but he wasn't sure. Sometimes his recollection of the nights bled into one another. He'd struggled to fit his key in the lock. Aware that he was drunk he looked at the familiar door and hallway, orienting himself. Yes, he was at his door. But he couldn't get the key into the lock. He heard footsteps inside and wondered who had broken into his apartment. The trio that materialized from the shadows at his back pummeled him and laughed. He lowered his chin, crouched, and let his fists go. He was aware that in other brawls he'd often felt joyous. Then he was bouncing, somersaulting down the stairs. At the bottom of the stairwell he managed to get to his feet, and marveled that he hadn't broken any bones.

He didn't know how much time had elapsed as the police helped him to his feet. He tried to tell them that someone had broken into his apartment. They didn't seem interested as they hustled him out of the hallway toward the curb and the patrol car. Several residents of the building had gathered in the hallway and they spoke excitedly in Spanish and English, but the police were no more attentive to the complaints of his neighbors than they were to Ben's insisting that a crime had been committed. Handcuffed, out on the sidewalk, Ben noticed that it was getting light. It had been dark when he entered the building; now a large cop pressed his head down with sufficient force but half solicitously so he wouldn't bump his head as he was thrust into the back seat of the patrol car.

When Ben had thought of purgatory he must have been mumbling to himself as the stout man standing close by began to answer him, spouting information and observation, spinning an odd, and Ben found, an interesting context for what had been Ben's involuntary remark: something that had escaped like a moan. The man's bald head shone in the fog of cigarette smoke. He rocked in a prayer-like motion Ben remembered from a former life. The lilting sing-song of the man's voice turned every declarative statement into inquiry. Ben recognized in the man who would introduce himself as Morris, a species of Jewish polymath he felt related to in some familial way. Morris said, "You won't find it named in the Bible, but in the thirteenth century the Roman church officially recognized purgatory. It's not a synonym for hell, but a place of temporary suffering where one can expiate one's sins, get clean. Hell, according to ancient apocryphal texts is not south of us, but in the third heaven. Anyway, better to be in hell with a wise man than in paradise with a fool. No? How do you do, I'm Morris." Ben wiping tears from his eyes shook Morris' hand. "I know," Morris said, "you're not crying, it's the smoke."

At each meeting someone told the story of how he or she got there. Morris had introduced Ben to Jeff. Morris and Jeff, at subsequent meetings, told their stories. The three Jewish drunks had found one another, their camaraderie initiated upon hearing certain familiar inflections of voice and a related humor when describing catastrophe. Ben wasn't ready to tell his story. There were many parts he didn't know, absences when he'd been ambulatory for some portion of time, and afterward, no matter how incredulous, he was forced to depend on the accounts of various witnesses: the adventures and misadventures attributed to him were often plausible, and sometimes frightening. He listened for clues to what was his life. Often there was evidence beyond what acquaintances had told him: like the face he encountered in the mirror that he had to acknowledge as his own, as there was no one standing behind him. The battered looking cousin looking back at him, was him. After a span of days and an interval of weeks listening to the stories of others he seemed to remember more, pieces of his history all at once at hand. But the prerequisite for this recall required listening to the confessions of men and women in which, no matter how different the particulars of the narratives (or the narrators) Ben was able to identify his own insane imperatives.

The swelling of his right hand receded. When he sweated

his perspiration no longer stunk of booze. The cowl of skin beneath his left eyebrow hooded the eye's autonomous introspection; and the welt on the bridge of his nose slanted down, like the short arm of a clock, forever fixed at five, the onset of happy hour at the bars in the city. If his nostalgia for the illusory freedom of not giving a damn became too enticing, he fished chocolate kisses from his pocket, peeled the tin foil from each chocolate, and jammed the fistful of candy into his mouth. Somehow the taste of chocolate mitigated the memory of the longed for first rush of a boiler-maker. The meeting began. The Christian drunks recited the Lord's Prayer while the Jewish drunks remained silent. Morris waddled over to Jeff and Ben, and the three, startled to find themselves alive and in the cellar of a church said in unison, "*Nu*, we're all here." "To have a synagogue," Morris whispered, "we need a quorum, ten adult Jewish males. But because it's not always possible to find the ten to make a minyan, exceptions are allowed, for instance a circumcision or a wedding. A wedding without ten adult male guests, would be maybe, a rush job at City Hall. We could think of this like a circumcision, no? A covenant to begin a new life? According to tradition Abraham circumcised himself. Sometimes you got to improvise."

When Ben was able to announce at a meeting that he'd gone thirty days without drinking he received applause. When he announced he'd gone sixty days without drinking he received applause and Morris asked if he'd tell his story. Ben said he wasn't ready.

Now there were days when Ben felt a calm as deep as intoxication. Selfish as a miser hoarding his wealth, he desired to talk to no one. He skipped meetings and was glad he didn't have a telephone. Neither Jeff nor Morris knew where he lived. Morris had said, "Not even the Angel of Death can scare some alkies. These are the low bottom drunks. They have to wreck body and mind before they die. You're lucky to have gotten here so young." Ben didn't feel young, or old. He felt himself concealed, hidden from time until the evening hours when solitude became desolate; he was not subject to the mere passing of the day, but the end of an era as every night he entered a new dark age. The one room apartment with the dilapidated armchair, convertible couch, bookcase, small table with a hot plate on it, and the bathtub with the door lid on it, which also served as his desk and occupied most of the kitchen alcove, seemed spartan during the day, and at night, squalid. On the bathtub desk was a typewriter and a pile of manuscripts. If he succumbed to reading what he'd written during the day, he found that the stories that had seemed the very tissue of his being were revealed at night as counterfeit, and he was ashamed. When he stopped taking night classes at City College, and managed to get himself fired at the warehouse so that he could collect unemployment checks and have four unencumbered months to write, and read what he pleased, he'd felt that he'd committed a brave and necessary act. Even the first week of nights felt pretty good. But as he was overtaken with revulsion for the language he'd put on paper, he had to get out, not only to assuage his disgust, but to find some redeeming act.

Ben, taking to the street, fingered the six ten dollar bills in his pocket. He walked past a liquor store and a bar without going in; the delay was akin to foreplay; the treasure of the sixty days promised that when he put down the first double shot of whiskey and the beer chaser the heat would spread through his chest, warming his heart and like the first time, he'd taste a levity that promised freedom. Whatever happened, events would have their own meaning and he could live there, if he were brave enough. Moreover, he might live again in the dream of eloquence he couldn't repudiate.

The ritual required the laying of a foundation. The next time he passed a liquor store he went in. In an alleyway between a tenement and a garage that was closed he drank the pint of whiskey. Now when he sat at the bar he could sip beer moderately and savor the "varieties of religious experience."

At the bar he decided to reinforce his foundation and ordered a double shot of Jamieson and a beer chaser. Mickey the bartender stroked his gray mustache with his thumb, paused and said, "Kid, do yourself a favor and disappear." Ben wondered whether he owed Mickey an apology. He couldn't remember, but said, "Sorry for any trouble I might have caused." Mickey sighed. To Ben's left a comfortable six feet away there were two men still in their work clothes drinking beer and discussing how the welfare system, supported by the taxes of hard working people assured that the lazy and irresponsible could remain lazy and irresponsible. At a table in a corner, adjacent to the bar, a middle-aged woman bundled in a winter coat despite the mild weather stared into her drink as if reading tea leaves. At a distance to Ben's right sat a woman whose attractiveness drew the attention of the other two men at the bar who agreed that if it were not for the idle poor they could be rich. Mickey replenished the handsome woman's drink and said, "Helen, I didn't forget," and dropped an olive in her martini. Ben became aware that as in childhood what claimed his interest left him staring, bereft of discretion. Looking directly into her eyes he had inflicted an unwanted intimacy. As though he were a subway exhibitionist flashing his nakedness, now in the glare of the woman's contempt, he lowered his eyes and she reached into her purse and put on a pair of sunglasses.

Ben bought himself another double shot of whiskey. He gulped the whiskey and sipped the beer. The heat the booze brought to his head was different from the inflammation the woman's hateful glance had brought to his face. Ben sensed that every man's fate gained glamour by simply being near her. Her presence gave momentousness to the evening. It was not merely time that had punished her beauty, but something else: perhaps innocent bravery, a capacity for tak-ing on the world that revealed the paucity of what any man might offer. He wanted to tell her these things, tell her his appreciation, his gratitude. Now he was able to lift his head and look at her again; blameless he was moved by the need to make an honorable gesture. But the sunglasses masked her. Whatever she thought or felt was rendered opaque be-hind the dark lenses. Still, Ben thought he recognized her, felt that he knew her, or had known her. He remembered anonymity expressed as a principle at the meetings. She like all the others would have offered only her first name, and said, "And I'm an alcoholic." And like Ben she wasn't quite ready to quit; she desired one more dance with the Devil.

Ben sipped his beer. He seemed to recall aspects of her story, although he didn't remember her telling it. He might not have been attentive, sitting in the blue fog of cigarette smoke, having heard so many stories, so many calamities: the narrators petitioning the "Higher Power" that they referred to obliquely, as the nearly dead were absolved of sectarian passion in the democracy of ruin; they petitioned in the hope that they could be restored to life. Ben suspected that he probably saw her there, perhaps even heard her speak at the meeting in the church on the Upper East Side where, it was said, there was a better class of drunks and the men were required to wear ties; and he was not likely to see Morris or Jeff so far uptown; they had presumed to know him, warn him of the alcoholic's egoism, and the dangers of terminal individuality. Ben decided that the way to convey his respect was to at least appear oblivious to the lady's presence.

Ben looked at the clock. Morris and Jeff would be at the meeting that began during the supper hour. Morris, Ben thought, was a surprise. He would never have imagined roly-poly Morris as a former marine. Yet when he told his story, Ben learned that he had survived the most savage fighting in the South Pacific; but when he came home from World War Two a decorated hero, he came closer to death in the celebratory chaos of an unending party than he had on Iwo Jima. Obliging Morris couldn't say no and it seemed that every inhabitant in the city wanted to buy him a drink. Before the war Morris had dreamed of being another Gene Krupa. Now he was a math teacher in a high school for gifted students. Whenever Morris, the aging bachelor, spoke at a meeting he concluded with a sincere and general marriage proposal to every unmarried woman in the room. Jeff was a very different story. He had been the major strategist for a congressman whose political philosophy made an essential claim on his conscience. But as the years wore on, the politics left Jeff bereft of himself, except for self-loathing. He readily admitted that he remained in thrall to the glamour of being so close to power. A handsome man, it was difficult for him to remember a time when he was not unfaithful to his wife; his capacity for analysis and rhetoric seeped poison into his blood, which he doused with the palliative of endless martinis. While Jeff sickened, the congressman thrived. Jeff's wife remained devoted to him; but when his teenage daughter expressed a deep and abiding contempt for her father, Jeff staggered into the program. Now he worked for the civil service. He spoke slowly and carefully, purging from his vocabulary any superlatives. He was constantly on guard against heightened language and studiously matter of fact. Ben had found Jeff's sobriety scary, a sort of inverted Faustian deal in which only devotion to the mundane might yield salvation.

Ben placed a ten dollar bill on the bar. He'd planned to move on when he'd drunk that amount in beer. But as he'd begun to retrieve the events that would make the medium of time he could once again inhabit, he thought it best not to cut off the fuel for the enterprise. He swallowed a mouthful of beer, closed his eyes, and knew that he'd have to do what he'd dreamed. As he placed another ten dollar bill on the bar Mickey leaned over and whispered, "You don't have to be a hero, and turn everything into fuckin' tragedy." Ben heard tenderness in Mickey's voice. The expression of concern touched him and he said, "Let me buy you a drink." The bartender said, "Thanks, not while I'm working." And so, to commemorate the moment Ben bought a round of drinks for the four patrons; three of whom raised their glasses by way of saying "thanks". The fourth, the careworn beauty keeping her eyes secret behind the dark lenses acknowledged no one, as Mickey topped her drink. Ben glanced at her and thought, she is a woman to whom evil things have happened. Perhaps the dark glasses provide respite from seeing the world too clearly. Awash in sympathetic magic, Ben willed something like hope, like prayer, in her direction. And it was then that he began to feel that even his failures were glorious, the striving a source of unending desire: the story he'd attempted to write (The Adventures of An Autodidact) and had judged a failure was still alive in him. Now a man of means, grateful, he was ready to hug everyone in the bar.

There was a shift in the population. A steady flow of men in suits, carrying attaché cases were arriving. The guys with lunch pails and thermoses were leaving, the bar had become crowded. The Friday night festivity felt more like New Year's Eve, something unruly and defiant in the celebration. Crowded as the bar was, the stool to Helen's right remained empty. Tiny meteors of neon light streaked across the dark lenses of her sunglasses. The patrons, except for the sanctuary of space surrounding Helen, were packed two deep at the bar. In addition to Mickey, a second bartender had come on duty. He was completely bald and massive with a Fu-Manchu mustache that made him look like a wrestler who always played the role of the villain. As he served martinis and manhattans to the patrons on either side of Ben, Ben cried "A moscow mule." From somewhere in the bar another voice cried, "A horse, a horse, my kingdom for a horse", and there was laughter. The huge, quick bartender covered half the length of the bar, served drinks, returned, reached over Ben's head and served the patrons standing behind Ben, and then set the moscow mule in front of Ben. He gulped it down. The bartender moved away toward patrons signaling with empty glasses. The mass of bodies squeezing Ben on either side ejected him backward and now he was standing behind the second row of drinkers pressing in toward the bar, and he had to take a leak.

In the lavatory that looked like a whitewashed cave, he took a long piss. He rested his chin on top of the tall white urinal, and held on to the sides like a man clinging to a raft, adrift in the ocean. He rested for a while, and then made his way to the only vacant seat at the bar, next to Helen. She said, "The seat's reserved." Ben sat down, "I'll give it up whenever the party arrives." "You better be quick about it," she said. Close by Mickey wiped the bar and the man sitting in front of him said, "The greatest sacrifice I've made for my kids is not blowing my brains out, and God forgive me, I've resented them for it." "Al," Mickey said, "I don't start hearing confessions until midnight." Helen removed her glasses and studied the man. Ben wondered, was she the woman who had earlier in the evening, said, "Are you going to live your life like a drunken sailor so you won't be mistaken for Shylock?" – or had that happened another night, in another bar? Looking at her he was a little afraid. Did she see through masks, even the mask that said, here are the secrets of my heart laid bare? Helen was staring at him. He was startled. She was older than he'd thought, and more careworn, but still beautiful; she'd always be beautiful. The contrast between her pale skin and black hair was stark. The fine bones of her face and neck suggested that even in the construction of her skeleton, her maker had already intended her to be beautiful. But when the door to the stockroom and rear exit swung open and another bartender emerged, a fluorescent light splashed a glare over her head and shoulders, and for a moment Ben could see the crone peering through the face of the beautiful woman. "Miss," he said, "May I buy you a drink?" She smiled. "How can I say no, you're such a sincere boy, and you're still trying to say yes in a big way." Mickey frowned and moved toward a patron waving an empty glass. Ben, embarrassed, almost blurted that he was old enough to vote. The unspoken assertion made him feel ridiculous and he tried to remember and assure himself that during the two months that he'd attended AA meetings, he hadn't revealed much about himself beyond saying, "My name is Ben and I'm an alcoholic." Helen's voice sounded familiar and remote. It was a cultivated voice, the pronunciation crisp, the timbre grated with a cigarette smoker's huskiness. Could she have been an actress at some time? During the long evening he'd imagined Helen's life. He thought that years ago she had probably come to New York to study and become an actress. That hadn't worked out. She could have worked as a model. Then Ben remembered the two times he attended AA meetings at the church on the Upper East Side where all the fancy drunks went, and he had been required to wear a tie. A woman had told her story, and it was Helen's story. The woman had been forthcoming and defiant in her account of the things that finally compelled her to desire sobriety. For a long time, she said too long, she had worked as a waitress. She had also modeled in the Garment Center, and worked as an actress; but she'd waitressed years longer than she had modeled or acted. "And oh," she said, "for a month I danced at a topless bar. The guy who owned the place figured I owed him favors. That's when I hit bottom."

Ben paused in his conjecture of Helen's life, embarrassed, as if he'd been prying and blundered into the truth. He'd also reached where he wanted to be. One sip less and he wouldn't have arrived. One sip more and he would have overshot his destination. He sat still. Perhaps he could fine tune the moment with the littlest of sips. Carefully, he brought the glass to his lips; the drop of beer lolled on his tongue and the moment opened: time a residence where he could abide, and he concluded that quite aside from the haunting sense of déjà vu Helen incited, they were, after all, strangers. Nevertheless, the feeling persisted that she was not a stranger. He swallowed and Mickey was there, in front of him, bending over the bar. "Ben, I been servin' poison for years, and you're one of the youngest, most far gone drunks I seen." "Mickey," Helen said, "You're all heart." Ben emptied his pockets, putting his keys, wallet, a five dollar bill, two singles, and seventy-eight cents on the bar. He figured that he could afford two more beers and a tip for the bartenders. Mickey poured beer into the glass he tipped expertly and placed it in front of Ben. He removed a dollar and some change, turned, rang it up in the cash register, turned again and scooped up the rest of the money, Ben's keys, and wallet and said, "Keep this in your pocket." Ben said nothing. Mickey removed a wallet from his back pocket, opened it like a book, and laid it on the bar. "Look at this." He pointed to a photo of a stout girl with a pretty face wearing a graduation cap and gown. "My daughter Mary, she's in law school, makin' somethin' of herself. It costs. You ever think about the future?" Ben thought, what if this is my last drink? The notion was momentous and he looked at Mickey and Helen as if he'd already said "goodbye". Mickey picked up a damp cloth, wiped the bar around Ben's elbows and wrung drops of water out of the cloth that dripped into the sink beneath the bar.

"Hey," Ben said, to demonstrate he was alert and not as drunk as Mickey might think, "That guy's trying to get your attention." Mickey looked and quickly came out from behind the bar and elbowed his way through the crowd toward the man. Helen frowned. The tall, middle-aged man with white hair wore a blue suit, white shirt and white tie. He wasn't carrying an attaché case, or waving an empty glass. Without effort, he looked over the heads of everyone at the bar and waited as bulky Mickey plowed through the patrons and arrived open-mouthed. There was something deferential, Ben thought, in the way Mickey bent his head to hear what the man was saying to him. Mickey had been nodding yes and smiling before the man had said a word. Helen, irate, slapped a ten dollar bill on the counter, took her pack of cigarettes from the bar, and made her way to the rear exit. Mickey lunged after her. Midway, he stopped, and turned. He made an imploring gesture with his hands and seemed frightened by the indifference of the white-haired man.

Mickey ran through the corridor to the exit door. Ben ran after Mickey. Outside the full moon illuminated the parking lot. Ben trotted in the maze of cars. He heard the wind carrying their argument down the pathway of cars. Helen yelled, "Go to hell." Ben chased after her voice, came to the end of the path, rounded the corner and continued in the labyrinth. The quarrel modulated, soft, loud, rushing on the breeze within the footway between automobiles. Helen said, "It's my night off, and I never do business from a bar." Ben spied the profile of a lunatic running beside him; his heart lurched, and he fell. On his feet again he recognized the guy as he looked at his reflection on a car window. He continued at a brisk pace. His forehead hurt. A fragment of conversation he'd had with Mickey months ago came to mind and all at once Ben hated him, because Mickey counted on a God who could forgive anything. The full moon cast an icy sheen on the roofs of the cars. Ben slowed his pace. He reached a place where the column of cars made a right angle and turned into that path. And there was a man staggering toward him, waving and shouting, "hello, hello," as though he'd been searching for Ben, and was overjoyed to have finally found him. When they were face to face, the young man, disheveled and plainly drunk said, "I can't remember where I parked the fucking car," stumbled on and hollered, "If you find it give a yell, it's a new blue Chevy." The fading resonance of the man's voice caught in its passing other voices, a man stating calmly, "Bitch," and the woman's voice countering, "Bastard." Ben hoisted himself over the hood of a Buick, slid down into the next lane, and saw them at about the distance of a runner rounding third base, and headed for home plate. They appeared to be jitterbugging. Ben stopped; he felt like an intruder. With the searing clarity of an insomniac, he saw them from some recall of dread, recognized them not from their faces but the circumstance that locked them together. They submitted to the dance wearily, oddly graceful. Bull-like Mickey caught Helen's hand, drawing her to him, and punched her in the stomach. She draped over his arm. Ben bolted, outrunning running away. He didn't know what he was going to do until he dropped and slid over the asphalt as though he were stealing home plate, the asphalt shredding his pants, taking skin; feet first he torpedoed Mickey's knees and Mickey crashed face forward.

Ben stood panting, his ass burning. Helen's nose was bleeding and she was bent over clutching her stomach. Mickey rolled over and sat up. His face was a mess. Slowly Helen straightened up and wiped blood from her lips with the hem of her dress. Ben shivered in the mild night air. He was receiving messages from his scorched ass. This had happened before. He couldn't remember the particulars, but knew that it had happened before, and the woman had said, "I'm a moral person, I believe in Hell." Helen walked to Mickey and kicked him in the head. He fell backward, his skull making an awful sound banging off the asphalt. He lay still. Helen said, "Get his wallet." Ben couldn't move. "Okay, Lancelot, I'll do it myself." She went through Mickey's pockets, removed his wallet, took the cash, and tossed the wallet.

She grabbed Ben's hand, tugged, and they were off. He was amazed at how fast she could run in high heel shoes. She wobbled and reeled, never slowing her pace, and didn't let go of his hand until she'd led him out of the maze.

They walked in circles wheezing. After a time he was breathing normally. He saw the high-rise apartment house across the street. There was a canopy over the entrance. On either side of the canopy was a scrawny, invalid looking tree, leafless and trussed with wires to a circular wrought iron base. Most of the windows in the apartment house were dark. The isolated windows of light made him long for the snug life he imagined living inside. The night was inexhaustible. He was tired of his revel, surfeited with magic, and he wanted to rest.

Helen stood, her face thrust close to his, "You figure I owe you somethin'?" Her voice had shed all refinement. It was low-rent, and ready for trouble. Ben said, "No." She said, "No is right," and took a step back. Her nose was still bleeding. She wiped it with her sleeve. She surveyed him from head to toe, and said, "I got to get away from this city, like right now. If you have any sense you won't go back to Mickey's joint, ever. Understand?" Ben nodded yes. She said, "I doubt it," turned and looked for a cab. Seeing none she walked away as fast as she could. Ben watched her. She was halfway down the street when she turned and hurried toward him. He saw her getting closer and thought he'd embrace her. She stopped short of bumping into him, and he thrust his hands in front of him to cushion the collision. Helen grabbed his hand, and pressed cash into it. "Remember," she said, "what I told you. Don't go back to Mickey's. He's an ex-cop and so are his partners. They work both sides of the street. Believe me; you're lucky you're still breathin'." She put one hand on his shoulder, balancing herself as she lifted the shank of her right leg behind her, reached back and removed the high heel shoe and let it fall to the sidewalk. Then she removed the left shoe the same way. Ben felt the warm impress of her hand on his shoulder, the weight of her resting on him; his guts swooped. Dizzy and lucid, he thought, how can she leave like this, after what we've been through? He thought he heard her say yes, though her lips never moved. Still, he knew she was only dispensing balm, condescending to him. And this long good-bye had him close to blacking out. Then he remembered how anxious he'd been when he was fifteen, because he expected to die in a nuclear holocaust before he ever got laid. And she was gone, running down the street with a shoe in either hand.

He plodded home sick, but didn't throw up. His knees and ass burned, and his back ached. He walked the deserted streets and looked for a cab, now that he had money. He saw neither a cab nor automobiles, except for the cars parked at the curb. He passed two bars that were closed. He knew it was ridiculous, but he still wanted her, and wanted to differentiate himself from every man she had known. He reminded himself that she was available for a price. He didn't want to think about the defeats that had left her with a respect for money; and he called himself dumb for not offering her refuge for the night. She wouldn't take the chance of going back to her apartment. She'd probably go straight to Grand Central Station, or Port Authority. But he could have kept her safe at his place. Mickey didn't know his address or his last name. At his apartment she could have cleaned herself up, taken a bath. She would ask him for a towel. Perhaps summon him to wash her back. He would touch her. She'd consider putting his yearning to rest. But maybe their conversation would lead them to a place where she would tell him her story, and he would have to choose between that intimacy, or getting laid. It was a difficult choice. After thinking about it long enough to have his agitation become an itch simmering near his crotch, he longed to give up this perplexity. Scratching, half mad, he recalled Mrs. Bickford, the nurse at detox who took care of him when he was sick. She was an older woman who stayed at his side through the worst of it, cleaning him up, whispering encouragement. The first day was hideous. When his shaking had become intermittent and he'd stopped vomiting, she continued to sponge his forehead and whispered that he should pray to Jesus for help. She repeated this again and again, trying to convince him that such help was forthcoming if only he had the faith to ask. He trembled and stuttered that he was a Jew. Mrs. Bickford was thrilled with the news. Ben's attention flickered in and out, but after a while he gathered that his existence was a symptom of the apocalypse, and thus the coming of Christ. Mrs. Bickford was overjoyed.

He staggered to the door of his apartment wanting to believe that Helen was inured to degradation, or there was something in her, in spite of all, that remained inviolable. The itching had stopped. He managed to get his key in the lock, pushed on his door, and stumbled into the dark. Dizzy, he made his way to the large worn armchair at the center of the room, and lowered himself into the chair. He leaned his head on the back cushion and sat very still. If he moved he'd spew all over himself and then he'd have to sit there and stink. He heard traffic moving in the street and water gurgling in the pipes in the wall. He thought it must be getting close to morning. But the window facing him remained dark. Sunk in the bog of the chair he rested, closed his eyes and drowsed.

His wooziness passed. He opened his eyes. It was still night. Something he couldn't remember nagged at him. He wasn't reconciled to what remained unconsummated between himself and Helen. He wanted to turn on the lights, but couldn't get out of the chair. From his chair in the void he could see out the window into the window of the apartment across the alley. He wondered why the couple didn't pull down the shade. Did they want to be seen? Were they exhibitionists whose desire was inflamed by arousing strangers? The lights in their apartment burned brightly and Ben couldn't deny that he was aroused. He wanted to see better. His eyes burned. The woman's back was arched; her thighs clamped the man's sides. The features of her face squeezed with excruciating feeling, squashed any individual trait from her face. Her mouth was a hole. As Ben stared and his vision became more acute, he saw that the woman was struggling.

The man was beating her, then Ben was falling inside an elevator cage. He plummeted down the shaft and heard the guttural roar, knew the savage importuning that consumed every sound on earth; the most bestial histrionics barking from a human mouth; and Ben could see between the bars of his cage the infinite bone white field strewn with howling infants, their heads cracked eggs oozing brains.

He awoke and heard screaming. The apartment was dark, and he was alone. He commanded the screamer to shut up. The scream became a child's nagging whimper and he had little patience for it. He was soaked with sweat. Stuff drooled from his nose. He couldn't stop shaking. Awake in the dark he was no longer falling. If he could get out of his chair, he'd use the fifty-bucks Helen had given him, and get a hair-of-the-dog; hell, with fifty bucks he could buy the whole dog. Remy-Martin – why not? He sweat and shivered, and the here and now became the last peek at the story he'd been writing. The language was inadequate. He couldn't abide this failure. There was then, no work for which he was suited. This being so, he was unworthy of love. On and on it went. He thought and thought. Reason, fear's accomplice, every iota of life's business a downfall. Bits of light speckled the window. The radiator under the window gonged. He was ready for sleep. And as if he had known always that he could be acquainted with his soul only by journeying through the things of this world, and he stumbled upon this, the most fearful thing, the portly Jew in his soft flesh, the most provisional of garments, waddling among worlds, one of God's comic adjectives, his face an overgrown garden.

The Patricide: a novella

The memory insinuates itself, and again I'm back there, trying to exonerate myself. The hot summer day. The mothers stacked on the tenement stoop. Mama perched on the top step. Pregnant Aunt Zelda, her huge belly resting on her lap, sits close to Mama. She glistens with sweat, mouth gasping, her eyes closed. The other women are distributed below, on the descending steps. Somebody's grandma sits on the middle step fanning herself with a newspaper, nodding yes to everything she hears. Next to the Babushka is a very young mother to be, a child herself, who looks frightened. One lady cradles an infant in her arms; another near the pavement reaches down and rocks a baby carriage. Me and my kid brother Josh are trying to hit a shiny new penny with a pink rubber ball. I'm eleven, Josh nine. We stand a half dozen paces apart, facing each other at the borders of the box sketched in chalk on the sidewalk. In the middle of the box is the penny we take turns trying to hit with the pink ball, while each of the women take a turn narrating the travail of childbirth. The woman with the baby in her arms recalls how, in the throes of labor she cursed her husband. The lady rocking the baby carriage says that eventually she couldn't hear herself screaming and wonders if that deafness is in some way related to the amnesia that allows her to long for another child. Stout Mrs. Kozckiewicz, the landlord's wife and janitor, emerges from the cellar having pushed open the large metal doors of the bulkhead built into the sidewalk. She's hauled the last of the cans of trash from the cellar, lined them up at the curb, the brimming garbage cans haloed with buzzing flies, she pauses, wipes sweat from her eyes and says, "Five I got. The first four came two at a time. My husband the landlord says, 'In and out, and boom, you're big as a house.' I don't know whether he's braggin' or complainin'. But just in case, when he gets that look in his eye, I bring out his vodka and that makes him sleepy, thank God." Meager Mrs. Cheechko, who has diminished with the birth of each of her six plump babies, so that her house dress hangs like a shroud over her skeletal body, says of her husband Stanley's mysterious vanishings and appearances, "He comes through the door with the bottle of milk I asked him to get three months ago, and says, 'Hello, heart of my heart. I'm home.'" I say to him, "Drop dead." He says, "I'm not in the mood." Aunt Zelda exhales in sympathy, puts her hands on her big belly and nudges the weight on to her right thigh. Then, from the summit of the top step, I hear my mother announce, "My Ben was a miracle. He came so quick. I was on a gurney in the corridor of the hospital when he crowned. The nurse said it was the easiest birth she'd ever seen. And when I took him home, what a doll! He nursed, he slept, no problems. My Ben was a dream! But his brother Josh, boy oh boy, then I paid. I was in labor all night. Josh tore me to pieces. And that was only the beginning. When I took him home, he cried, he screamed no matter what. From the minute he was born, I never had a minute's peace. But with my firstborn I got a little lucky," she says, lowering her voice, fearful of being overheard by the demiurge who can only create a conscience through punishment. I squirm hearing myself named in Mama's tribute and know Josh also listens. Maybe, that's why I chased the ball into traffic, dodging the car that almost hit me.

I can still hear Mama shriek; inside the shriek, I'm no longer the blessing that marks my brother cursed; but in less than a moment, Mama was on her knees in the gutter weeping, hugging my head to her bosom. Then she stood up, looked in the direction of the car that hadn't stopped, and in Yiddish wished cholera on the driver. In the same breath she recapitulated in a scream the event that had hardly passed and was already a legend, grabbed a handful of my hair, yanked me onto the sidewalk and remonstrated against heaven, "Just like his father, he'll put me early in my grave. God Almighty, he scared me out of ten years of my life." And with her free hand smacked me again and again, while her other hand clutched the hair on top of my head, as she pulled me up the steps. The women sitting on the stoop moved to the right and the left to make a clear path. Aunt Zelda called to her sister, "Don't aggravate yourself." Josh trailed behind me, and slipped the penny in my back pocket.

I remember being on fire. Josh had telephoned, spoke

mysteriously of a crisis, danger. I figured that he was behind on his rent again. "If you're short on cash, I can help." Josh said, "I have to go on the lam, the dough will help." I recall Doctor Stern's advice. Be patient, don't confront the story as a lie. Josh, sounding like Humphrey Bogart, insisted that we meet at three o'clock in the lobby of a hotel on the Upper West Side. I got there at two-thirty. At three-thirty he still hadn't arrived. At four o'clock I left, worried, and angry with myself for being angry. I crossed the lobby, stepped into the revolving door, walked and pushed on the glass partition, my vision filled with the image of Josh homeless again, haggard, selling his blood to buy cigarettes and coffee. In the revolving door, not seeing the street, I passed the lobby a second time and plodded on in the turning until the street came into view, and stumbled outside. It was November, a raw day. Still, I preferred to be above ground, and decided against the subway, walking the six blocks to the downtown bus. I told myself to calm down, smoked my pipe and thought, if only I could talk to Josh, I might find a way to enter his story, learn what kind of trouble he was in and straighten things out. Josh's last disappearance lasted two months and ended with his hospitalization. I considered calling Doctor Stern, paused at a phone booth, tapped the dregs of my pipe out on the curb and put it in my coat pocket. Again, I reviewed the various diagnoses of psychiatrists over the years, Josh always abetting the shrink's findings, adept at the latest terminology, reassured the doctors of their acuity, until he landed in the hospital to be hydrated and fed intravenously. Persuaded that calling Doctor Stern was a waste of time, I continued walking and smelled smoke. I looked for fire engines, remembered, and argued with myself. After all, I couldn't have been more than seven. I'd stood at the curb looking at the backs of the big boys standing around a large metal trash can from which the tips of flames swayed and sparks hovered in the spume of smoke. Snow was heaped on the sidewalk and the gutter, but within the circle where the big boys stood, surrounding the flaming garbage can, the snow had melted away, the asphalt shiny and black where the shadow of smoke drifted like a river; a radius of heat encompassed the boys extending their sticks in the flames, the illuminated spokes stabbing at the fire. Drowsy in the ring of heat, I saw the boys creating their own weather. Beneath the slate-gray sky my face was warm, as if I were basking under the summer sun. I heard the phrase "roasting mickeys", but even after one of the boys gave me the smoking potato impaled on the end of the stick, and I bit into the potato, my tongue juggling the hot fragrant lump, I wasn't aware that I'd been beguiled by the word and named the sparks flying up out of the flames "mickeys". When Mama called from the window four stories up, her voice reached me as if it had fallen from the moon, spiraling down in the snowy air. The urgency in her voice dissipated in the long journey down, "Ben, Benny, come home." I munched on the potato, slogged through the slush, and climbed the stoop steps slowly.

That Sunday morning in the kitchen, standing at the bathtub with Josh beside me, our parents at the opposite end of the railroad flat, in their bedroom, I heard sounds that weren't snoring as I held Josh's hand. In our underwear, enthralled, we watched the flames consume the cereal and sugar boxes, and wooden clothespins I'd placed at the bottom of the bathtub. I'd ignited the little world with a wooden match and then dropped the box of matches into the fire which bloomed bright orange, the flames fanning into blue veined leaves. Beads of light darted upward in the curl of smoke and disappeared in a black cloud. I heard the slap of feet, felt the vibration in the floor, turned, and saw the naked man running toward us, eyes mad, hairy as a dog, his sex swinging between his legs, and recognized Papa looming above us. I don't remember the words that flew from my mouth as my hand went to the faucet handle and unleashed water drowning the conflagration, but know that I'd screamed my innocence, and blamed my brother. Josh suspended above me, hung from Papa's hand, a sound like applause boomed with each whack on his ass, the back of his legs, Josh swung, bawling, dripping piss. Mama ran from the bedroom in her slip screaming "Maniac" at Papa, and he released into her arms the unclean thing wetting the floor, soiling them both.

I walked; the smell of smoke was stronger. People in the street hurried by me. I listened for sirens and guessed that the fire must be close by. I hurried along in a veil of smoke, felt intense heat on my hip, and as I realized what had happened a wing of flame burst from my coat pocket. I tore the burning coat from my body; the sleeves billowing smoke, the coat in flames fell from my hand to the pavement and I stomped the fire. Passersby glanced at the madman dancing in the flames.

I continued on my way to the bus stop. I was cold, and

smelled charred. The wind flapped threads of steam from my trouser leg. The inside of my pants pocket had burned away, and with my fingertips I felt the blisters on my thigh. The synthetic cloth of my topcoat must have been especially combustible and the embers from the pipe I'd jammed in my pocket, alive. The palm of my right hand was red and smarted.

I'd never confided to any of Josh's psychiatrists what had happened that Sunday morning; I tried to confess to Josh, but failed every time. In his unending narrative, what actually happened sank beneath the perpetual creation of the stories through which he needed to see his life.

By the age of ten I could hide in the anarchy at home; I'd learned when and how to duck, and I couldn't deny that I was the favored child. If I didn't glory in that, neither did I give up that estimable place, especially in regard to Papa. Long before I had knowledge of what went on in Mama and Papa's bedroom, I intuited something momentous and dangerous about the dark they entered each night, and I was prescient while Papa was bewildered and angry when the bedroom door was closed to him. When he kicked the bedroom door open, Mama brandishing a breadknife, forced him to retreat to the living room couch, where, she reminded him, he could sleep and expect to wake in the morning. He never doubted her sincerity. I could gauge, to the hour, when Papa's exile would become insupportable (rarely as long as a week) and he'd smash the place up, which broadened the scope and time of his exile, usually, two or three nights. Through some tacit agreement of my parents, I accompanied Papa in exile to the Russian baths where we slept blissfully in a dormitory of men wrapped in white sheets, like mummies laid out on cots. The blue light bulbs overhead provided perpetual nightfall that echoed with the snoring and belching of men who would never know such fulfillment awake.

I was already acclimated to the heat of the steam room. In the pine scented steam, I was attentive to Papa and the other lefties, explaining to one another the reasons for the dilatory pace of the forever imminent worker's paradise in the country their parents or grandparents had fled. After a good schvitz, discussion, and being hosed down, we feasted. The restaurant concession featured cantaloupe, herring, steak and potatoes. All of it in portions generous enough to provide ballast for the deepest sleep this side of the grave.

But beyond the profound creaturely pleasures was the event I longed for, guiltily: not the battle between Mama and Papa, but the expulsion that followed. Because almost always upon leaving the Russian baths, we'd rise early and after a breakfast of cheese and potato blintzes, make our way to one of the theatre palaces uptown, arriving before eleven, when the price of admission was sixty cents. In the velvety, bejeweled semi-dark of the theatre we sat in balcony seats as in sky-borne gondolas, floating beneath rosy bottomed cherubs and nymphs swimming in air. And from that heavenly perspective we waited for the band to rise, golden and shining out of the vertiginous well of dark way down below, the band rising and blowing "Sing, Sing, Sing". The culmination of Mama and Papa cursing one another, the promise of homicide, and Papa's busting up the furniture ended in music. Music that opened me beyond words, and still I wasn't dumb; and Papa, soaring beside me in the music, could have been my wild big brother.

I waited on the corner. The wind picked up. The cold made my eyes tear and through the blur I saw my bus coming. The insomnia that had kept me up for three nights was abating and I thought that when I got back to my apartment I'd be able to sleep. The passengers on the bus were elderly, except for one young mother clutching a girl of about three on her lap. I sat opposite the mother and child, smiled at the little girl, and the mother shielded the kid's face with her hand. A great wail hushed thought like the herald just before the end of everything. One, two, and three fire engines screamed by, and an ambulance and a police car, sirens howling. When the howling swooned and subsided, I looked out the window and saw that the pedestrians who had been frozen in place were walking again. I also noticed that the seat beside me remained unoccupied even though several passengers were standing. I looked at an old gentleman gripping the overhead bar, swaying on his feet and the old guy averted his eyes. An old woman whose girth occupied two seats glowered at me. She sniffed at the air indignantly and didn't turn away when I stared back at her. And then I knew. The stench of the arsonist. The stink of smoldering ruin drifted from me and filled the air. In the old lady's eyes I was one of the culprits torching the city. As if I were explaining to the elderly travelers the arguments I knew to be futile, I chose my words carefully: excuse me, but you're mistaken. I don't earn my livelihood igniting insurance fires. And if you look a little closer you'll see that neither am I one of the adolescent vandals setting the city on fire for the fun of it. And now talking to myself, without, I hoped, moving my lips, heard once more, as I'd heard it when I was twelve, in Hebrew school, the story that foreshadowed the most primal failure of all the kinds of love that fail. Tired, I leaned the back of my head against the window. A humming vibration in the glass fluttered into the back of my neck and shivered down my back. I was neither asleep nor awake. And the story that had been dormant was whispering to me again. Abel loved God's favor better than he loved his brother. He was implicated in Cain's being disinherited, alone, cast out. Cain's patrimony, wandering, and the founding of cities: every bad neighborhood, his work.

In a drowse and no longer argumentative I believed I loved my brother. The bus rocked me. Josh's guileless face expressed only the emotion that held sway at the moment. The paradox of his nakedly innocent face was the secret it held, even after he'd forgotten it, or it had mutated within the labyrinthine tales of his life.

⟿

Snoring at the bottom of a well: the sound floated upward and clarified itself into the shallow grind of a metal roller skate skimming pavement. I was riding my scooter. I'd made it. The footboard had a milk box chassis in front with handles shaped into a "v" nailed to the top; two metal roller skate wheels were hammered into the front and rear of the footboard. One leg planted on the footboard, the other pushing against the pavement, my leg was the engine. Josh squeezed inside the milk box chassis, his face on his knees, his arms hugged his legs. Cargoed fetus-like in the milk box, he smiled. We roared around the block speeding past the tailor's shop, grocery, and stoop fronts on the way home. Josh's eyes were blissful, blood flowed from his nose. I'd turned my back. Forgot him. For how long? Ten minutes? Twenty? "Who did it Josh? Tell me, please?"

A day or two later, Josh, as though recalling the distant past said, "It was Frankie Tomanaro, he did it." Frankie, I knew, was in the eighth grade, two years older than Josh and a head taller. When I confronted him in the schoolyard, Frankie said, "Pickin' on your brudder? Who's your brudder?" I figured that Frankie couldn't keep track of the kids he bullied, and repeated "Just lay off my brother." Frankie shoved me and laughed, "You wanna pick a fight, go ahead, do somethin'," and shoved me again. Then, as if I were about to leap from roof to roof, as when the other boys and I played Follow the Leader, and Buzzy Pizzaro was the leader because he had more heart than anybody – and the first time I leaped I did it with my eyes closed and landed on the roof of the building next door, bouncing and skidding, skinning my knees and bruising my shoulder. Buzzy had seen that I'd closed my eyes. He said, "It don't count if you can't look at what you're doin'." I jumped again with my eyes open. If anyone but Buzzy had said that the second jump was necessary, I wouldn't have done it. When Frankie shoved me the second time, I swung and kept on swinging.

Although my eyes were open, the effort felt blind. But it was alright; I tasted blood in my mouth, and the mix of fear and exhilaration that at first felt like jumping off the roof became a zone of focus, and I let my fists fly, alternately hitting and missing the presence in front of me. And then something surprising: Frankie sitting on the ground, looking scared. My surprise grew out of an assumption I hadn't questioned; Frankie, like many of the tough guys was in the class of those designated slow in learning. I'd believed that God, in compensation, had granted them invincible prowess.

Several days later, Tommy Genco and Miriam Schwartz told me that Frankie hadn't hit Josh. It was Lena Volpi. Beautiful, amazonian, Lena Volpi; at fourteen she was taller than most of the boys her age and a better handball player. Her thick black hair hung down her back in a single braid. Her skin had the sheen and color of bronze and her eyes were an unnerving glacial blue. When Tommy mentioned her name I blushed. I'd recently dreamt of Lena and awoke wet with a fluid my body had never before produced.

Tommy and Miriam explained that when Lena asked Josh to move away from the wall of the Esquire Boot Polish Factory where all serious handball challenges were answered, Josh just stood still and smiled. Tommy and Miriam said that Lena who had challenged Whitey Costa, the handball champ of the block, had asked Josh to move in a nice way, more than once, and he just stood there until Lena smacked him.

I followed Josh into the kitchen and asked him why he said it was Frankie who hit him. Mama had her head out of the kitchen window conferring with Aunt Zelda, who leaned out of her window, draped bed sheets over the clothesline to dry, and nodded yes with several clothespins clenched between her teeth. Josh was responding to Mama's diatribe, apologizing for kicking her so hard when he was in her belly. "Josh," I said, "Miriam and Tommy told me it was Lena who hit you." Josh, in a trance, repeated Lena's name, and confused by my confusion, said, "What?" I repeated the question and he continued to stare at me, unable to fathom what it was I found so difficult to understand. I guessed at the truth. What Josh required from me was loyalty, and the acceptance of the truth beyond the mere appearance of things. If he were not allowed to tell his own story, he couldn't be anything other than what Mama, Papa, and the doctor knew him to be. I had begun to grasp this as Josh had begun to absorb Mama's declamatory style. And over days, months, and years I gained understanding, although what I understood presented practical difficulties. The truth Josh's portentous silence presented in the kitchen was that Lena Volpi wasn't merely beautiful, she was beauty. Worthy of worship, her prerogatives exceeded the norms of lesser others. Moreover, Frankie Tomanaro was a bully and the retribution inflicted on him was just and timely. Why quibble?

I had rushed Josh home and into the kitchen. Josh's nose was spewing blood. Mama recited one of her blood is thicker than water stories as she wiped blood from his face. She tilted his head up and swabbed inside his nostrils with a thin stick with the absorbent cotton nub soaked in the cauterizing medicine. Without the burning medicine the bleeding wouldn't stop. Mama was quick, efficient. She unbuttoned

Josh's blood stained shirt and filled me in on my early history. The sing-song of her voice burrowed into me. Now I remember it as though it happened. She said, "Remember, you're almost fifteen, already a man." I was almost fourteen. Whenever she mentioned my age, she made me a year older, as though she'd begun counting when I was a seed seeking harbor in her womb. She computed the years of my life using her own algebra; days, months, years, factored and translated from the instant I was a sperm propelled by my father, shedding his rabid virginity, weeping and screaming that Mama, who was fifteen, had ignited the blaze that made his virginity torture, and only his breaching her hymeneal barrier, could restore him to understanding – such as it was. Mama, from that first coupling, from the first searing touch became pregnant. Within hours she regarded the event as rape accomplished through imposture. At least once a month, until the day he died and on the day he died, she reminded Papa that he'd concluded his courtship by violating her. She also repeated the story that sealed symbolically and in fact my obligation to care for and protect my brother. My agreement had been expressed from some depth of being of greater authority than conscious choice. Mama reminded me: "You were eight then. Your brother was six. He stepped on a nail. Everything happens to him. We were in the doctor's office for the tetanus shot. Josh was crying. You stepped in front of the doctor, wouldn't let him give Josh the injection. You yelled at the doctor, 'Go home and stick needles in your own kid.' We had to drag you out of the office." I understood, with that act, I'd agreed to protect my brother. I'd vowed implicitly. There could be no shirking.

I asked Josh not to go around the neighborhood challenging the promising psychopaths, telling them, "Watch out my brother's going to beat you up." Before hulking Billy–the-Moose grabbed my shirt front with both hands and shook me as if I were a pillow case he was opening, Moose, chagrined, said, "Your kid brother tells me you said you were gonna wipe up the street with me." Even if I could have thought of something to say, he'd knocked the wind out of me. Mr. DeSapio, Moose's prospective employer, sat at a table under a green canopy sipping espresso in front of the Sons of Calabria Social Club and said, "Billy, enough." Billy let me go; nauseated, my back aching, I was grateful for the reprieve. For the next week it hurt whenever I sneezed or laughed. I tried to explain to Josh why he shouldn't call out the junior thugs in my name. Josh said, "Are you afraid?" I said, "That's right, yeah." A look, close to reproach colored his face. I wondered if he wanted to see me hurt. But the more I thought about it, I came to believe that what moved Josh was his desire to corroborate something limitless, because I was also a myth his mind made heedlessly.

Oblivious to the other passengers on the bus, and haunted, because I shared with my brother a powerful need for making stories, I talked to myself. Speaking on my behalf I noted that I worked obsessively to get my stories written. Unlike my brother, I was aware of augmenting fact, reshaping actual events and shuffling time to get at the essence of a story. But Josh's output was torrential. There wasn't any way he could recall the volumes he spoke, and he was every bit as serious as I about his stories, even though the story he was speaking at any given moment annihilated the stories that preceded it. Josh's regard for each story in its time was ecstatic. His telling had the force of accomplished performance art, and there were times when I was charmed.

Home at last I stripped and collapsed, naked on the couch, and with a length of twine I tied a sock stuffed with ice cubes around my blistered right thigh. Noise from the street, that in my best moments reached me as dissonant and remote music, kept me from sleep. Three stories below, the kids were playing Kick-the-Can, one of the variants of Hide-and-Seek. "Tap tap, Louie" one of them yelled."One potato, two potato, three potato, four, my mother said pick this here one." That's how it had begun and Louie was it. But Louie got to kick the can as far as he could, run as far as he could and hide again, because the kid who found him had to retrieve the can, bang it on the curb and yell "Tap tap, Louie, tap tap, Louie" before he and the others could give chase in the crepuscular remains of evening, a serene delirium bathing their cries as the dark filled alleys, cellars, and the recesses beneath stairwells. Soon, I thought, soon, some of their mothers will call them home.

After I forgot the idea of sleep, intervals of sleep took me throughout the night and some portion of the morning. Startled in that sleep, as if waking, I heard my heart thumping and noted that I'd painted the blistered, uneven walls off-white and plastered to achieve a stucco effect. And I'd torn up layer upon layer of old linoleum and sanded, stained, and varnished the wooden floor. I'd framed the

Vermeer reproduction, an interior within the interior of my lair, where the mother-to-be stood, thoughtful, by the window, in quiet, meditative light; and I hung it on the wall, above the waist-high bookcase I'd assembled out of pine boards and cinder blocks that ran the length of my one-room apartment. Lying on the convertible couch, beneath the woolen blanket, I worked my fingers under the sock stuffed with ice cubes and felt the blisters on my thigh growing numb. I assayed the round oak table piled with manuscripts, two wooden kitchen chairs, and a large beat up but comfortable armchair. I'd bought everything at the Salvation Army except the two kitchen chairs, which I found in the street. The old gray refrigerator provided by the landlord looked like a monolith covering the deeper recesses of a cave dwelling. I heard the radiator hissing, and mice squealing from either under the radiator or behind the refrigerator. Still it was home, and not without charm. Moreover, it was here I'd gone eight months without a drink and written my first published story.

In a doze, I spied on myself, pestered by the promise I couldn't keep. Josh had begged. "No matter what happens, no more hospital. If the cops take me there, you get me out." My fortissimo snoring made my eyes ache and announced the recall of something oddly reassuring. I was in the sixth grade, Josh in the fourth. It was a warm spring day and the water in all the school's drinking fountains had been turned off because a second little kid had his front teeth broken when he bent over to drink from the fountain. A bigger kid had come up from behind and shoved the little one's face into the metal

spout. Sonny Ryan who was in my class said, "On account a'
that, the fuckin' principal turned off the water in the fountains. I think your brother got his teeth knocked out." I raced
across the schoolyard to where the fourth graders were taking
recess, and found Josh milling around with the other kids. He
smiled at me, with all his teeth.

Noon, my morning: after checking the calendar and con-
firming that I was right, it was Sunday, and although the
bookstore was open it was my day off. I glanced at the
manuscript on the table. For some minutes my confusion
felt like money in the bank, and I relished my second sip of
coffee and a smoke. I wondered if I could muster the resolve not to answer the telephone. Neither I nor Dolores,
Josh's social worker, had seen him for almost three weeks,
although we received cryptic phone calls; Josh sounding alternately like Humphrey Bogart confounding the under-
world hunting him, or desperate and oracular, he made plain
that we were the privileged humanity upon whom he was
trying to impose truth. And Mama was certain to call. She
was in the ninth month of widowhood, worried about Josh,
and I was running out of plausible lies, reassuring her that
Josh was well in spite of her not hearing from him. "Ma," I
said, "he's gone to that dude ranch in the Jewish alps. You
know how he loves horseback riding. And I think he's got a
girlfriend." She said, "I hope to God. So maybe they went to
the Catskills like you say, but how my son the cowboy is
gonna support a wife, I can't imagine. Your brother only
visits or calls when he needs money, so maybe he's okay."
"Ma, maybe he found a rich girl." "From your mouth to

God's ear. Benny?" "Yeah Ma." "Your father called me on the telephone. He didn't say anything, but I could hear him breathing." "Ma he's dead already nine months. How do you know it's him?" "I can smell his breath over the phone, he's still drinking, and believe me, even down there, he's having a good time. You know how he loves heat. Better than the Russian Baths even, and he don't have to tip the attendants."

I called all the hospitals in Manhattan and checked with the police. I didn't expect to learn where Josh might be, but the odds of my being able to work on the story would be enhanced if I first made the effort I knew to be futile. On two previous occasions Dolores, ostensibly a social worker, had found Josh after he'd disappeared for three weeks, and later on for two months. Dolores didn't say much about herself, but did divulge that once upon a time she had been a novitiate. In an expansive mood, smiling, she described herself as an escapee from a nunnery. Most of the time she was a stark presence, and moved as though wading through hurricane winds. She'd grown up in the Red Hook section of Brooklyn. I guessed she was about thirty, but she could have been older, or younger; it was hard to tell; exquisitely made, her face and body might have made her a beauty; but something inside erased any suggestion of sensual allure: for Dolores Kelly love was a principle, and endless work. Whatever her eccentricities, Josh and I were the beneficiaries of the history that made her. She was kind, fearless, streetsmart, and always on the job. I was more than a little in awe of her. I suspected that eventually, if I confessed to anyone it would be Dolores, and I'd reveal that when I was a boy I'd set a fire at home, been a coward, lied, and blamed my brother. Josh took a beating because of me. I also knew that I would provide the information that I was seven when I set the fire. Dolores would undoubtedly reply that at the time of the incident I was also a child. And because I knew that what I wanted most was to have Dolores declare me innocent, when she did, I'd be incapable of believing her. But she wouldn't quit. She'd try to convince me. I counted on that. She had told me that my brother needed to take everything I could give. She also confirmed my sense of the importance of finding a way to honor Josh's experience. She suggested that I respond to the aspirations of Josh's stories without becoming lost in the plausible, implausible, and contradictory facts.

～

On the sixth ring, I picked up the phone. Josh said, "I'm sick of being a hostage to bourgeois expectations. I'm going to join the Merchant Marines and see the world." I said, "I can't argue with that." "Ben, I'm just telling you so you'll know. Understand?" And he hung up.

The last time Josh called I made the mistake of asking if he was behind on his rent. He ranted, "Hirschorn, the slum lord, he acts as if he doesn't know where his next meal is coming from. Ben, there are hypocrisies so profound they metastasize into delusion. Whose side are you on? You got to decide, man, are you with the exploiters or are you going to resist?"

Monday at about noon, Dolores phoned me at work to

tell me that Josh abandoned the rent controlled apartment she'd found him, and quit his job as a shipping clerk at the textbook company where he'd worked for four months. Wednesday, as I was about to leave work, she telephoned and said that Josh had called her twice that day. She asked where he was calling from and if she could call him back. He said he was calling from a phone booth because the phone in his apartment had been bugged. He wasn't sure whether it was the FBI or the KGB. She asked to meet him and said she could help. Josh said he wouldn't expose her to that danger, and the next time he was sure he wasn't being followed he'd call her again, from another public phone.

Friday evening I dozed in my armchair with *Anna Karenina* on my lap. The ringing must have commenced the instant time was invented, and I knew it would continue until I was deaf and dumb. I pried myself from the chair, the book fell to the floor, and I stumbled to the telephone on the kitchen wall. Josh laughed and said, "I hope I didn't wake you. But I feel I owe my brother an explanation." "You don't owe me anything. Why don't we meet for coffee?" "Ben it's after one in the morning and the only places open are the bars, and you can't go there. Just listen." "I'm listening." "It's like death. Worse. I've lost the world – like coherence, the possibility of meaning. Know what I'm saying? When I had discussions with Professor Espinoza, I was able to articulate things I didn't know I knew. You tell me! How can I be reconciled to such a loss. Could you? Are you paying attention?" "I'm here Josh." "I'm not so sure. It's a long night's journey into morning and it's getting dark. It was like Professor Espinoza was translating my life for me. I know the word is not the thing. Empirically speaking, a word can have, like, a hundred meanings, depending on the weather, a belly ache, a hard-on. But Professor Espinoza had the wit to narrow it down to the image or concept that was me. That's not just conversation. And that's the news of the day that will remain news. As in days of yore and even before yore. Now you can go back to sleep."

I struggled with a recalcitrant sentence. I knew the phone was going to ring, and speaking would deplete the place where language renewed itself. The night could last long enough, if I worked as if I had all the time in the world.

"Ben, I thought you'd never answer. I called before also, nobody home. Hope I'm not interrupting." "It's okay, Josh." "Really?" "Really." "Well, what I was afraid would happen, happened. But it's not my fault. Professor Espinoza's daughter Emilia was coming on to me. The kid's fifteen. I told you about her." "No Josh, you never mentioned that Professor Espinoza had a daughter." "Okay, so they were living me with me. They're from Nicaragua and they're in the country illegally. Professor Espinoza is disillusioned with the revolution at home. He spoke truth to power so naturally he's a refugee. U.S. officials aren't sympathetic because he's a socialist. What's worse, for a while he had a government post and he knows stuff that could embarrass a number of governments, so now also he's a fugitive. And I swear, I never touched his daughter. But they took off. It's my fault they had to run away? I'm asking you!"

I knew what Josh was asking. He needed a place to stay

again, and he was waiting for my answer. I couldn't get the words out. I was thinking how long it would be before Dolores or I could get him settled in a new place. Maybe I could write in Adam's Cafeteria, it was open until midnight. My one room apartment could accommodate a man and a woman, if they were in love, and didn't entertain. Josh and I had crowded the place. It had gone on nearly three months. He didn't mind sleeping on the cot. I tolerated the clutter, but when he appropriated parts of my life and told them to me as his experience, however fantastical in his version, I tried to change the subject. He recognized what I was trying to do, and looked desolate, ready to take off and hide. So I begged, "Please don't leave me hanging here, you said it was a turning point, what happened?" Josh exultant, said, "Benny, you won't believe this, but I've given up drinking. I've been scared sober." And he regaled me with what I'd confided during one of the occasions when I felt compelled to speak to him about my experience as an act of faith, a prerequisite for true fellowship, such rituals overwhelming me time and again. Josh described what he called the nadir of his five year misadventure with booze. He'd found himself wandering in a blizzard in a city he didn't know, and he was all busted up. He didn't know how that had happened. The only sound in the city embalmed in ice was the wailing wind. Finally he'd overcome his embarrassment and trudged through knee high snow drifts and asked a man bundled like a north pole explorer, what city he was in. Without halting his trek, the man turned his inflamed face to Josh and spoke, the wind looping the syllables, "Schug-cog-oh." I'd actually wound up in Albany, upstate New York.

At the same moment I heard myself say, "Josh, why don't you stay with me," he'd begun counting like a referee standing over a fallen fighter, "One, two, three,..." I don't know if I beat the count of ten. He laughed. I tried to sound jolly. "So how about it Josh? What do you say? I've got a new single mattress, it's much more comfortable than the cot. Josh, you still there?"At last he said, "Good of you to offer, but it won't work. They can track me to your place. I refuse to put you in danger." His voice was confident, tolerant, and worldly. "Ben, on the night before Professor Espinoza and Emilia ran away, she tip-toed into my bedroom and whispered, 'I hope my being a virgin isn't an obstacle.' Like I said, I didn't touch the kid. I hope that in my old age, I don't regret my virtue. Go figure."

Josh smiles because he doesn't consider it his job to keep tabs on all the rampant stuff living in his head. I imagine his face epitomizing the phases from comedy to tragedy, and his performance, if it is performance, gives way to the masks that become his face. Too often what he initially finds funny, bottoms out into what terrifies him.

Now I wait, hope, and stare at the telephone, as if my worry could summon Dolores' voice. Usually, she calls every couple of days to keep me apprised of her efforts, or suggest some practical thing I could do. She hasn't called in a week and when I call her office she's out. The last time Dolores called, she told me that Josh's landlord, Mr. Hirschorn, had called her. The man was hysterical. He said that Josh had invited two street derelicts to live with him.

The other tenants in the building were threatening to move. They said they could smell the drunken old man as he rode in the elevator. The old guy panhandled, cornering people in the hallway, and had been sick in the vestibule, the mess puddled below the mailboxes. The old man's companion was a woman young enough to be his daughter, and she shrieked denunciations at the tenants, whom she called. "Parasites" and berated beings only she could see. Josh had also been keeping pigeons in the apartment, and Mr. Hirschorn said it was going to cost a fortune to make the place habitable again.

I grab the receiver on the first ring and Dolores says, "West Side Community Hospital; he's okay." "Okay?" "Yes, definitely, he's getting better." "What happened? "He asked to see you." "Yeah, yeah, of course. How bad is it?"Dolores' pause is rhetorical. Her silence says, just get here. Then, "I'll wait for you." I know that despite her reassurances she finds optimism superfluous, and while she doesn't exaggerate the odds in Josh's favor, she's withholding the worst. The information she's willing to provide now is meant to imply that the story will continue; there is a future, and I'm supposed to take comfort from those particulars.

I thought I'd take a cab. Panting as though I'd run a marathon, I dug into my pants pocket for the ten dollar bill I'd put there. It had vanished. I searched all my pockets. The tenner was gone, so was my wallet. I checked the pockets of my windbreaker, found my keys, pipe and tobacco, a pack of Luckies, and the chocolate kisses I could resort to if a strong desire to pick up a drink was gaining on me. I decided to dip into the money I'd put aside for rent, went to the bookshelf and removed "Moby Dick", where I'd stowed my nest egg. I flipped the pages and shook the book. The money wasn't there. I told myself to calm down. My head hurt. I ate the chocolate kisses, gulped two aspirins, and lit a cigarette. Perhaps I was mistaken, I might have reached for Melville and grabbed the *The Naked and The Dead*. I flipped the pages. I shook *The Magic Barrel, Death In Venice, The Air-Conditioned Nightmare*, tasted the gall of a repressed scream, and greenbacks spilled from *Woman of Rome*.

At the door, ready to leave, I couldn't find one of my shoes. I swore, searched, found the damn shoe, cursed it and all inanimate things which had taken to hiding, revealing the shallowness of my sanity. I struggled into my windbreaker and ran.

It was drizzling. I couldn't find a cab. People were coming home from work, headed for supper. The street lights turned on. Lights appeared in the tenement windows. I slowed to a trot, going west on East Tenth Street. On the corner of East Tenth and Avenue A, the savory aroma from an Italian bakery melded with the smell of the rain. I slowed my pace to a brisk walk. Approaching First Avenue I passed the wheeless chassis of an automobile parked at the curb. The thieves must have decided that the tires, radio, and other parts were worth more than the whole car. I was soaked, and felt the need to apologize to the living and dead: my brother, Dolores, Mama and Papa, and the panhandler at my back who put the bite on me as I rushed by and dropped the coins that missed his hand and rolled off the pavement. He got on his knees to scoop the money from the gutter. I stopped and helped the bum gather up the coins. I figured that on foot I could make it to the hospital in a half hour. But if I could grab a cab, I'd be there in fifteen minutes, and chances were better on Second Avenue.

In the middle of the thoroughfare, I waved my arms, yelled and whistled at the cabs that sped by. Vehicles passed dangerously close, the driver's faces smears, they honked their horns, their curses swallowed in the wind and catarrhal hum of wet tires on wet asphalt. A Lincoln Continental went by so close I was shocked to find myself on my feet, as if holding my breath had made the inch that left me standing. Something had granted me a reprieve, a matador's lucky progress to the opposite curb. I wanted a drink, ate the last chocolate kiss, and headed for the shelter of a shoe store lobby. I stood there dripping. The brilliantly lit windows on either side of me displayed men's, women's and children's shoes on ascending transparent pedestals; at first glance the shoes appeared poised in air, as if all those who had been so splendidly shod had already ascended to paradise. I thought about Mama's obsession with shoes, the hackneyed syndrome of her shoeless, often hungry childhood. She can never have enough shoes. Mama's still working as a manicurist in a barbershop in the Garment Center. With the money she earns, she buys more shoes, which she adds to the stores in her two closets, and stashes under her bed; and she makes gifts of shoes to relatives and friends. The largesse of shoes, her obeisance to continued prosperity.

I smoked a cigarette, awed that I wasn't crapped out in an

ambulance, and realized that I was only one block from my favorite restaurant. Max, proprietor, chef, and lone waiter in the little place that is usually as crowded as a subway car during rush hour, has the most loyal and forbearing clientele. The first time I wandered in I was lucky to find a vacant stool at the counter. Long lean Max, harried, dripping sweat appeared before me scowling, and put a bowl of soup in front of me before I had a chance to look at a menu. "What is this?" Max, outraged by my question, said, "None of Your Business Soup." I said, "But…" He said, "Eat it, if you don't like, don't pay, and get lost." The soup transcended delicious, in itself and with the two thick slices of buttered rye bread, it was the most gratifying meal I'd ever had. Out on the street again, I could believe I'd never go hungry, and my loneliness was transfigured into solitude. I've tried and haven't yet persuaded my brother to join me for a meal at Max's place.

The week I discovered Maxie's Soup and Greens, Josh commenced four months of unprecedented prosperity. The auspicious time coincided with his finding employment walking dogs for the well-off residents of the Upper West Side. Josh was amazed at how lucrative this work was, and it didn't feel like work. He enjoyed strolling along Riverside Drive with the dogs, loved them, and claimed they were his ideal companions. "Like Diogenes," he said. The cash from dog walking came to him on a daily basis and supplemented his monthly Social Security Disability check. During this time of affluence, he didn't need me or Mama to bail him out; he ate most of his meals in restaurants, went to the theatre, and traveled around the city by cab. In spite of all I knew I hoped that Josh had at last found a way of sustaining himself that would lessen his need for flight. He appeared happy. I was beginning to believe that whatever the anomalies of my brother's inner life, he was after all functioning in the world and seemed to be moving toward some optimal health, shaped by the confluence of his needs and capacities, however eccentric. His face took on its Harpo Marx aspect, giddy and angelic. I'd come to think of my pessimism as a moral failure. Responding to Josh with a generous measure of good faith, might allow his good fortune to continue. I was superstitious enough for this notion to be compelling, and thought that one day, I might be truly religious.

A cab pulled up at the curb in front of the shoe store. The driver rolled down the passenger side window, thrust his apoplexied face toward the rain and hollered, "What you waitin' for, yesterday? In the taxi, justifying myself, I yelled, "West Side Community Hospital, go!" The kamikaze ride delivered me to the emergency entrance of the hospital, pumped up, and amazed again that I was alive.

I shoved through a crowd haranguing a nurse behind a counter, passed an old man on a gurney, dead or dying, and burrowed by a grinning young man in a wheelchair holding his hand to his bleeding gut, telling a cop, "You should see the other guy." A security guard grabbed me as I pushed a door I wasn't supposed to enter. We grappled, and it took seconds for us to untangle, before the guy pointed at the door I could enter.

Dolores was waiting for me at the end of a long corridor.

At first I didn't recognize her. She was wearing an olive drab trench coat that came down to her ankles, hefty orthopedic shoes, and a gray slouch hat. The interrogating glare of the overhead fluorescent lights, prophetic of the worst, rendered anything I might say moot. As I came closer I saw the chronic forbearance straining Dolores' face – the austerity something like beauty – shocked to see it always for the first time. She handed me a towel to dry my soaked head, took my arm, and led me past a visiting room where I glimpsed a man pacing and a woman weeping – on to a small ante-room at the end of the corridor. We were the only people there. Dolores sat down in one of the bright yellow plastic chairs and said, "Sit." The chair was uncomfortable. My right leg, from the knee to the sole of my shoe pressed down on the floor, the shank of my leg bobbed up and down; the only way I could stop it was tensing my leg mus-cles. My right hand rode my right knee. I'd intended to say that the reason my leg was shaking was because of too little sleep and too much coffee. The pervasive hospital odor was reminiscent of the purgative smell that made my eyes sting and water when I visited Mama. Dolores gave me a tissue. I dabbed my eyes and saw Mama's bathroom: the pink wall paper with white swans and emerald water lilies, from which a brass hook protruded, hanging from it, a red, rubber en-ema bag, and the curled tubing with its pink nozzle. Mama believed her health depended upon at least one enema a week. Dolores was reiterating how Josh and other street people had been rounded up by the police and brought to the shelter because of the spell of dangerously cold weather.

Josh told her he'd only consented to go because it was a place where the FBI wouldn't think of searching for him, and even though he was a fugitive he wasn't going to give up his anti-nuclear activity, and he hoped he was causing the Supreme Commander sleepless nights.

The meaning of Dolores' words faded in and out; a haze in my head shrunk the scope of my vision, as if I were looking through a key-hole. I thought I heard her say "salt." "Please" she said, "sit down." I didn't know that I was on my feet, and had no idea what I'd do – but I was in a hurry. She whispered, "Attempted sexual assault, and he was beaten and robbed." "Who was it?" "Ben, we're not having any of that." "Goddammit! Who?" "Ben, lower your voice." A large man in white filled the doorway. Dolores waved him away. "Ben, listen, we don't know who they are, and there's a lot to do. I can't do it all myself." I thought she, or the police, must know who they are. I'd need a piece; something reliable would cost more than a week's pay, more than what I'd put aside. The switchblade I'd carried during the drunk years and pulled on two occasions when I was stalked by a bunch of kids figuring they'd roll me, but backed off when I got my blade out – the shiv was still in my dresser drawer; but it wasn't enough. I'd need an equalizer. Dolores, holding my gaze like a snake charmer, said, "That's not who you are." And I thought, yeah, there's truth in that. But often I'd been who I wasn't – to be sure, under the influence, and that had authenticated something. It was lavish, and tonic to vacate myself. Moe Rifkin could help. He could get me what I needed – might even make a gift of it, as another token of his citizenship, in what he called the real world. He was the only one from the old neighborhood I'd kept in touch with. We saw each other once or twice a year to talk about what we were reading. Moe said he saved up all he wanted to say for the better part of a year, but he'd been most articulate in the discussions he had with me in his head. More than a year ago we discussed Dostoyevsky. His talk, as always, was urgent and brilliant; if he hadn't been a brilliant talker, he might have been a writer. He was also a math whiz and a dangerous person, affiliated with some of the most dangerous people in the city. And Moe Rifkin was a gambling addict. Every moment of his life was the penultimate moment —a matter of life or death, and he was addicted to that too. We'd been best friends, but I was uneasy – no – afraid of being beholden to him. I'd let the year pass without contacting him; and I'd been relieved that he hadn't called me. He'd probably surmised as much. But without Moe, how could I arm myself?

All the while, Dolores in my face, her incantatory mumble making another kind of claim, and suddenly I'm hostile, because hers is a face I can't fall in love with. And I would prefer that falling to the embrace of all and everything. "Ben," she said, "if you really want to help your brother, you have to focus on the things he needs. Josh can't remember what happened at the shelter, and you shouldn't ask him about it. It may surface at some time – meanwhile he's on a new regimen of meds, and it seems to be working. When you see him, no hugs; he shies away from touch. But he's as talkative as ever – an encouraging sign. The doctors said that the first day he was here he didn't speak at all, and they considered sending him to Bellevue. He's been here three days. I've known for two. I'm sorry I didn't call you right away. But Josh isn't my only client. I've been dealing with multiple emergencies, and I wanted to have things in place so Josh can be released. He wants to leave, and he can, in a couple of days, but I need your help. I found an apartment for him in a half-way house. United Christian Charities bought an old hotel on the Upper West Side. Maybe you've heard of it, Friendship House? There's staff, including security guards, a nurse, and a psychiatric social worker. The residents are re-covering addicts, teenage mothers learning to be mothers, their little ones, and people with various psychiatric prob-lems – like Josh. The subsidized apartments are very nice, three rooms, and the rent is nominal. I had access to some emergency funds from Social Services and the first month's rent is taken care of. Consider it a loan." "Thank you." "Now listen, Josh's furniture is still in the basement of his old place. You know where it is?" "I've been there, often." "Okay, I need you to move his stuff into the new apartment. I'll give you the address. Carlos Santiago, the superintendent at Friendship House, will help you with the hauling. You can offer to pay him." "I'll take care of it." "Okay then, you'll have to rent a truck, maybe you know someone who owns a pick-up. Ben?" – "I said I'll take care of it."

We turned right, into a corridor of administrative offices, walked by a nurse's station and turned left into another cor-ridor. Here there were rooms with patients groaning, and the beeping and humming of sophisticated machines. The hallway was crowded with wheelchairs where old people sat, their heads tottering on the flaccid stems of their necks. Fearful, they stared into a void. Dolores and I maneuvered around the wheelchairs heaped with human wreckage. Our progress was slow; they couldn't get out of our way. We squeezed by. Dolores sighed. I'd never heard her make such a sound. I thought I saw in her expression the temptation to default, as if the suffering and dying surrounding us were all her work, and she could never get to it all. But she put her hands on her hips, stared into my eyes and summoned me from reverie. "Ben, Josh's face is healing, but he still looks pretty bad. He's in the room at the end of the hall. He's sharing it with another patient. I have two more clients to see while I'm here. If I don't hear from you tomorrow, I'll assume you're taking care of business. Good luck – and oh, don't forget to deal with Josh's former landlord, he's threatened to take Josh to court."

I heard laughter as I entered the room. Josh in a long green gown and slippers, one knee on the floor, arms flung out in the posture of a minstrel importuning, sang, "It's us Ma, the wretched refuse of your teeming shore." A doctor stood behind Josh trying to examine his bandaged head. "Please," the doctor said, "be still." The nurse standing beside the doctor with a cup of water in one hand, and the other, palm up, laden with pills, said, "Open." Josh stood up, opened his mouth, and stuck out his tongue. One at a time, the nurse put a pill on the tip of his tongue – he swallowed and made an exaggerated gulping sound. The nurse held the paper cup to his lips. Josh burped ecstatically, in appreciation of a feast. The overhead fluorescent lights made his shaved head and the bandages across the top of his skull shine. The misshapen left side of his face was the color of an eggplant, and his upper lip was swollen and cleft. A surge in my gut rose into my chest and my ears were ringing. The nurse said, "Are you all right?" I didn't know if she was talking to me or Josh. He said, "I gotta be crazy to keep from going insane." The doctor peering into an otoscope he held to Josh's ear said, "I concur." In the room's one window, a full moon shined blatantly, invisible clouds shed rain, and a fat middle-aged man in bed with his leg in traction begged, "Please no more, it hurts to laugh." Josh gestured toward the window; the moon travelled at his behest. I swore to myself that if Josh assumed that something in his disposition made him curator of nocturnal heaven, and it helped him heal, I'd never question his claim. He said, "Look," the spectacle of the moon illuminating rooftops, and the night-washed sky floating in the window was something he'd provided. Like me, Josh was present and elsewhere, and I saw the resemblance – a face nearly transparent with inwardness and such disregard for the world's business that realists were bound to be provoked.

Looking into my brother's face as a mirror, I saw the attributes that marked us both. Josh's glance swept his audience and all that lived beyond the window. He said, "It's a matter of religious freedom – you hear what I'm saying?" He tilted his head toward the doctor and explained in a tone of waning patience, that his every adventure – and for that matter misadventure – was the irresistible expression of his spiritual vocation. He didn't expect medical professionals to understand that, wedded to the myopic study of symptoms as they were. I'd heard it all before. "Big brother," he said, "they don't understand, can you explain it to them?" The doctor, a young man with bloodshot eyes, alert, although he looked like he hadn't slept in years, said, "Josh, I don't doubt it. Now we have to continue on our rounds. See you gentlemen in the morning." The nurse had her back to me and was making some adjustment to the bed with the man with his leg hoisted in traction, who sat, as on a throne. She said, "I hear that Joshua will be leaving us." I said, "I hope so," and took a step in Josh's direction. He circled away from me. "Josh, in a couple of days you'll move into your new apartment. Dolores said it's very nice, three rooms on the Upper West Side, two blocks from Riverside Drive." Josh waved goodbye to the doctor and nurse and said, "The news is, ladies and germs, I'm tired of living in this nut house of a city. I want to live in the country." The man with his leg in traction shouted, "Where you gonna go? Long Island? There's nothin' out there but trees and cemeteries. When you leave New York, you're goin' nowhere." Josh said, "I'm thinking New Jersey. Like a farm. I can learn. I'm serious, even if I have to get up five o'clock in the morning to jerk off a cow." "Josh," the fat man said, "try Central Park. They got trees and plenty kinds a' animals in the zoo."

~

In bed, longing for sleep, I argued whether or not to call Moe. I decided I would and with the decision felt sleep com-

178

ing, until misgivings aroused me, and I decided I wouldn't –
until scruples made me think I must. Stupefied, I quarreled
with the homuncular advocate espousing homicide. I argued
that if I kneecapped the bastards who jumped Josh, justice
would be satisfied, although blowing the degenerates away
was a clear civic good.

I dreamt I was walking in the old neighborhood. I was
grownup and also the boy I had been, and I couldn't find my
way home. I recognized the buildings and storefronts, but
couldn't remember the number of my building. I asked
passersby for instruction, but they shunned me. I continued
on my way, lost.

The next few nights I dreamt further episodes of the
same dream. Josh and I were kids again. He was invisible,
but I could feel his hand in mine. I was confident that if
only I could get my bearings I could protect him from further harm. Then a man who identified himself as Moe
Rifkin's cousin told me that Billy-the-Moose had heard what
I was saying about him, and he was after me. Moe's cousin
said, "Watch out, you're in trouble." In the dream, and when
I woke, I was anxious. Nevertheless the morning felt like a
reprieve. I slept in two and three hour intervals; close to
morning, or waking in the middle of the night, a span of
dreamless oblivion was sufficient to get me through my
work day. But I was ashamed. The fuckers who had assaulted Josh were still above ground, breathing. I had spasms
of nostalgia for my life of not that long ago, when I could
pick up a drink and find the violence that might leave me
busted up, but cleansed, justified, and ready to re-enter my

old life as if I or it were now endowed to see itself as the wondrous new thing it always had been. But I couldn't dispel a reasonable doubt about the elixir – the cost of folk medicine was exorbitant – one could die of it.

One morning I awoke after living several lives and needed to rest. In one of those lives, I had been able to make a wise decision. Recuperating over my morning coffee and a smoke, I hadn't any idea what the wise decision had been, but felt myself cradled in a sweet, postcoital void. Slowly, I awakened to a day like jumping off the roof at Buzzy Pizzaro's command; in wingless flight I fell into the eternity between heartbeats, and being a good working stiff applied myself to the tasks at hand.

I rented a truck. Carlos Santiago helped me move Josh's furniture and other belongings to Friendship House. When I attempted to pay him, he refused the money. There was neither anger nor resentment in his refusal. I'd felt awkward offering him what could be taken for a gratuity, because of Señor Santiago's natural dignity. There was something princely in his bearing. He appeared to be in the youth of his old age, a vigorous sixty or seventy, tall, lean, gray haired, with a neatly trimmed white mustache and goatee; and he was very strong. I followed his lead when we maneuvered the couch, bed, dresser, and arm chair up cellar steps and through narrow doorways. He drove the truck with Buddhist serenity through the bedlam of New York traffic. We didn't talk much and were comfortable with the silence. The only ostentation about Señor Santiago – that made me stare from time to time –was the gold crucifix, big as a fist that hung from his neck. It reminded me of a conversation I'd had with Moe when we were teenagers. We had a terrible a crush on Annunziata Fellini, a beautiful young widow garbed in black, who wore a crucifix too large to be tucked under her blouse; even under her coat it swelled, like Golgotha, heaving on her bosom. Moe, paraphrasing a writer whose name I can't recall said, "Imagine a contemporary Jesus, executed because he's too good for this world. Those who commemorate him wear necklaces from which, a miniature electric chair dangles." And Moe and I, standing on the corner outside Gertie Appelbaum's candy store were engulfed in the same fantasy, and considered being young widow Fellini's second husband – even if it meant dying young, as had been the fate of Salvatore Fellini, who'd barely made it to his twenty-fifth birthday and died of a fever of unknown origin. Sal had occasionally played stick ball with us younger boys on Saturday afternoons. Moe and I acknowledged, simultaneously, and without having to think about it very long, that each of us was willing to die at twenty-five, because being married to Annunziata for ten years was sufficient bliss for any man. But then we began to argue about who would be Annunziata's second husband, neither of us wanted to be the third; although, if that were the only opportunity, number three couldn't resist and would have to acclimate himself to the long wait, and a certain anonymity and diminution in the widow's romantic feelings, because by then, husband number three would be perceived as some universal aspect of the species. I don't know who threw the first punch. It began with wrestling and then got serious. We staggered around each other. My nose was bleeding and Moe spit a gob of blood on the sidewalk, a demented luminescence widened his eyes and Moe said, "Would you convert (to Christianity) to marry Annunziata?" It gave me pause. Moe said, "I wouldn't hesitate." It was a Saturday, so then we went to the movies.

Traffic was heavy, the glare coming through the windshield and reflecting off the gold crucifix hanging from Señor Santiago's neck made me blink. "This," he said, brushing the cross with the tip of his pinky, "I wear it to comfort my wife. Our son is in prison for taking the life of another boy in a street dispute. Alberto was not a bad boy. My wife prays for his freedom. Alberto has been in prison almost twenty years, and is now a monster. While his mother prays for his freedom, I pray for the world, should he be freed. This is one of two secrets I've kept from my wife in the half century of our marriage."

It occurs to me now that Señor Santiago was neither instructing nor confessing — the two secrets he kept from his wife notwithstanding — telling the truth was a courtesy. He hadn't signaled the prospect of some greater kinship, and if he was exemplary, he didn't will it. I don't know if Señor Santiago's story pardoned me from the obligation to commit manslaughter. But the hauling and lifting helped.

And I pacified Josh's former landlord. Mr. Hirschorn kept the one hundred and sixty dollar security deposit Josh had paid when he moved into the apartment. The rent had been eighty dollars a month. Mr. Hirschorn said he needed another hundred to cover the expense of cleaning, repairing, and painting the apartment. He swore he wasn't making a profit. I didn't dispute his word, gave him another fifty dollars and promised the fifty still owed at the end of the month. Mr. Hirschorn put his hand on my shoulder, and moaned, "Oy, a mensch." I took the compliment in silence. He said, "Enough already," returned the five tens I'd given him, and confessed, "When I was young, I was a Socialist, goodbye and good luck."

❧

Christmas was approaching. Ding donging everywhere. In the elevator emitting 'Silent Night' and carrying me to Josh's room, two lovely teenaged mothers cradled babies in their arms, another bent to a toddler in a stroller. The perfume wafting from the girls filled the ascending elevator. I'd been wondering if my reminiscence of violence had been what AA folks call "stinkin' thinkin'" – that is the dalliance that precedes picking up a drink. Still, when I thought of the humiliation Josh suffered, I winced, and couldn't expunge murder from all the chambers of my heart. But paroxysms of sanity were coming more often and lasting a little longer. Inhaling the scent of the beautiful young mothers, I imagined a robust grace that would allow me a sweet and fulfilling life with any one of them, all the way to my brother's door.

Josh's face was healing. The swelling had receded and the bruised skin under his left eye down to his upper lip had faded to a jaundiced yellow. The bandages had been removed from the top of his head, and his hair had grown a

183

quarter of an inch covering the stitched furrows crisscrossing his skull. After much urging from Dolores, Josh promised to avail himself of the free dental care at NYU's Dental School. Despite performing my duties in a fog, I'd been promoted to manager at the bookstore, received a significant raise and was able to help Josh with money. He'd telephoned Mama and promised to visit her soon. His apartment on the eleventh floor had a large window in each of the three rooms, and the place was filled with light. The refrigerator and gas range were new, the furniture worn but not shabby. He seemed very much at home.

Josh was cordial and shook my hand as if we'd just been introduced. But as I listened attentively and didn't interrupt, and he became immersed in the tale he was telling, he looked directly at me, and I put my arm around his shoulder. We laughed and the distance between us diminished. Although Josh could go on for hours without a thought of pausing, I said, "Wait, I have to go to the bathroom," and "By the way, are you interested in starting up your dog walking business again?" He considered it briefly. When I left he let me hug him.

But at the outset of every visit, Josh would shake my hand as if meeting a stranger, remained formal and distant until I'd listened to an hour or more of his adventures as he inhabited or was inhabited by various personas. Shadowing Josh's metempsychosis, I was glad to find myself still haunted by brotherly love, but desperate to return to my own story.

At the door we embraced. I'd started to move toward the elevator. And there was Señor Santiago, toting a toolbox and girded by a belt holstering wrenches, hammers, screw drivers and pliers. He moved as if all he carried was weightless. He gave me a friendly nod, as I was part of the known world. The face of the gaunt young man Señor Santiago had been listening to was hammered by the worst that could befall a human being; but still feisty, and wanting to make a favorable impression, he called after Señor Santiago, who was stepping into the elevator, "I wake up dead in the morning, but I get out of bed anyway," Josh was saying, "The thing is, I'm twenty-two years old and still a virgin. I don't mind much, it's only that there must be like, you know, a mission, a purpose, and I can't figure out what it is. It's not just a philosophical question for me, know what I'm saying?" I said, "I think so." "Like, Buddha got laid before he went on the road looking for wisdom. Confucius was a pragmatist and I bet he got laid. Only the Jewish wunderkind, Jesus, was supposed to be a virgin, like his momma. Know what I mean?" "I hear you." "Ben, I think, yeah – my problem with girls is I'm too intense, it scares them off. And I know that sometimes my imagination gets too big, it makes me nervous, especially when it puts bad pictures in my head. Well, at least we were able to save Carnegie Hall. They were going to turn it into a luxury apartment house. Ben, I had an army marching out there. Jesus! I'm tired of being precocious."

The insomnia began to yield manna. Hours when the city was quiet and I, punch drunk and pixilated wrote the groans and crooning airs my sleepwalking soul vented.

The phone rang at three in the morning and I didn't answer. After first light and a brief nap that occurred between the time I'd made coffee and let it percolate into smoldering sludge, I awoke to the stink and wondered whether it was Josh or Mama who called. If it had been Josh, he would have called again; if he was in trouble Dolores or the social worker at Friendship House would call. When Mama telephoned, the calls came in clusters, usually early in the evening, and more frequently now she didn't remember that she'd called only an hour ago. But her long term memory remained prodigious; she sounded alternately jubilant or frightened. I worried that she might be at the onset of Alzheimer's. Still, Monday through Friday, at the barbershop, she manicured the fingernails of the Garment Center bosses.

The phone rang at four in the morning and rescued me from a sentence I'd never be able to finish. "Hello firstborn," she said. "Hello Ma." She said, "Who's this?" "Me, Ma, you dialed my number." "Ben, life is shit." And she hung up. I called her back. She picked up the phone and yelled, "Who calls at such an hour?" and slammed the receiver down.

The phone was ringing as I came through the door. "Hello stranger. Ben, you there?" "Yeah Ma." "I'm alone here, like a dog." "I was there last Saturday, we had lunch. I'll try to make it this Saturday." "You'll try?" "I have work to do." "What? The scribbling?" "Yeah, the scribbling." "Listen Ben, come. I'll make you lunch, and have I got a story for you! Your brother I bribe with money, with you, it's stories. But you should hurry. I'm down to my last bag of words, and I ain't gonna live forever." "Okay, Saturday then." "Saturday is good. Listen, you hear anything from your brother, him I only see when he needs money. Which now and then is often." "He's fine Ma." "Fine he'll never be. Oh yeah, I almost forgot. The reason I called, I got for him the opportunity of a lifetime. I want you should talk to him. At least you he listens to sometimes." "What is it?" "Ben come. Saturday, I'll tell you everything."

⸺ɷ⸺

The train climbed out of the dark and I saw through the window, buildings, streets, people, and clouds traveling backwards, as I was carried back to the realm where the future exists only in longing, and the present is subliminal. And I remembered Laura Providencia as I rocked toward Mama. Beautiful Laura Providencia had been in my English class at City College. Before I dropped out to scavenge as much time as possible for my writing, we'd gone out twice, once to a movie, and another time to a coffee shop in Greenwich Village. We kissed twice, and talked and talked, astonished that we'd found a language to access elusive aspects of our histories. But on both occasions, Laura smelled booze on my breath. She said that if I could stay off the sauce for a year, she'd be willing to see me again. Given all we talked about I knew she had good reason to utter an ultimatum, and she meant what she said. The memory of Laura Providencia had become as fleeting as conjecture of a former life. Perhaps because when I'd been with her, in proximity to such beauty, I'd had to will myself to believe that what was happening was happening. And in retrospect I'd balk at the prospect of having to revamp my soul—

which I couldn't resist if I laid eyes on her again. Maybe I resembled those old Jews before the re-creation of Israel, who cried "Next year in Jerusalem" – a millennial longing so consuming that it was impossible to believe that such desire could, or should be fulfilled. The wages of insomnia granted that recall, and what I'd rather forget. I'd been more success-ful than my brother in deceiving Mama. During the drunk years I abstained when I visited her, and hurried to the first bar I could find when I left. It could be that she didn't want to know, couldn't bear to know. The resemblance to my father would spawn a repugnance for her first-born she couldn't survive.

The brisket filled the entire plate. There was a large bowl of mashed potatoes and gravy and a salad. I'd eaten the her-ring entrée and a bowl of barley soup. "Ben how come you're not eating bread?" I swallowed, and thought that among other things, my presence had the function it always had; I was a sounding board for God's ears. I felt like a kid again, waiting and listening in the interval between the sighting of lightning and boom of thunder, anticipating the moment when Mama's recitation would become a scream. But the brisket was deli-cious, as were the mashed potatoes laced with butter, garlic, and fried onions. I ate as if I were going to The Chair. The look of gratification on Mama's face as she watched me eat was lascivious. We blushed. She began telling me the story she'd told thousands of times. In one telling, when I was about twelve, Mama in the course of petitioning the Almighty, began to beat on my shoulders. I wanted to hear the end of the story, and if the thumping was the price I had to pay, that was okay. Now she told it again, as she always had, hoping to find her way back, and discover the questions that would fit the answers she had to believe.

She was at the dance sitting alone, the couples dancing slowly around her. In this rendition I had swelled her belly into a hillock that was difficult to camouflage. I envision a semitic Hester Prynne, complicit in her public humiliation. The disgrace she'd felt wasn't ameliorated by the whole mortified world she described; ragged, hungry kids seeing their parents powerless, and shamefaced men lined up in the city streets at soup kitchens. The whole needy world in concert with her degradation confirmed her sense that the time on earth allotted to her would be rife with disaster; lighter moments were aberrations not meant to last.

Her nausea had abated during the evening, but she couldn't forget that I was there. She glanced at her stomach and tried to convince herself that she wasn't showing. The dancing couples glided around her. She sat in a straight-backed wooden chair near the phonograph. It was humid, the air thick with cigarette smoke. She smoothed the flounce of the pleated dress that she hoped curtained her belly. She imagined that her flushed face and swollen middle made it plain (as it had to her mother) that she was a girl in trouble, one who must marry in a hurry. She thought that among her sisters she was the one who, without complaint, had been willing to sacrifice to lighten her mother's load; but when her mother saw her sick in the morning and knew why, she looked at her daughter with contempt. Grandma worried that she couldn't marry off this daughter without a dowry; unlike her dark and beautiful sisters, Molly was plain with rope-like red hair and a Mediterranean profile. In her care and worry, and now disgrace, Grandma had grabbed Mama's offending nose, screamed "Mieskeite," pulled her around the kitchen, and whacked her with her free hand until they both wept.

Mama loaded my plate with a second helping of brisket, and said, "But I understood how hard her life was and forgave her." I thought, why am I hearing this now? Does she want me to forgive her? Haven't we lived in a place where forgiveness is beside the point. "Your father said I was beautiful, up on the roof it was, after he proposed marriage. Beautiful, he said, but he was crazy."

I regarded the things in this telling that were news. Saul, the crazy man, had sent his mother as an emissary to speak on his behalf, and had her deliver the shoes, dress, and coat he'd bought for Molly. She marveled that he'd gotten the correct size dress, coat, and shoes. And as Saul assumed, it was the first time Molly dressed in clothes that weren't hand-me-downs. His mother presented him to his future mother-in-law as he had asked – as a serious working man. He had just turned sixteen. His mother said that Saul was an only child conceived when she was certain that her child-bearing time had passed. When she and her husband were young, in Poland, that land of hardship and pogroms, her body had refused to harbor life. But here in America, the miracle of her Yankee Saul, burst into life. It was true she said, that he had an excitable nature; but also, he was his parent's salvation. Her husband, a man too good for this world and a nebulous presence – although he persisted in bed – had never been much of a bread winner. But Saul, even as a boy would go out into the street and find a way to earn. At twelve he worked for a fruit and vegetable vendor; at thirteen he had his own pushcart, at fourteen he earned more at the rag factory. "A Rabbi he's not, but with Saul, your Molly won't starve."

I watched Mama prepare a bowl of borscht for herself. She dropped a tablespoon of sour cream into the blood red liquid. This was a dish she ate with eyes closed. She sniffed the vapors. As a boy the odor of borscht made me gag. Although I was no longer nauseated, I wanted to get away from the smell. But it may have been that smell that prompted the conflation of surmise stewing for decades; I saw myself as a twelve year old: me and Papa, zoot-suited, Sunday after the war, on our way to music, passing through the rubble of the destroyed kitchen, Papa saying, "But I never laid a finger on nobody, right?" I agreed, and we stopped in the hallway for a moment, where Papa had a half pint of vodka stashed in the mailbox. And what I saw next I may have dreamed, or imagined, and associated with the time of Josh's birth. Mama staring at Papa as he walked naked, in the kitchen, not quite awake, shortly after the operation on his hernia. The lower right side of his abdomen after surgery, took on in relief, the swollen, livid shape of his sex; and it must have seemed to Mama the mocking emblem of nature's hustle, Papa its instrument, disguised as a provider. And years later, Josh, partaking of the shrink's vocabularies, whispered in my ear, "She never survived her childhood."

Mama paused over the borscht and said she and Papa

were on the roof. They watched the sun go down. She let him hold her hand. He asked if he could touch her breast. She said no. He declared, in anguish, that he too was a virgin. She said no again. In his mind he was only asking for a small advance on his conjugal rights. He said, "Please." She said, "No means no." He trembled, walked to the edge of the roof and said he was going to jump. She had no doubt that despite his dramaturgy, he would jump. She said, "Wait, next time."

During the early evening just before he and Molly left for the dance, he delivered groceries to his future mother-in-law's apartment. Also he had sent his mother to deliver another new dress for Molly, since she had given the other dress to her sister Esther. This had hurt Saul, and he considered enduring the pain an aspect of courtship. Molly watched him struggle to control his rage. She took his arm and by the time they arrived at the dance, he simmered down. Climbing up the steps to the loft, he heard a radio playing Count Basie's "One O'Clock Jump"; a great joy took him, and he wished the tune were the national anthem. At the dance Molly discovered that the occasion had been sponsored by the Communist Party. Their people were proselytizing and looking for volunteers to help organize the textile waste workers.

These specifics of my father's courtship – Papa begging to touch Mama's breast – the gifts of clothing and groceries, and the dance having been sponsored by the Communist Party, I'd never heard before. I had heard ritually, as though commemorating births, deaths, and the New Year, the litany of Papa's bad behavior at the dance. What astonished me was that given Mama and Papa's torrential expressiveness, any fact could be withheld; how could anything remotely resembling discretion exist? But now, here were these things I hadn't known. I thought that perhaps in such a case secrets must live in incomprehension; the more revealed the deeper the mystery.

Mama told the story and laughed. The laughter palsied her body and she accepted that she had to pay for the levity which had wormed its way into her memory. She was still sitting alone at the dance. I was balled up under her heart, giving her indigestion. I saw myself in gestation, an embryonic submariner peeking through Mama's navel, watching Papa inform her that now that they were only a couple of weeks from their marriage, she had to have his permission before dancing with anyone but him. But because they were among progressive people, if a colored man asked her to dance, she should dance with him. Mama looked askance at her husband-to-be, and said, "I'm not dancing with a *shvartze*." In the kitchen Mama paused and fastened her eyes on me, so that I might give sufficient thought to the unreason her was life subject to. Peeking through Mama's blooming belly button, I'd seen the men who had been waiting to recruit Papa for organizing work whisk him away. Mama repeated that they wanted to unionize the rag factory, "And they needed somebody crazy enough to go into the shops, and they'd heard about *Meshuggener* Saul. I thought, in a couple of weeks I'll be a widow, and you a bastard."

Saul had disappeared into a back room with a group of

men who surrounded him and spoke urgently, waving their arms. Someone put "I Can't Give You Anything But Love" on the phonograph and couples slow danced around Molly. A group of young men and women, who didn't dance, stood close by and argued that the music they were listening to wasn't authentic people's music. Standing among them, was a handsome, elegantly dressed black man listening and smiling, and Molly changed her mind and wished that he would ask her to dance. But he remained where he was, entertained by the argument.

No one asked her to dance and no one invited her to join in any of the discussions of the various groups arguing loudly at the edge of the dance floor. Mama said again that Alvin Vasser was quiet, refined, and he would never have been so inconsiderate as to leave her all alone for such a length of time. Alvin, as I already knew, had appeared ghostly white and thin among the dancers. She said that she was shocked to see him, and explained that Alvin's pallor was the result of his sympathetic capacity. Alvin threaded his way between the tightly packed dancers, and stood before Molly, speechless. And while Alvin the druggist's son sometimes hovered in proximity on their street and had taken month's searching for the right words, Molly had been overtaken by events that she now thought foreordained. Also, Saul had grabbed Alvin and threatened him, and Alvin faded. I have no idea how Mama had gotten the photo of Alvin. But in a number of my parents' fights, Mama had taunted Papa with it, and later he found the photo and tore it to bits. In retaliation, while he was at work, Mama found Papa's hidden bottle of schnapps and the half-pint of vodka he'd stashed in the mailbox, poured both bottles into the kitchen sink, and set the empty bottles like trophies on the drain board. Papa got home from work and stood dumbfounded, gaping at the empties. Mama sat at the kitchen table, patiently fitting the pieces of the photo of Alvin together and gluing the reconstruction onto a square of cardboard. Papa bellowed like a gored bull, grabbed hold of the rim of the sink with both hands and yanked and pulled at it while Mama taunted him, calling him "Tomashevsky", an actor known on the Yiddish stage for the most heart-rending expressions of agony. The wall cracked, chunks fell, the dry plaster sifted down, and the sink fell, suspended a foot above the floor, by two twisted pipes spouting water. And that night, I chased after Papa in the street with the five dollar bill Mama gave me, so that Papa and I could spend the night at the Russian Baths.

At the dance, Alvin stood before her, astonished and trembling. Mama wondered if she had looked that stricken when Saul had stepped to the edge of the roof. In the kitchen she acknowledged to God, and me, inadvertently, that something about Alvin made her feel, however fleetingly, reckless. "I Can't Give You Anything But Love" concluded. Someone put an up tempo swing number on the phonograph. The jitterbugs rushed to the floor, bumped Alvin sideways, up and back, but he remained, upright and disoriented. Mama saw how the art and athleticism of the jitterbugs allowed the music to fling them around, and recognized that the abandon of the dancers was the self-mockery of the body's inevitable surrender. Along with Benny Goodman's high pitched clarinet, she also heard the young men and women who refused to dance, shouting that jitterbugging was a symptom of the decadence of capitalist society, a self-induced soporific sparing the dancers the awareness of historical necessity. They smoked cigarettes furiously, and several of the theorists maintained that the swing music was simply a means of attracting young people, like the free doughnuts and coffee. The arguments raged.

And Alvin was still there, spectral in the fog of cigarette smoke. The jitterbugs flopped in chairs and leaned against the walls huffing and puffing. Someone put a languorous fox-trot on the record player. Molly lifted herself out of the chair and smiled. She placed one of her hands at the backside of Alvin's waist, and clasped his other hand. Alvin looked terrified. She said Alvin couldn't dance, but it didn't matter, the floor was crowded and they were held in place; the encumbrance of me blooming between them. She tried to soothe Alvin's nerves, and assured him that he was learning to foxtrot. She said that until recently, she had only danced with her sisters.

The dancing couples toppled all around them; some ran for the exit. A crush of bodies pressed forward in the smoky blue air. The crooning song screeched into caterwauling. A wide swath like a tornado wind had passed, made an aisle to the one door that led in and out. Alvin vanished. Molly heard screaming and saw the phonograph flying through the air. Saul's intention had been to throw the phonograph at Alvin's head, but Alvin's flight had been so swift that Saul pivoted, throwing the music out of the window, wishing that the phonograph and the shattered glass from the window would rain down on Alvin in the street, running for his life.

Saul looked at the dancers rising from the floor, and those running for the door. He didn't quite understand the pandemonium. He had bumped into some of them in his pursuit of Alvin. He'd expressed himself, now it was over. Not a big deal. Had someone yelled "Fire"? But there wasn't a fire, no reason for panic. Arthur Luchinski, who had been given the task of explaining the more arcane and inevitable workings of history, also explained that in revolutionary times elemental forces were unleashed. Arthur studied Saul and authenticated him as the truest specimen of proletariat, and as such, allowances were made for Saul's periodic eruptions. Arthur had run to Saul's side and said, "Take it easy, be calm." Saul said, "I am calm. Why is everybody leaving?" Arthur said, "Well, for one thing, we don't have a phonograph." "Oh yeah, right. Artie, when Molly and me got here, I heard a radio playing downstairs, in an apartment at the front of the house. Why don't you borrow the radio and invite the people who own it to the party."

Mama said that Luchinski the Explainer had returned with a radio, set it on a table, and tuned the dial to the "Stardust Ballroom". Most of the dancers had fled. The coffee and doughnuts were gone. A thick fog of cigarette smoke hung in the air. A half a dozen proselytizers preached to three neophytes; two true-believers bludgeoned one another with outrage. Saul had run to the door and made himself a barricade closing off the escape of three couples bottlenecked where they attempted to exit. He pushed them back with his arms extended, herding them back to the floor, exhorting them to dance. He pushed one couple closer together. He pleaded and shoved, set another pair spinning, and hummed encouragingly "Melancholy Baby".

"So we were married and Saul went into the shops and made speeches. The bosses offered him a lot of money to join their side. He wouldn't listen. They warned him. They sent a tough guy to heckle him when he was making a speech. The tough guy's interruptions aggravated your father and he jumped off the loading dock with a baling hook in his hand and chased the tough guy. So the bosses hired two tough guys, and they gave your father the Socialist such a beating he pished red for a week. I tried to explain to him, your heart's in the right place, but this activity is for a bachelor, not a responsible married man with a family. But him, you couldn't discourage. All right, I admit, no matter what, in all the years he was a provider, but he didn't exactly leave me a rich widow, so now, at this time in time of life, with aching bones and stones in my gall bladder, five days a week I ride the subway to manicure the nails of the big shots. The salary is *bupkes*," she said, wrinkling her nose as if the odor of the goat droppings was rising from the palm of her hand. "But the tips is very good. How about desert? I got rice pudding." "Mama, I can't." "You can say no to rice pudding?" "I'm full." "Full?" She puzzled over "full". "So Ma, "what's the deal with Josh?" "*Oy!* Your brother. Where's my head? Okay. You know how things hit his emotional gland, then he feels too much, and can't cope. If I try to talk to him, he won't say yes and he won't say no. He'll just disappear. That's why I need you to explain to him." "Explain what?" "You remember my cousin Meyer, the diamond cutter? He's a lot younger than me, on account of he was a change-of-life baby. He was here when we sat shiva for your father. You remember him?" – "Yes, yes." "Well, I've been after him for years to teach Josh he should become a diamond cutter. Finally he said "yes" and Josh should get started with him before Meyer changes his mind. You wouldn't believe the money diamond cutters make. Josh is handy, he could learn. If he had a trade, a wife, he'd be like a person. Without, what's to become of him? Ben, I'm not going to live forever. And then what? He should sleep in the street – beg like a bum? He's your brother, you only got one. As God is my witness, if you walk away, your brother is as good as dead. Ben, you don't want that on your head – so while I have breath, I plead, for your benefit also."

The journey home seemed interminable. I looked forward to returning to my manuscript, and letting time dilate. Mama had gone on and on saying the same thing, with slight variations. But she wasn't speaking to me exclusively. Her repetitions had morphed into prayer, as if only the exhaustion of her voice might get the attention of the Almighty. Mama, trying to summarize the infinite, her drone one note below a scream, managed to keep one eye on me, while her blood pressure tugged the other eye into a gibbous white marble resting at her temple. "They'll find your brother dead in the street – you can live with this?"

—◦◦◦—

199

And at the door she thrust a jar of barley soup into my hands and said, "Enjoy." Christmas and the New Year had passed. Still the windows and doors of the tenements were wreathed with colored lights, Lilliputian nativity scenes ensconced in store windows, inflatable Santa Clauses and his reindeer tethered on fire escapes, and here and there a window with a menorah, the eight candles no longer kindled. The holiday rush at the bookstore was over. I'd worked long hours, seven day weeks when necessary, and hadn't yet taken any part of my annual two week vacation – that was the argument I presented to the owner, Bernie Fine. He reluctantly agreed to my taking a week off, said that he'd assume my responsibilities, and if he had questions, he'd telephone me at home.

I stocked up on groceries, cigarettes, and pipe tobacco – sharpened the points of seven pencils and opened the manuscript to the page I'd abandoned. Too excited and strung out, I decided to rest, and flopped on the couch. I reminded myself that first and foremost was the will to preserve the interior habitat where the most primal work could begin. It required courage, even ruthlessness. The infernal instrument was ringing again, and again I didn't pick it up. The stuff that gave rise to the tale that had been taking shape was still with me; the facts in themselves mythic, but my confidence in those actualities was giving way to other words, breeding the apologies I'd offer to Josh, Mama, Dolores, and my boss, Bernie Fine, an aspiring writer who didn't write, and may have promoted me to manager because I provided the literary talk he found indispensable. When I wrote well, I winnowed from my reading authors whose voices were uncongenial or distracting to the story finding itself under my hand. Now I couldn't stifle my own officious babble, and questioned the conceit that allowed me to presume that I could create something that might be worthy of existence. And it wasn't midnight, but one in the afternoon.

I took my befouled self to the street and walked west toward Greenwich Village. Strolling past a number of bars, I congratulated myself for not going in, and noted that my desire for a drink was modest. My neighborhood, the Lower East Side, had recently been christened the East Village, and as I found myself standing in front of what had once been my favorite bar, and was now a coffee shop, thought it auspicious, and entered.

The coffee shop retained the subliminal light of the bar it had replaced. On each round table a hurricane lamp contained an electric, flame shaped bulb. On the adobe-like walls were reproductions of Munch's "The Scream", Van-Gogh's "Sunflowers", and a bullfight poster, illuminated by small lamps above the frames, shaped like drooping tulips. There were only four other patrons: one young couple holding hands, intent upon each other, a man reading a newspaper, and an old guy munching a cannoli. At the rear of the place, what had been the bar supported glass enclosed shelves of pastries, flanked by two espresso machines, and a soapstone statute of a bald, pot-bellied sage, smiling in his sleep. Beyond that a door, slightly ajar, issued vapors of freshly baked bread, pastries, and cake. The pretty, blond waitress wearing what looked like an antique nightgown, brought the espresso to my table. I heard someone call her "Jean". She seemed to glide in an aura of contentment and good cheer. Jean's womanly body animated her loose fitting gown. But she had the face of a kid just barely entering adolescence. I sipped the espresso; it tasted of brandy. I may have looked surprised. Jean said, "Irish coffee," as if this was something we'd agreed upon. I wondered whose child she might be – perhaps she was an orphan, or a runaway, and I couldn't bring myself to say, "You've made a mistake." True – I had thought of an Irish coffee, but dismissed the idea without a struggle. I do remember asking for the second Irish coffee, and the cordial or two, perhaps three, that followed.

Jean, orphan or hippie – a term as new to me as the East Village – asked if I was feeling well. I said I was fine. She said I looked sad and asked for my astrological sign. I said I didn't know. She asked what month and day I was born. I told her. She said, "You're a Virgo," looking worried and solicitous, and I was agog. Why hadn't I thought of it before? Go home. Tear the phone from the wall. Smash the damn thing. Done. There was barely an interval between the thought and the deed – I was already on my way – the gift of revelation a moral imperative that fulfills itself. I was joyous. Jean said, "You look like you're gonna cry."

I left her a tip sufficient for a week's groceries. She followed me out into the street. "Mr. Man," she whispered, "alcohol is gross," hugged me, and pressed an envelope into my hand. I was moved. She smiled and said, "Have a good trip."

The apartment felt familiar and somehow new. The one

room with the kitchen alcove, the orange crate storing the portable phonograph and records, arm chair and convertible couch, the table piled with manuscript, the humming refrigerator, and tacked to the wall, above the book shelves, Vermeer's mother-to-be, thoughtful, basking in the doting sunlight coming through a window – a refuge prepared by my prior self waiting for me to arrive. And on the wall in the kitchen alcove, next to the sink, the diabolical instrument, ringing. I took a hammer to it. The thing was sturdy. I hammered away, cut the cord with a large kitchen knife, pounded until the thing was debris at my feet, buried by chunks of plaster and white dust. From a crater in the wall, a length of phone line hung like a severed umbilical cord. I dropped the hammer. Grateful, choked with tears that never came, I relished the quiet. It hadn't been necessary to speak at the check-out counter of the supermarket. I paid for the six-pack of beer without saying a word. The same at the liquor store; I paid for the fifth of Jamieson and nodded in reply to the cashier's "Thank you". No talk, no lies. The blessed quiet would restore me – a physic cleansing contaminated language. After a sufficient duration of silence, I could listen to music. But that would have to wait. I'd know when the time was right. In the street, I'd filled my corncob pipe with the reefer Jean had given me and puffed my way home. What a generous girl. Such an intimate gift.

What if Josh knocked at the door? He rarely visited. But he might. The superintendent's visits were also rare. Cesar had come twice in the past six months, once because of a plumbing problem, and again because neighbors were banging on their radiators because of the lack of heat. Although Cesar had a key and could have let himself into my apartment, he'd knocked at the door. He told me, as he had the other tenants, that he'd turned up the thermostat in defiance of the landlord's instruction. It would soon be warm. And however it came to pass, good Cesar is still "El Super".

I locked the door. If anyone knocked, I didn't have to answer. I turned off all the lights except for one table lamp that glowed like a birthday candle. The radiator hissed. I heard a woman crying, a man exclaiming joyously in Polish, a lamenting ballad in Spanish, a woman announcing "pork chops", and a kid bouncing a ball on the floor above me. The walls wheezed asthmatically, words disembodied from meaning shimmied in the air, all of it the remnants of what had been one language, and if I were patient and listened attentively, I'd recover that language. I raised the bottle to drink to the prospect of my spiritual progress.

The stairs boomed under the feet climbing toward my door. Fee, fi, fo, fum – rumbled in my gut, and I was fearful of the knock that might come to my door. I lit up and smoked some weed to calm myself. The footsteps thudded by my apartment and on up to the fifth floor. Then I remembered. My neighbors, the Komarinskis, Stanley and Ludmilla in the apartment next to mine, one or the other might knock. Once, sometimes twice a month, Stanley got drunk and collapsed on the second or third floor landing. If he collapsed on the second floor landing, Mr. O'Reardon, an amiable and aging bachelor, who lived in 2B, would help Stanley up the two flights and deliver him home. But if Mr.

O'Reardon was not at home, or Stanley had crawled to the third floor landing, collapsed and bawled for Ludmilla, he'd have to lay there a long time. Ludmilla would open the door, study her husband, curse him in Polish and English, and return to her apartment, leaving the door open.

And I'd carry and drag Stanley up the stairs and into his kitchen, where he'd sleep it off on the floor. On some of our epic climbs, Stanley was still on his feet but too wobbly to go on unassisted. I'd put my arms around his waist, entwine my fingers, making a lock of my hands, and we'd thrash our way up in a ferocious embrace; after a half a year of grueling ascents, I learned to parse Stanley's drunken speech. I discerned "DP". The "P" sprayed from Stanley's lips felt like tears on my cheek. I recalled Cesar referring to Stanley as "*refugiado*", and it came to me that "DP" was the acronym for "Displaced Person". Stanley and Ludmilla were refugees from World War Two. Neither of them young. And Stanley, taciturn sober, when smashed divulged that his wife stabbed him with a fork because he refused to father a child. Mrs. Komarinski, on the advice of Mrs. Meshchanki had tried to ply Stanley with a tumbler of Manischewitz wine and a glass of raw egg to incite his desire. Stanley gulped the wine but refused to drink the egg. That's when his wife stabbed him. On the steps Stanley bawled, "After everything we went through on the other side – the hiding, starving, murder, she wants to bring a child into this stinking world. God in heaven, can you imagine such selfishness."

Someone flushed a toilet and the plumbing gurgled in my ears. The smell of frying bacon had oozed in with the morning light. And now it is getting dark again. Two women have stopped near my door and one of them can't stop laughing. Is she laughing at me? The other woman says, "Tia Amina was a virgin and widow, that's why many men desired her." Her companion says, "I heard she had to marry in a hurry, but I don't believe it." "*Si*, that is only *chisme*. Poor woman, so much supervision, her father, mother, the four brothers, it is a miracle if she and Hector had a minute alone. Recuerda? After the wedding ceremony, Hector running for the bus so he could be killed in Korea?" "Pero, one should not forget – God is merciful. After all, her brother Rafael did find Jose for her. True, he's much younger than Amina, and even Rafael says Jose is *un jibaro*; but Amina says a country boy knows which hole to put it in. And no one who sees her can deny she's happy. When do they arrive?"

The voices of my neighbors dwindle as they continue down the stairs and discuss arrangements for a party. I'm almost content. I have no desire to go out, dredge my soul to be genial, make noise with my mouth.

The knocking at my door won't quit. I murmur, "Nobody home, nobody home." "Please" she says, "I've been trying to reach you for two days." I plug my ears with my fingers and listen to my heart beat. The throbbing keeps count of the time left to me. I unplug my ears. "If I didn't need your help, I'd leave." I open the door an inch and peek. The face is a cloud of smoke. She pushes the door. I can't push back and she is over the threshold. Smoke streams from Dolores' nostrils, clouds from her mouth rise to her eyes. She squints. A cigarette hangs from her lips. She looks like a comic book gun moll. She's probably taken up this vice to deepen her empathy for her addict clients. After all, there are only two ways to know something, from the inside or the outside. And I've long thought that her devotion to social work is the bulwark against having to vindicate divine providence. Once, we slipped into a theological discussion. I think because my swearing had upset her, but she quickly changed the subject, as if metaphysics were a contagion leading to moral turpitude. "Oh Ben," she says, clearly disappointed in me. The smoke drifts from her face and spirals into script I'm unable to read. Dolores sniffs the marijuana in the air; she eyes the empty bottle and beer cans on the table. Her only reproach is "Oh Ben, – can you walk? How about some coffee?" "I don't want coffee. I can walk, but I'm not going anywhere. Please close the door." She slams the door and recoils from the noise she's made. "Ben, this is something that can't be put off. Maybe we can get something to eat on our way." "On our way?"

It's dark, not many people on the street, and I've never felt so exposed. Smog enshrouds the moon. We've taken a bus and now we're walking. We haven't stopped to eat, and she's trotting ahead of me. I shout at her back, "Can we slow down?" She stumbles, looks at me, and allows herself to frown. On the bus she disclosed nothing more. And I couldn't bring myself to ask. She's breathing hard, leaning forward. "Ben, your mother's been phoning me all week. Josh gave her my office number. She tried to reach you and couldn't, and she's panicked. Josh has taken off again. He's been gone ten days. Yesterday I found out where he is, and I met with him." "So what else is new?" "Ben, what's happening is going to be hard for you to hear. But your brother is very grateful to you. You have no idea how grateful." "Really? Couldn't we grab a cab?" "We can't get there by cab." From a grate in the sidewalk, the stink of debris swept from the bowels of the city is gyred up by a subway train. "Ben, in some ways this is a familiar pattern. Josh balked at taking his meds. He said it was interfering with his poetry." "I know, he showed me some poems when we met for lunch. It couldn't have been more than two weeks ago, he was fine." "It's more like three weeks and Josh isn't fine. Your mother repeated in each of her phone calls that an Uncle Meyer…" "Cousin Meyer?" "… Okay, Cousin Meyer agreed to take Josh on as an apprentice. Josh went to see Meyer and wrangled an advance on his salary and never showed up again. Ben, I know all this is the usual stuff, but there's more. Ah, here we are." We turn a corner: trash cans tipped over, garbage heaped on the pavement, a single room occupancy hotel, pawn shop, tenements, a liquor store, a check cashing place, and a bar. A man and then a woman run past us as if they couldn't be gone from this street fast enough. Dolores says, "This is it," and lifts a manhole cover. I step to the edge and look down what looks like a well, its darker night gapes in the sidewalk. Dolores is climbing down a ladder. "Come on," she calls, and I follow like a kid being dared. I descend, a fluttering in my gut, as if I were a kid playing Ring-A-Levio (the warlike variant of Hide and Seek, those who find me may take me by force, and I may use fists and feet to break free, run and hide again) on a strange hostile street; and I've found a place where no one can find me, but how will I find my way back.

Dolores fishes in the large handbag hanging from a strap over her shoulder. She hands me a flashlight, points the beam of her flashlight forward, and leads the way. Within the long cone of light dense with particles, living and dead, the glow a shade brighter than the murk I can see through, I recognize that the shape brushing the bottom of my trouser leg is a large imperturbable rat; its nose at the cuff of my pants. I kick and jump back – repress a scream. Dolores is up ahead of me, marching on. Her words are warped in an echo ricocheting in the gloom. I trudge forward wondering what I'd missed until my hearing acclimates to the percussive beats of the vowels. "Amtrak executives and Metro authorities said the colony living down here will have to be out by the end of the week. They say they're legally liable if anyone living here is injured. Some of these folks have been down here for years. Josh is the most recent resident. Lawyers for the corporation contacted the police and social services. If these people aren't out of here by Friday the police will move them out, and that could turn ugly." I soldier on, alert, coexisting with the rats nosing about the piles of trash and ancient stones. This journey could be a task my brother has set for me, Josh's recompense, justice that is his due.

I'm thirsty, hungry, and sleepy. Dolores looks over her shoulder and waves, signaling me to pick up my pace. I catch up to her. Dolores, who has always adhered to the principle of confidentiality concerning her clients, is oblivious to her words reverberating through the tunnel. "Yesterday my client Rob Lacy came to see me. I've been trying to coax him out of here for months. He said that he'd been persuaded to live up top again by the most inspiring human being he's ever met, and he's going to finally take seriously his God-given talent as an artist. Mr. Lacy is forty, looks sixty and has spent much of his life in and out of prison, and he's a two-time loser; one more conviction means a life sentence. I can't deny that for the year that he's lived in the subway, venturing out only at night to climb to the street, and rifle through garbage cans for fresh leftovers from the best restaurants in the city, he has stayed out of trouble. He informed me that his guru is a young man who has studied in the east, and is living below to take respite from witnessing the evil in the city. Guess who Mr. Lacy's guru is."

Cackling like shrapnel slices through the air. Dolores has again outpaced me. I'm busy watching where I put my feet, but uneasy as I am, I raise my gaze from my shoes. I can make out a tall man carrying a pail in one hand and a squeegee in the other. He is moving past Dolores and sounds like he's in a hurry to get home to his supper. The man speaking to Dolores is also addressing the powers that be – and himself. "He helped me to see I been a tough guy all my life and scared. Afraid of losin' things nobody can keep anyways. And this Joshua can be a friend to any personality – know what I'm sayin? All peoples, dogs, fishes, aliens from another planet."

I plod on. Dolores hurries, keeping a distance between us. The tunnel curves and for a moment I lose sight of her and panic. To my right, within reach of my fingertips is a wall, to my left about a hundred yards away, beyond wide fence-like girders, a train roars by, the all consuming clangor nullifying every other sense. The cars of the train have no beginning and have no end; at last, the din diminishes and I realize I'd given up hope of being sensible to anything but the annihilating shriek of the train. But I haven't stopped walking and I'm no longer studying where I put my feet. The tunnel has widened and the prospect is once more straight ahead, dim and infinite. I see three figures, two appear perched in mid-air, the other on the ground is shouting. Their words are embellished with unintelligible resonances.

I catch up with Dolores. She's shouting "Bravo" and now I'm able to differentiate between the stuttering echo and the words being spoken. She gives me a bag of peanuts and a canteen of water. I gulp the water, drink and drink and the canteen doesn't empty. I start on the peanuts. Up above, sitting on two ladders, two boys are spray-painting a wall. The graffiti artists wear miner's caps with small powerful flashlights affixed to the visors. At about twelve feet apart, the lights shining above their brows illuminate voluminous egg-shaped globes, in roiling yellow, pink, red and green intimating a dream of tropical paradise. The fronds of the palm trees, huge pink ears fan an edible sun. The artists laugh as they work and shout to each other in Spanish. Dolores claps. Her applause sounds like gun shots. Dolores can't be applauding the mural, the composition is too fluid and huge to take in all at once, her ovation must be for the process. From a distance I can't appraise, specks of light snow down from a grate in the sidewalk and extinguish above my head. I get closer and stand before the mural in the semi-dark like the proverbial blind man with his hands on some enormous living thing whose appearance, and manner of being he can only guess at. The swaying egg shapes provide intermittent flashes in this blind man's imperfect dark, allowing visions of God's promised plenty.

The graffiti artists call "Adios" and "dios, dios, dios" rings in the gloom. Dolores is chasing after the sound of squeaking wheels. I chase after Dolores. I've had enough of this. If I could find my way out I'd be gone, and being gone would contradict that where I am is inevitable. If I could backtrack to the graffiti artists and ask them for instructions on how to find my way out – or maybe they'd be willing to escort me out of the tunnel, up into night in the city, whose lights are light enough. I pause, lose sight of Dolores and chase after the sound of squeaking wheels – fall into filth, scramble to my feet, and continue to run as if I could out-run my stinking self.

Dolores is within sight, walking beside someone wearing a beret, olive-drab fatigue jacket, red skirt and combat boots. This person is pushing a shopping cart; the roof a web of clothesline, and inside the cart, an orange cat, an eyeless doll, clock, and a plastic bag stuffed with laundry. Dolores says, "Please Billie." Billie's face is painted white; he or she is wearing elegant kid gloves. Billie says "Shut up Buster" to the whining cat. The alto voice might be male or female. I can't tell. Perhaps Dolores knows. My guess is that we are not meant to know Billie's color or gender; identity itself, a vanity Billie can forego. "Please," Dolores pleads. Billie has sauntered to the left some fifty yards, and jumped off the curb of a shoulder-high barrier. The beams of our flashlights scour the white mask mumbling what sounds like a prayer. Dolores genuflects and yells, "She's scavenging near the third rail. Billie, careful!"

Slowly she climbs back over the barrier, smiles, and walks towards us carrying a rusted shovel. "Lady social worker, no harm comin' to me down here, this is my home and I don't intend to go nowhere." She taps Dolores's shoulder with the shovel as if knighting her. Dolores says, "Thank you, this is Joshua's brother Ben." Billie stares at me. I'm related to celebrity. "You Joshua's brother? For real?" "For real." "You read the Good Book?" "I read a lot of good books." "Well if you read the onliest Good Book, you know Cain killed his kid brother, 'cause even though he was first born, it was little brother who was favored." What difference would it make if Billie knew I was the favored one? She says, "Lissen, Joshua's a wise and sweet boy; he can park his shoes under my bed anytime he want. And me and him ain't goin' nowhere. Stayin' right where we made our homes, understand?" I nod to indicate I understand. She takes the shovel from Dolores and gives it to me. She says, "Sorry, he needs it," pushes the cart, the wheels squalling, the orange cat in the shopping cart, watchful. Her back to us, she waves goodbye.

Dolores doesn't move – too much happening all at once, the debacle in which her clients will be hurt, imminent. "If Josh would move out," she says, "I think most of the others would follow." I know I should be glad to have the opportunity to reciprocate, help her, but I can't hide that I want to be gone; my life depends on it. Dolores looks like she's about to apologize. The two of us stunned, stare at one another. And

I see a little girl suffused with disabling good will, enamored of the miraculous. I'm certain that something terrible happened to that little girl. The wound unremitting and never less than an ache, goading her beyond loving humanity in the abstract. "Your brother is really grateful to you." "Yes, you told me." "No I didn't, not really, not everything. June Mallory, I told you about her – the psychiatric social worker at Friendship House; she spoke to Josh a number of times about the importance of taking his medicine. Especially now, that on top of everything else, he's been diagnosed with type-one diabetes. About a month ago I phoned you; I told you Josh would have to have tests. Do you remember?" "Yes, I remember." "Well, it complicates things, doesn't it? And Josh's sneaking alcohol into his apartment, locking the door, drinking, and passing out – -he might as well be playing Russian roulette. It's to his credit that he found his way to AA meetings on his own. But he stopped going, and if he continues to drink, it will kill him." I can't look at her. The skin at my temples contracts. Can she see my shame? I can neither explain nor dispel what has dogged my life. Behind the miasma veiling my eyes, I know what I feel is mean, as I now know that Josh is an alcoholic, as I am an alcoholic, as our father was an alcoholic, and our paternal grandmother diabetic. When Dolores first told me that Josh was an alcoholic, I was incredulous, and couldn't rid myself of the idea that Josh willed his alcoholism in the process of appropriating what I'd confided to him. Whatever the mysterious facts of Josh's most recent crisis, I'll hear my life fall from my brother's mouth as something fabulous, clichéd, and grotesque. I'll recoil, distance myself, and try to will my good faith, but my words will be tainted with condescension, pushing Josh to improve upon reality already surreal. I have to face the truths Josh has told and I've dismissed. Josh's surreptitious boozing compounded by his diabetes must have left him crapulous, coming to in strange places, not knowing how he got there, or how much time had passed. No matter if Josh's recounting of his besotted journeys are stuffed with the particulars of my drunkalog, as I told it in the times of overwhelming kinship. What other truths has Josh told through the years that I've dismissed? Well, the social workers and shrinks have also missed things, made mistakes – Josh, a plethora of fascinating symptoms, obscured pedestrian and dangerous diabetes.

Here in the tunnel under the earth, the beam of my flashlight penetrates the entombed air, and Dolores, as though exhumed, but impervious, (the sepulchral dust coating her, all in a day's work) has mustered the resolve to tell me what she finds so difficult to say. What would change if I told her that the last time I saw Josh, the stories he told were witty, and concerned with practicalities. I'd been elated, teetering on the brink of optimism. It was like falling in love. I felt my face slipping into an imbecilic grin, making Josh smile, until his smile collapsed into laughter. I'd never seen anyone laugh like that. An agony of hilarity – Josh's laughter wracked him inside out. "June," Dolores says, her tone like a school teacher reminding a dreaming student that he must be present when he's present, "wasn't having much luck with Josh. She asked me to join her because Josh said that I was one of the two people he could trust. We were in her office – June, me, and Josh. We persisted, trying to persuade him how important it was that he take his medication and get back to AA meetings. He refused to sit down. He just stood there looking past us. I said, please Josh, and pushed an arm chair behind him. He put his hands up in front of his face to ward off blows, staggered backward, and fell into the chair. And he slipped into a trance and began to shiver and cry. He wet his pants, and begged your father to stop. Ben I heard it, and I've heard it before; it was the voice of a terrified child. Later, when he came out of it, soaked, but calmer than I'd ever seen him, he retained pieces of the memory that had emerged, and was able to say, 'if it wasn't for my brother, it would never have ended.'"

I glance back in the direction from which we'd come. If only I dared to run. I'd have to keep the flashlight. I thought Dolores was about to tell me that Josh had recovered the memory of being assaulted in the shelter, but she's talking about something else. "Recovered memory," I tell her, "There's a lot of that going around." "Yes, and June and I agree, Josh has as complete a set of classic symptoms as either of us has ever seen, but a promising sign is that he's capable of being grateful to you for putting an end to it. Ben, I know this can't be easy for you. I've felt for a long time that you've withheld things you couldn't talk about. I understand. But if you hadn't intervened, your father's sexual abuse of your brother would have continued. Josh told us how you warned your father that if he ever touched Josh again, you'd kill him."

I'm lightheaded. An invisible membrane sheathes the senses through which I'd known the world. Hermetically sealed inside my skin I peer out, where some rendition of my life is taking place. I say, "Never happened, and I never threatened to kill my father." Dolores looks at me with a kind of militant pity. I must confront Josh about the terrible story he told about our father. But if I confront him with the lie, he'll deny it, the lie already taking on the attributes of truth within him – or maybe he's forgotten it – as he's moved on and is now Captain America saving the western world. I wonder whether the story Josh told about our father was vengeance, or some exigency, like having to meet with Dolores and June about not taking his meds – or not paying his rent made it necessary to create some greater catastrophe to obliterate from his mind the event which is more humiliating to him than the end of the world. Hell, Josh invokes the Apocalypse to explain why he hadn't visited Mama.

I'm less afraid of the dark. Except for the peanuts, I haven't eaten in a long time, and my stomach growls. I remember what I must do if I'm ever to live my own life. Whatever the disparities between what I know to be my history, and what Dolores is telling me, eventually I'll be able to use it all. Already I begin to feel the distancing that will make new work possible. Funny that my salvation should be a by-product of what Mama calls my scribbling. Dolores is trying to decide which of the brothers is crazier. I may have smiled, because she is smiling at me, as if we've overcome an impediment. "Ben, there isn't much further to go. Are you coming?" I shrug. "Ben, I have to go. It's straight ahead, you can't miss it. Scrap wood and cinder block huts with tin and tarpaulin roofs. You'll see lights, they've siphoned electric power. You could be there in twenty minutes. I know Josh would be glad to see you." Dolores' eyes entreat me and she continues on, the beam of her flashlight poking about in the dark.

The deafening rush of a passing train turns me, obliterating every contingency, leaving me dumb. The beam of my flashlight wavers. Standing still, I try to orient myself. Which way is out, and who is the father Josh described? I recall the countless drafts I'd written of a story drawing on what I took to be Papa's character. Through the endless versions of the father I created, I went far away, and that distance lingered. There are times when I'm reminded that after the endless drafts of that story I could no longer distinguish between the stories Mama and relatives told about Papa, and my own inventions. Had Mama actually said, "They gave your father the Socialist such a beating, he pished red for a week." Had I heard something like it elsewhere and appropriated it? Papa had been an organizer; he had been roughed up. This I learned from friends of the family and relatives. But had Papa, brandishing a baling hook really chased the thug who had heckled him? It's possible that Uncle Herman, who worked in the shop with Papa, told me about the beef Papa got into with the trucker who'd blocked the loading dock, and Papa lost it and went after the guy with a baling hook. Have I confused the events, taking particulars from one and applied them to another? – I no longer know. The facts are there to be harvested in the service of archetypal truth, and now there are a number of things I recall that I can't swear happened. And what about Dolores? She's certain the accusations Josh made about Papa are true. Consider her scruples and acumen. But Josh and I grew up in the same house; if any such crime had been committed I would have known. Then again, what is theoretically possible, is possible – and now Papa's alleged crime lives in my head like a virus. I turn and walk in the direction I hope will take me to light. Squinting into the distance ahead, my most acute vision returns darkness, except where the air looks like it's crawling with worms. I stop – must calm down so I can think things through before I take another step. One thing is certain; my brother is the ghost who will shadow my every word, for as long as we both live.

Fomite
Burlington, Vermont

Fomite is a literary press whose authors and artists explore the human condition – political, cultural, personal and historical – in poetry and prose.

A fomite is a medium capable of transmitting infectious organisms from one individual to another.

"The activity of art is based on the capacity of people to be infected by the feelings of others." Tolstoy, *What is Art?*

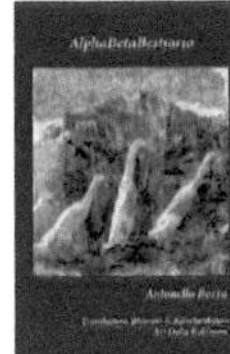

AlphaBetaBestiario - Antonello Borra
Animals have always understood that mankind is not fully at home in the world. Bestiaries, hoping to teach, send out warnings. This one, of course, aims at doing the same.

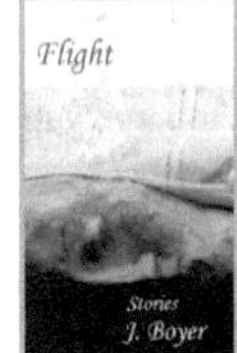

Flight and Other Stories - Jay Boyer
In *Flight and Other Stories,* we're with the fattest woman on earth as she draws her last breaths and her soul ascends toward its final reward. We meet a divorcee who can fly for no more effort than flapping her arms. We follow a middle-aged butler whose love affair with a young woman leads him first to the mysteries of bondage, and then to the pleasures of malice. Story by story, we set foot into worlds so strange as to seem all but surreal, yet everything feels familiar, each moment rings true. And that's when we recognize we're in the hands of one of America's truly original talents.

Improvisational Arguments - Anna Faktorovich
Improvisational Arguments is written in free verse to capture the essence of modern problems and triumphs. The poems clearly relate short, frequently humorous and occasionally tragic, stories about travels to exotic and unusual places, fantastic realms, abnormal jobs, artistic innovations, political objections, and misadventures with love.

Fomite
Burlington, Vermont

Loisaida - Dan Chodorokoff

Catherine, a young anarchist estranged from her parents and squatting in an abandoned building on New York's Lower East Side is fighting with her boyfriend and conflicted about her work on an underground newspaper. After learning of a developer's plans to demolish a community garden, Catherine builds an alliance with a group of Puerto Rican community activists. Together they confront the confluence of politics, money, and real estate that rule Manhattan. All the while she learns important lessons from her great-grandmother's life in the Yiddish anarchist movement that flourished on the Lower East Side at the turn of the century. In this coming of age story, family saga, and tale of urban politics, Dan Chodorkoff explores the "principle of hope", and examines how memory and imagination inform social change.

Still Time - Michael Cocchiarale

Still Time is a collection of twenty-five short and shorter stories exploring tensions that arise in a variety of contemporary relationships: a young boy must deal with the wrath of his out-of-work father; a woman runs into a man twenty years after an awkward sexual encounter; a wife, unable to conceive, imagines her own murder, as well as the reaction of her emotionally distant husband; a soon-to-be tenured English professor tries to come to terms with her husband's shocking return to the religion of his youth; an assembly line worker, married for thirty years, discovers the surprising secret life of his recently hospitalized wife. Whether a few hundred or a few thousand words, these and other stories in the collection depict characters at moments of deep crisis. Some feel powerless, overwhelmed – unable to do much to change the course of their lives. Others rise to the occasion and, for better or for worse, say or do the thing that might transform them for good. Even in stories with the most troubling of endings, there remains the possibility of redemption. For each of the characters, there is still time.

Loosestrife - Greg Delanty

This book is a chronicle of complicity in our modern lives, a witnessing of war and the destruction of our planet. It is also an attempt to adjust the more destructive blueprint myths of our society. Often our cultural memory tells us to keep quiet about the aspects that are most challenging to our ethics, to forget the violations we feel and tremors that keep us distant and numb.

Fomite
Burlington, Vermont

Carts and Other Stories - Zdravka Evtimova

Roots and wings are the key words that best describe the short story collection, *Carts and Other Stories,* by Zdravka Evtimova. The book is emotionally multilayered and memorable because of its internal power, vitality and ability to touch both the heart and your mind. Within its pages, the reader discovers new perspectives true wealth, and learns to see the world with different eyes. The collection lives on the borders of different cultures. *Carts and Other Stories* will take the reader to wild and powerful Bulgarian mountains, to silver rains in Brussels, to German quiet winter streets and to wind bitten crags in Afghanistan. This book lives for those seeking to discover the beauty of the world around them, and will have them appreciating what they have – and perhaps what they have lost as well.

The Listener Aspires to the Condition of Music - Barry Goldensohn

"I know of no other selected poems that selects on one theme, but this one does, charting Goldensohn's career-long attraction to music's performance, consolations and its august, thrilling, scary and clownish charms. Does all art aspire to the condition of music as Pater claimed, exhaling in a swoon toward that one class act? Goldensohn is more aware than the late 19th century of the overtones of such breathing: his poems thoroughly round out those overtones in a poet's lifetime of listening."
John Peck, poet, editor, Fellow of the American Academy of Rome

The Co-Conspirator's Tale - Ron Jacobs

There's a place where love and mistrust are never at peace; where duplicity and deceit are the universal currency. *The Co-Conspirator's Tale* takes place within this nebulous firmament. There are crimes committed by the police in the name of the law. Excess in the name of revolution. The combination leaves death in its wake and the survivors struggling to find justice in a San Francisco Bay Area noir by the author of the underground classic *The Way the Wind Blew:A History of the Weather Underground* and the novel *Short Order Frame Up.*

Fomite
Burlington, Vermont

When You Remember Deir Yassin - R.L. Green

When You Remember Deir Yassin is a collection of poems by R. L. Green, an American Jewish writer, on the subject of the occupation and destruction of Palestine. Green comments: "Outspoken Jewish critics of Israeli crimes against humanity have, strangely, been called 'anti-Semitic' as well as the hilariously illogical epithet 'self-hating Jews.' As a Jewish critic of the Israeli government, I have come to accept these accusations as a stamp of approval and a badge of honor, signifying my own fealty to a central element of Jewish identity and ethics: one must be a lover of truth and a friend to the oppressed, and stand with the victims of tyranny, not with the tyrants, despite tribal loyalty or self-advancement. These poems were written as expressions of outrage, and of grief, and to encourage my sisters and brothers of every cultural or national grouping to speak out against injustice, to try to save Palestine, and in so doing, to reclaim for myself my own place as part of the Jewish people." Poems in the original English are accompanied by Arabic and Hebrew translations.

Roadworthy Creature, Roadworthy Craft - Kate Magill

Words fail but the voice struggles on. The culmination of a decade's worth of performance poetry, *Roadworthy Creature, Roadworthy Craft* is Kate Magill's first full-length publication. In lines that are sinewy yet delicate, Magill's poems explore the terrain where idea and action meet, where bodies and words commingle to form a strange new flesh, a breathing text, an "I" that spirals outward from itself.

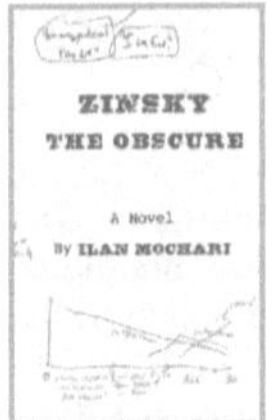

Zinsky the Obscure - Ilan Mochari

"If your childhood is brutal, your adulthood becomes a daily attempt to recover: a quest for ecstasy and stability in recompense for their early absence." So states the 30-year-old Ariel Zinsky, whose bachelor-like lifestyle belies the torturous youth he is still coming to grips with. As a boy, he struggles with the beatings themselves; as a grownup, he struggles with the world's indifference to them. *Zinsky the Obscure* is his life story, a humorous chronicle of his search for a redemptive ecstasy through sex, an entrepreneurial sports obsession, and finally, the cathartic exercise of writing it all down. Fervently recounting both the comic delights and the frightening horrors of a life in which he feels – always – that he is not like all the rest, Zinsky survives the worst and relishes the best with idiosyncratic style, as his heartbreak turns into self-awareness and his suicidal ideation into self-regard. A vivid evocation of the all-consuming nature of lust and ambition – and the forces that drive them.

Fomite
Burlington, Vermont

Visiting Hours - Jennifer Anne Moses
Visiting Hours, a novel-in-stories, explores the lives of people not normally met on the page---AIDS patients and those who care for them. Set in Baton Rouge, Louisiana, and written with large and frequent dollops of humor, the book is a profound meditation on faith and love in the face of illness and poverty.

Love's Labours - Jack Pulaski
In the four stories and two novellas that comprise *Love's Labors* the protagonists Ben and Laura, discover in their fervid romance and long marriage their interlocking fates, and the histories that preceded their births. They also learned something of the paradox between love and all the things it brings to its beneficiaries: bliss, disaster, duty, tragedy, comedy, the grotesque, and tenderness.

Ben and Laura's story is also the particularly American tale of immigration to a new world. Laura's story begins in Puerto Rico, and Ben's lineage is Russian-Jewish. They meet in City College of New York, a place at least analogous to a melting pot. Laura struggles to rescue her brother from gang life and heroin. She is mother to her younger sister; their mother Consuelo is the financial mainstay of the family and consumed by work. Despite filial obligations, Laura aspires to be a serious painter. Ben writes, cares for and is caught up in the misadventures and surreal stories of his younger schizophrenic brother. Laura is also a story teller as powerful and enchanting as Scheherazade.
Ben struggles to survive such riches, and he and Laura endure.

The Derivation of Cowboys & Indians - Joseph D. Reich
The Derivation of Cowboys & Indians represents a profound journey, a breakdown of The American Dream from a social, cultural, historical, and spiritual point of view. Reich examines in concise detail the loss of the collective unconscious, commenting on our!contemporary postmodern culture with its self-interested excesses, on where and how things all go wrong, and how social/political practice rarely meets its original proclamations and promises. Reich's surreal and self-effacing satire brings this troubling message home. *The Derivations of Cowboys & Indians* is a desperate search and struggle for America's literal, symbolic, and spiritual home.

Fomite
Burlington, Vermont

Kasper Planet: Comix and Tragix - Peter Schumann

The British call him Punch, the Italians, Pulchinello, the Russians, Petruchka, the Native Americans, Coyote. These are the figures we may know. But every culture that worships authority will breed a Punch-like, antiauthoritarian resister. Yin and yang – it has to happen. The Germans call him Kasper. Truth-telling and serious pranking are dangerous professions when going up against power. Bradley Manning sits naked in solitary; Julian Assange is pursued by Interpol, Obama's Department of Justice, and Amazon.com. But – in contrast to merely human faces – masks and theater can often slip through the bars. Consider our American Kaspers: Charlie Chaplin, Woody Guthrie, Abby Hoffman, the Yes Men – theater people all, utilizing various forms to seed critique. Their profiles and tactics have evolved along with those of their enemies. Who are the bad guys that call forth the Kaspers? Over the last half century, with his Bread & Puppet Theater, Peter Schumann has been tireless in naming them, excoriating them with Kasperdom.... from Marc Estrin's Foreword to Planet Kasper

Travers' Inferno - L.E. Smith

In the 1970's churches began to burn in Burlington, Vermont. Travers' Inferno places these fires in the dizzying zeitgeist of aggressive utopian movements, distrust in authority, escapist alternative life styles, and a parasite news media. Its characters – colorful, damaged, comical, and tragic – are seeking meaning through desperate acts. Protagonist Travers Jones is grounded in the transcendent, mystified by the opposite sex, haunted by an absent father, and directed by an uncle with a grudge. Around him: secessionist Québecois murdering, pilfering and burning; changing alliances; violent deaths; confused love making; and a belligerent cat.

Views Cost Extra - *L.E. Smith*

Views that inspire, that calm, or that terrify – all come at some cost to the viewer. In *Views Cost Extra* you will find a New Jersey high school preppy who wants to inhabit the "perfect" cowboy movie, a rural mailman disgusted with the residents of his town who wants to live with the penguins, an ailing screen writer who strikes a deal with Johnny Cash to reverse an old man's failures, an old man who ponders a young man's suicide attempt, a one-armed blind blues singer who wants to reunite with the car that took her arm on the assembly line – and more. These stories suggest that we must pay something to live even ordinary lives.

Fomite
Burlington, Vermont

The Empty Notebook Interrogates Itself - Susan Thomas

The Empty Notebook began its life as a very literal metaphor for a few weeks of what the poet thought was writer's block, but was really the struggle of an eccentric persona to take over her working life. It won. And for the next three years everything she wrote came to her in the voice of the Empty Notebook, who, as the notebook began to fill itself, became rather opinionated, changed gender, alternately acted as bully and victim, had many bizarre adventures in exotic locales and developed a somewhat politically-incorrect attitude. It then began to steal the voices and forms of other poets and tried to immortalize itself in various poetry reviews. It is now thrilled to collect itself in one slim volume.

My God, What Have We Done? - Susan Weiss

In a world afflicted with war, toxicity, and hunger, does what we do in our private lives really matter? Fifty years after the creation of the atomic bomb at Los Alamos, newlyweds Pauline and Clifford visit that once-secret city on their honeymoon, compelled by Pauline's fascination with Oppenheimer, the soulful scientist. The two stories emerging from this visit reverberate back and forth between the loneliness of a new mother at home in Boston and the isolation of an entire community dedicated to the development of the bomb. While Pauline struggles with unforeseen challenges of family life, Oppenheimer and his crew reckon with forces beyond all imagining.

Finally the years of frantic research on the bomb culminate in a stunning test explosion that echoes a rupture in the couple's marriage. Against the backdrop of a civilization that's out of control, Pauline begins to understand the complex, potentially explosive physics of personal relationships.

At once funny and dead serious, *My God, What Have We Done?* sifts through the ruins left by the bomb in search of a more worthy human achievement.

Fomite
Burlington, Vermont

As It Is On Earth - Peter M. Wheelwright
Four centuries after the Reformation Pilgrims sailed up the down-flowing watersheds of New England, Taylor Thatcher, irreverent scion of a fallen family of Maine Puritans, is still caught in the turbulence.

In his errant attempts to escape from history, the young college professor is further unsettled by his growing attraction to Israeli student Miryam Bluehm as he is swept by Time through the "family thing" – from the tangled genetic and religious history of his New England parents to the redemptive birthday secret of Esther Fleur Noire Bishop, the Cajun-Passamaquoddy woman who raised him and his younger half-cousin/half-brother, Bingham.

The landscapes, rivers, and tidal estuaries of Old New England and the Mayan Yucatan are also casualties of history in Thatcher's story of Deep Time and re-discovery of family on Columbus Day at a high-stakes gambling casino, rising in resurrection over the starlit bones of a once-vanquished Pequot Indian Tribe.